The Fallen Angel

HELEN GOLTZ

The Lady Mortician's Visions, book 8.

PUBLISHED BY: Atlas Productions

First published 2025.

Copyright © Helen Goltz

Cover design, as always, by the wonderful Karri Klawiter, Art by Karri.

PLEASE NOTE: This book is written in British-Australian English.

Contents

Dedicated to the ladies in my family who have read every volume – Lisa, Raylene and Bev. What forbearance!

For dog and animal lovers everywhere: no animals, including Julius's big hound Rufus, ever get harmed, dog-napped, threatened, injured or die in these stories. Rufus lives on forever. So, read on in peace, dear reader. I proudly support the WSPA (World Society for the Protection of Animals), the RSPCA, and Animals Australia. I thank them for their continued efforts to make the world kinder to animals.

PLEASE NOTE: This book is written in British-Australian English.

Chapter 1

BRISBANE, AUSTRALIA. MONDAY, *18 December, 1891. Fine and sunny, 32 degrees, humid.*

Miss Phoebe Astin looked quite the picture wearing a red taffeta frock, amongst the decorations that adorned her workroom. Her white apron partially hid the dress, which was fitted at the bodice with wide sleeves and a full skirt. She wore her long blonde hair pulled back from her delicate face but loose, making her look like a Christmas angel.

Several weeks before, Phoebe, assisted by her sister-in-law, Violet, and the kitchen manager, Mrs Dobbs, had wrapped the stair banister in ropes of evergreen sprigs fashioned with red berries cleverly made and decorated at the local market. A tall Christmas tree stood in the corner, with paper decorations of little dolls and candles, and the occasional oddity that her brother Ambrose snuck onto a branch to surprise her, like a banana that bore no connection to the festive season. Had it not been a funeral home with a body in the process of being prepared for presentation, the picture would have been a traditional Christmas scene.

Phoebe smiled to herself as she thought about how generous her eldest brother, Julius, had been with the Christmas decoration budget this year. He was normally more restrained given the nature of their business, which was perpetually in mourning. Perhaps having a wife, hearth and home had mellowed him.

'Ah, lovely,' a voice said, and Phoebe looked up from the young lady she was preparing for viewing to find her favourite spirit visiting.

'Uncle Reggie, it is good to see you. It has been at least a week.'

'I'm a very busy ghost, my dear great-niece,' the suave Reginald Astin joked. Brother of Phoebe's grandfather, Randolph—the first face customers encountered at the front desk when entering *The Economic Undertaker*—Reggie had met with an unfortunate riding accident aged forty and remained forever handsome, cutting a dashing figure in his riding attire.

'I wish Christmas lasted all year. The decorations give the room a lift, don't they?' Phoebe said with a glance around.

'Indeed, they do, but I was referring to you as being lovely, dear Phoebe. I could put you at the top of the tree and declare you an angel!'

Phoebe laughed. 'Thank you, Uncle. I am dressing to match the decorations. I found two wonderful sellers in the marketplace, and I confess, I have detoured on my walk home several times to peruse their Christmas ornaments.'

'They do wonders with tissue paper,' Reggie teased, noting the abundance of colourful balls and fringes adorning the lamp and the pot that housed Florence, the fern. He approached Phoebe's worktable and looked at the young lady lying upon it. 'Goodness, she can't be much older than you.'

Phoebe glanced at the identity card beside the lady. 'True, Uncle. This is Miss Charity Buckley. She met with an unfortunate accident close to the marketplace. A sad time of the year to commit her family to mourning. I have changed her into her favourite dress as requested by her brother.'

'A tragedy indeed. She's a lovely young miss, and had the perfect name for Christmas,' Reggie said, looking upon the petite brunette with the pretty features wearing a cream embroidered dress. He moved around Charity and groaned. 'Oh, I see.'

Phoebe nodded. 'I believe they found Miss Buckley on the side of the road. A horse and cart may have struck her while she was crossing, and perhaps they did not know of the accident; she was left to die alone.'

'I hope they did not know,' Reggie said warily. 'How will you disguise the injury?'

Phoebe indicated a red cape. 'I shall place it around her when I have finished Miss Buckley's hair and face. The mourners will only see her fringe and face then and, given the season, she will be as pretty as a picture.'

'Ten minutes, Phoebe dear!' a voice called from upstairs, advising it was nearing the time. The body was to be finished one hour before the viewing, lest anyone arrive early.

'Almost finished, Grandpa. I will ring the bell when done,' Phoebe called back.

Reginald sighed upon hearing his brother's voice.

'Does it pain you, Uncle?' she asked, concerned.

'I miss him,' Reginald said, and then, being of a similar nature to his great nephew, Ambrose, he cleared his throat and resumed his cheerful countenance. 'I shall leave you to your work, dear niece, and go easy on the Christmas decorations,' he said with a wink. 'We won't be able to find you in here shortly.'

Phoebe laughed and returned to her work, quickly finishing her preparation for Miss Charity Buckley's viewing. Summer in Brisbane, Australia, did not allow the deceased to remain above ground for long, and she knew her two brothers would struggle in the humidity and heat at a funeral they were officiating this morning. The dark black suits were far from comfortable, and Julius bemoaned the season and all who had the audacity to die in summer.

With a last brush of powder, a comb of Charity's fringe, and the draping of the cape, Phoebe stood for a moment to observe her work.

'There you go, Miss Buckley,' she whispered. 'You are as beautiful in death as in life. It was an honour to serve you, and I wish you a safe journey to the afterlife.'

Phoebe returned to her desk, rang the bell, and moments later, she heard her grandfather summoning one of the men from the stables. Soon, the business would run on a skeleton staff for Christmas, and Phoebe hoped they did not get a rush of business. Hurried footsteps crossed the floor above and started down the stairs. Claude appeared.

'Hello Claude, Miss Buckley is ready.'

The tall, quiet employee, who was second in charge in the stables and often stepped up to partner Julius when Will partnered Ambrose, came to her side.

'She looks beautiful, Phoebe,' he said, having finally agreed to address her as such after several years of insisting on formality. 'Shall we then?'

The pair moved the table closer to the recently installed pulley system and opened the door. As Miss Buckley was only small, Phoebe lifted the corner of her stretcher as Claude did the same, and they slid Miss Buckley across and into the opening. Claude closed the doors.

'I shall go pull her up,' he said, departing as quickly as he arrived, and Miss Buckley would soon arrive in the very room where her viewing with family and friends would begin in an hour.

Phoebe turned to clean up. It had been a while since a spirit had required her help, and that of her beau, Detective Harland Stone. The last time was when Miss Alma Thornton, jilted at the altar, had found her deceased fiancé was, in fact, not deceased and was still duping young ladies of their fortune.

'It is a good thing,' she said to herself. Much better that spirits go to the other side rested. But Phoebe spoke too soon.

Chapter 2

Tall, strikingly handsome Julius Astin had mastered the art of looking impassive while keeping an eye out for any funeral attendees needing assistance, and an ear to the word—'Amen'—that would indicate the priest's delivery was over. It was in this perfect state of suspension that he stood in his dark suit and hat, oblivious to the admiring looks of the ladies present, and looking cool despite the heat at just after 10am that morning.

While the priest delivered the last prayer in a booming voice, 'Into your hands, Father, we commend our sister,' aged family members hard of hearing added their own comments to the service.

"She was a caring and compassionate soul," a gentleman announced to everyone.

'If she were that caring, she would have died in autumn,' Ambrose muttered to his brother. Julius ignored him, as was his practice when working.

'And so giving,' a woman tutted.

'What I'd give for some cloud cover,' Ambrose sighed.

'She'll be back to haunt you, Frederick, be sure of that. She said many a time that you were quite a handful when younger and caused her grey hairs,' a craggy voice declared, and muffled laughs and hushing sounds followed.

'Watch out, Freddie,' Ambrose continued to commentate.

'Amen.' The priest made the sign of the cross.

'Amen to that,' Ambrose sparked up, seeing the end was near, and feeling Julius nudge him into action.

The men of *The Economic Undertaker* took their positions and lowered the small, lightweight coffin containing the deceased into the grave. Nearby, the gravediggers, Mr Redford and his son, waited to fill in the plot.

'Thank God we only book funerals between 9am and 11am in the summer,' Ambrose grumbled. 'I am sure that any closer to midday we would expire. I can see Lilly's headline now,' he said, thinking of Phoebe's close friend, reporter Lilly Lewis. 'Undertakers perish in extreme heat. Discount funeral packages offered in commemoration.'

'That might work better than advertising,' Julius agreed. He allowed himself a smile now that the mourners were on their way out of the gates, a sea of black umbrellas above their heads to ward off the sun, and one white umbrella that a wayward guest had displayed determining the heat won out over appropriateness.

'This afternoon's funeral is at Saint Patrick's, and the burial is in the church grounds. There's plenty of shade. We'll survive,' Julius assured his brother.

'The good Lord has sent us a warm one today,' the priest said, joining them and fanning himself with his notes.

'Can you do something about it, Father?' Ambrose asked. 'Organise cloud cover for the hour while you are in attendance?'

'Leave it with me, son,' Father Taylor said with a nod. 'I'll work on it. Julius, might I have a word?'

'Of course, Father,' Julius said, and gave Ambrose the payment for the gravediggers. He followed the elderly priest to a nearby gazebo and joined him in the shade. 'Is there something I can assist you with, or do I look like I need to confess something?'

'Always the latter,' Father Taylor said with a chuckle. 'No, I heard you are good friends with the young detective, the new one in town... not so new anymore, I suppose.'

'Detective Harland Stone? Yes. He is also dating my sister, Phoebe.'

'I saw him escorting Miss Astin at the Christmas market; I'm sure he is a fine, upstanding young man.'

Has something happened?' Julius asked, concerned.

'A crime, perhaps.' The priest reached underneath his long black cassock into the pocket of his dark trousers and produced a letter. 'I received this. Might you read it and give me your opinion?'

Julius studied the holy man before him for a moment and opened the folded page. He read the lines:

'Forgive me, Father, for I have sinned.
She broke the fifth, and I broke the sixth. She was deserving, and
I will do so again.
No one escapes divine retribution.'

Julius folded the note and looked at the priest. 'Fifth and sixth... commandments, I assume?'

'I believe so. The fifth commandment is honour thy father and thy mother,' Father Taylor said.

'And the sixth?' Julius asked. 'Thou shalt not kill?'

The priest nodded. 'This was not a confession offered in the confessional box, so I can pass it on to the detective. I have nothing more, so I doubt he will be in any position to act upon it.'

'Where was it left?' Julius asked. 'At St Mary's?'

'Yes. Late yesterday afternoon, on my chair in the confessional. I looked around after finding it, but there were very few people in the church other than those coming for confession or the ladies working on the altar table flowers. I knew everyone in attendance and do not believe anyone among them was responsible for the letter.'

Julius nodded. 'Yet if the crime has taken place, the person is likely a Catholic and perhaps a church-goer at St Mary's. I shall give it to Harland this day and let you know what he says.'

The priest waved his hand dismissively. 'There is no hurry, and there may be no course of action to be taken. I have done my duty in passing it on. Thank you, Julius. I shall see you at the next funeral, and I'll work on the cloud cover in the interim,' he joked with a glance above to the source of the request.

Julius chuckled and pocketed the letter for now. He returned to retrieve the hearse and horses from nearby in the shade of a bank of trees at South Brisbane Cemetery, and found Ambrose waiting. He gave a wave of thanks to the Redford men, senior and junior.

'What is the matter? Did the priest feel you needed an extra blessing?'

'Yes,' Julius said in jest, boarding the hearse and taking the reins; Ambrose leapt in beside him. 'He offered me a blessing and a prayer for patience and perseverance when dealing with my brother.'

Ambrose scoffed and nudged his brother. 'Tell me what he really wanted.'

'He has a letter for Harland, a confession of sorts to a crime but left in note form, so Father Taylor is not obliged to keep it to himself. I will take it to Harland this afternoon after the second funeral.'

'A church crime?' Ambrose said. 'What could it be? Has someone robbed the donation plate or slurped the holy water?'

Julius glanced at his brother as he steered the horses through the gates of the cemetery on the return route to *The Economic Undertaker.* He said dryly, 'A lightning bolt will strike you dead any moment, and I hope the sender does not misfire and take me by mistake.'

Ambrose chuckled. 'How series is this crime?'

'Someone has admitted to breaking the Sixth Commandment.'

'Honour thy father and thy mother? I hardly think that's worthy of Harland's time,' Ambrose scoffed, and Julius rolled his eyes.

'That's number five. Number six is "Thou shalt not kill".'

'Oh,' Ambrose said, and nothing more.

The office of Detectives Harland Stone and Gilbert Payne was quiet for 10am in the morning. Both detectives were immersed in administration; Gilbert collated notes to be filed while Harland completed a report for the inspector.

'This is our second Christmas working together, Sir, but I don't recall it being this quiet last year,' Gilbert said. 'I would have thought with the pressure to buy gifts and make the children happy that theft would be on the rise.'

'That is how it was when I was on the beat, Gilbert,' Harland told his protégé. 'As there were more festivities with gathered crowds, there was more pick-pocketing too. Increased alcohol consumption caused more violence, and the season's financial pressures fueled increased theft.'

'Then we best not look a gift horse in the mouth for the current peace,' Gilbert said.

Since their last newsworthy crime—the theft by the vanishing grooms—the detectives worked unsolved cases, and in collaboration with reporter Miss Lilly Lewis, successfully located several missing persons. However, one family was displeased to have their "loved" one returned. Their most reason case unearthed a deceased gentleman wrongly claimed by another family and buried thus, closing that case. Harland was finishing the report on the last case at this very moment.

A knock on the door had both detectives looking up. Sergeant John Henderson from the front desk stood in the doorway. The sergeant managed the constables and community traffic with an efficiency second to none.

'Detectives, there is a gentleman present who claims he may be a witness to a crime. The other detectives are engaged and suggest he be sent your way.'

'As expected, Sergeant, please show him through,' Harland said, knowing laziness was more likely the excuse and the hope to have a break over the coming festive week; Harland did not mind. He turned to Gilbert. 'You never know where our next exciting case may come from, so let us look on this favourably.'

'Yes, Sir,' Gilbert said with a smile.

Moving to the meeting table, Harland greeted the thin, nervous-looking man who arrived at their door in a suit that was also thin and threadbare in sections. The senior detective introduced himself and Gilbert.

'Walter Lomer,' the man said, shaking the offered senior detective's hand. 'I'm sorry to be interrupting you both. I'd be guessing you're busy and all,' he said nervously, twisting his hat in his hand and sitting.

'We're never too busy to speak with members of the public who help us maintain the law, Sir,' Gilbert said earnestly, and Walter nodded his thanks.

'The wife said I should come because I saw something, but it might be nothing. I'm not the type who tells tales, but you know, if it were my girl, I'd want someone to help.'

'Of course, very conscientious of you, Mr Lomer,' Harland said and welcomed the man to be seated. 'Perhaps start at the beginning and tell us what you saw.'

Once the three men were seated, Walter Lomer said, 'Well, I've got a stall at the Christmas market selling my eggs there. The hens have been laying well this year. The wife was with me earlier in the evening, but I sent her home to the children while I packed up at the end of the night.'

'Where are these market, Sir?' Gilbert asked, taking notes.

'Just on the other side of the Victoria Bridge in South Brisbane. When you cross the bridge, you can't miss us.'

'I was there just the other evening,' Harland said, having walked Phoebe home that way and partaken in a little Christmas shopping.

'Right you are then,' Walter said. 'So I was heading home with my horse and cart, with my wares in the back, and I saw in the distance two women walking along. I greeted them as I passed and tipped my hat. One woman was about my age, I'd say, and the other a young lady.'

Harland nodded. 'Had you seen either before?'

'Well, that's the funny thing. I'd seen the younger lady earlier because she bought half a dozen of my eggs for her brother; he was partial to them. A pretty young thing she was too; my wife served her. She had a Christmas bonnet, which she'd decorated herself, or so she told my wife.'

'And what concerns you about the ladies, Mr Lomer?' Gilbert asked.

'Well, the senior woman seemed to grip the arm of the young one rather tightly. I thought at first she was ensuring the young woman did not stray in front of my cart, or maybe the older woman needed help, but she wasn't leaning into her; she was definitely tugging the younger along.'

Harland nodded for Walter Lomer to continue as the visitor hesitated as if reconsidering whether the information was important. 'What has you worried then, Sir?'

Walter exhaled and shook his head. 'Detectives, you could have knocked me down with a feather the next day when I saw in the late edition of the paper that a girl had been killed by a cart along that same street I was travelling.'

'What street was that, Mr Lomer?' Harland asked.

'Stanley Street,' Walter said.

Gilbert scribbled down the details. 'And you think it was her, the younger lady?' he asked, now leaning forward with interest.

'I didn't, but when we went to work that night at the market, everyone was talking about the poor young girl, and someone said, "Walter, she bought some eggs from you. The girl with the Christmas bonnet." Well then, my wife said I had to come because we were wondering when it happened and what of that woman walking with her?'

'Excellent questions, Mr Lomer,' Harland said. 'Our grateful thanks to your wife for encouraging you to come forward and to you for doing so. Where was the pair when you bid them goodnight?'

'I passed them not far from the bridge abutment near John Hunter's Boot Palace.'

'Could you describe the woman she was with?' Harland persisted.

'I can't say I took much notice. She was a head taller than the young lady and a solid woman. She had a dark coat on and a small felt hat with a brooch. I noticed because it caught the light. Her hair was an inch above her shoulders.' He thought for a moment longer. 'Nothing else I can recall.'

'Mr Lomer, you have been of great assistance, and it may be that this young lady did not meet with an accident. We shall investigate.'

'Will you?' Walter looked embarrassed by the detective's praise. 'A cart might have struck her once she parted from her lady friend, and there might be nothing in it.'

'Perhaps,' Harland said, 'but we will make sure that is the case for the sake of the young lady and her family.'

'That's what my wife said,' Walter said, rising and looking relieved to have done his duty.

There were handshakes all round, and Gilbert saw Walter Lomer out of the office and down the hallway to the exit.

Harland donned his jacket and grabbed his hat. On the return of the younger detective, he said, 'Come, Gilbert, a trip to the coroner is in order.'

Chapter 3

IN A LEMON DRESS with a fetching straw hat and matching ribbon, reporter Lilly Lewis stood on tiptoes to look through the square pane of glass in the coroner's door. She could see Dr Tavish McGregor was finishing up. He removed his apron, washed his hands and spoke a few words to his assistant, who would do the clean-up.

Lilly was no stranger to waiting for the coroner. In her former role as a daily writer for the births, marriages and deaths column—also known as Hatches, Matches and Dispatches—she was a regular visitor to the coroner's office in search of a story. Today was no different.

'Ah, my favourite reporter, Miss Lewis,' Tavish said in his Scottish brogue, his eyes lighting up on finding her waiting as he pushed open the door to return to his office. 'And looking resplendent.'

'Just like old times,' she joked. 'Fear not, good doctor; the editor has not relegated me to my old job, but I'm after a story. Even the sniff of a story will do.'

'Come this way then and have a cup of tea with me and I'll see what I can stir up, beside the leaves in the teapot,' he said and Lilly followed him into the next room where the whiskered, jovial doctor preceded to make tea. 'Where is your fellow reporter?'

''Tis the season,' Lilly said as if that would explain everything. 'Mr Cowan, the editor, is taking the holiday season leave as his parents are in town, and Fergus has done the same. He is taking his wife and son on the train to visit his parents in Bundaberg.'

'How exciting! And you are holding the fort?' Tavish did not wait for an answer before adding, 'We too are one of the businesses that do not close for the holidays.'

'At *The Courier*, there are quite a few of us without children that will work the holidays,' Lilly said and thanked him for the cup of tea. They moved to the coroner's small meeting table and sat. 'The acting editor, Mr Faherty, could not be more different from Mr Cowan.'

'Would that be Lionel Faherty?' Tavish asked.

'Yes. You have met him?' Lilly asked, surprised. 'He is not distantly related?' she asked as the thought just occurred to her.

Tavish laughed. 'No, fortunately, I'm not related to every Scotsman in Brisbane. I did, however, meet him at the Scottish club. Straight as an arrow he is.'

Lilly agreed. 'He does not smoke, his desk is clean, everything about him is neat, and he does not waste a word.'

Tavish chuckled at the description as Lilly continued. 'He is happy for the journalists to contribute stories of their own making for the festive week ahead. But there is little to report. Thanks to the detectives, my last story about the missing person buried by the wrong family went down well. I shall visit the detectives after I depart from here and see if they have any interesting deaths on hand.'

'No need, Miss Lewis, we are here,' a voice said behind her, and Lilly spun around to find Detectives Harland Stone and Gilbert Payne entering, hats in hand.

'Gentlemen! Do I have a dead person you are interested in? I have no new arrivals from last evening,' Tavish said, waving the pot at the men. Gilbert declined.

'Is it stewed as your tea normally is?' Harland asked.

'How ungracious,' Tavish rebuked him in jest. 'No, it is only mid-morning. The leaves have barely touched the pot.'

Lilly poured milk into a cup and passed it to Tavish to pour for the senior detective. 'Tell me you might have a crime that I can report, detectives. It would so make my day.'

Gilbert grinned, sitting beside her. 'Possibly so, Miss Lewis. But too early to tell yet.'

'We will soon know, Miss Lewis.' Harland sipped the tea and, appearing satisfied with its taste, asked, 'Tavish, is there a young lady in your rooms that a carriage hit on Stanley Street two nights ago? She had been to the Christmas market.'

'Ah yes, the little brunette with the terrible skull injury, begging your pardon, Miss Lewis,' he added as an afterthought.

'I am sure I have seen and heard worse, Dr McGregor,' Lilly assured him. 'What of her, detectives? Have you suspicions it was not an accident?'

Harland nodded. 'A witness has come forward and claimed to have seen the young woman in the company of another lady, but perhaps not willingly.'

'Ooh, well that changes things a bit, does it not?' Tavish said, rising and going to his files. 'A name?'

'We don't have one, Doctor,' Gilbert said. 'Only a description. Red dress, a bonnet decorated with a Christmas theme.'

'We ran the story in the newspaper,' Lilly said, recalling it, 'and she was unnamed then too.'

'Do not fear, it is a recent case so easy to find, and she has been claimed,' the doctor said, pulling out a file and rejoining them at the table. 'The young lady bought some eggs for her brother. I recall how the eggs were smashed on her pretty red frock, and her hat was crushed. Her brother took the hat home, very sad.' He stopped and skimmed his brief notes. 'Her name was Miss Charity Buckley.'

Lilly reached for her notebook and scribbled the name. 'What did the witness say, detectives?'

Harland gave Lilly a stern look, and she nodded.

'As always, our agreement stands,' she assured him of her discretion. 'I shall seek your permission before I publish my story if you allow me access to your investigation,' she added pleadingly, making the gentlemen present smile at her enthusiasm.

'It has worked well for all of you,' Tavish said. 'Why, you and Detective Payne must be the most celebrated detectives in town, and Miss Lewis has earned herself the title of one of the newspaper's best reporters.'

'We certainly received our share of Christmas gifts,' Gilbert agreed with a smile.

'All right then,' Harland agreed, as he always did after playing tough for a short while. 'I will speak with the girl's brother today, so you may publish this, Miss Lewis. A witness claimed to have seen Miss...' he hesitated.

'Buckley, Charity Buckley,' Gilbert said before the coroner could.

Harland nodded and continued, 'a witness saw Miss Buckley walking along the road with a woman who was holding the young lady's arm most forcefully. The other woman was older, middle-aged perhaps, and sturdy. What did you make of Miss Buckley's injury, Tavish?'

'As the constable who delivered Miss Buckley to me said she was found on the street and had been struck by a horse and carriage, I did not do an extensive study of her. Had they said they were unsure of her cause of death, I would have been more thorough,' Tavish said with frustration.

'Could you take another look for us?' Harland asked.

'Indeed, but she is with *The Economic Undertaker.* Ambrose collected her yesterday.'

Harland gulped his tea in one mouthful. 'We are off there, then. Let us hope she has not already been buried.'

Lilly leapt to her feet at the same time as the detectives. 'May I come, Detectives?'

'Could we stop you, Miss Lewis?' Harland teased.

'Get Ambrose to bring her back if need be,' Tavish called after them, as Lilly thanked the doctor for the cup of tea, bid him a quick farewell and hurried onward, a potential story calling her name.

Mrs Violet Astin bid two customers farewell and, while loitering near the door, decided to restock the stand of black umbrellas. She glanced next door, where mourners were arriving at *The Economic Undertaker* for a viewing. As the manageress of *Beyond the Veil*—a dress store that catered for brides and the mourning—and as the enviable wife of Mr Julius Astin, life had changed greatly for Violet since Julius and Ambrose had arrived on her humble doorstep to bury her grandmother. She was now married and in the family way, managing a store, and her brother was apprenticed to Julius's cousin, Lucian – life was settled and happy.

'Those umbrellas have been walking out the door faster than we can restock them,' senior dressmaker, Mrs Nellie Shaw said as Violet opened a box and removed another batch. 'This dreadful heat. So uncomfortable for a woman in your condition, Violet.'

'I think doing the midnight change or feed in the cold of winter will be worse,' Violet said, expecting the next generation of Astin any day now. She had not told Julius of her pregnancy until she was well along, at least ten weeks. Her mother had herself and Tom, but lost every child thereafter in the early days, and Violet feared raising Julius's hopes or making him anxious before she was sure a little one was on the way. Nellie Shaw had known right away.

'There are quite a lot of people arriving for the viewing,' Miss Mary Pollard, the talented young dressmaker who made Violet's wedding dress on display in the window, piped up from her seat with a view of all the comings-and-goings on the street.

'Half of them will most likely drop in for umbrellas after the viewing on their way to the funeral,' Nellie said. 'Let's hope we don't have a rush of in-house clients at the same time.'

The newest appointment to *Beyond the Veil*, Mrs Jane Moss, a young widow with unruly red hair, a full figure and impressive ability as a seamstress, looked up from her hemming. 'We have two ladies booked for fittings in thirty minutes. Mrs Shaw and I will be unavailable to serve while they are here.'

'Don't you fret, Jane,' Nellie Shaw assured her. 'We'll manage.'

'Of course we will,' Violet said, sure the business would be in expert hands in her absence with calm Mrs Shaw as manageress. She continued, 'Mary and I will have the clients equipped and out the door before you can say, "Shade anyone?" but not that quick that they don't notice Mary's designs in the window.'

Mary blushed with pleasure. 'Oh, the hearse is back; it is just turning into the backyard now,' she announced and then gave a small laugh, knowing what was to come.

'Uh oh,' Violet said, returning to her desk, and the ladies laughed. 'Prepare yourselves, ladies.'

As expected, shortly thereafter the back door opened and Julius peered in.

'It is all clear for the moment, Mr Astin,' Mrs Shaw assured him.

'Thank you, Mrs Shaw, and good morning to you, and Miss Pollard, Mrs Moss and my dear,' he said, finishing with Violet, and studying her with a look of concern upon his countenance.

'So romantic,' Mary said, blushing by the window.

'Should you be working in this heat, Violet?' he frowned, removing his own hat and wiping his brow with a white handkerchief.

'I think you will agree it is quite cool in here,' Violet assured him. 'You, on the other hand, must be terribly uncomfortable.'

'Ambrose has asked the good father to organise cloud cover for the next funeral,' Julius said and made the ladies laugh. 'How are you feeling?'

'Fine. We are all well today.' She saw his expression and humoured her husband. 'It is better for me to be here than at home alone, and Nellie is ready to step up at any moment.'

'I am, do not worry, Mr Astin,' Mrs Shaw assured him. 'We will ring the bell out the back the moment Violet feels the need to return home, and I will accompany her. Mary will go for the midwife, Charlie has the cart prepared, and no one will use the covered one so it is in place and ready. If you are at a funeral, Will or Claude will come for you, unless they are on leave and then Mr Astin senior will come for you,' she said reciting the drill that had been reinforced every day, sometimes twice for the last month or so.

'And if there are customers in the store, we shall fling them out of the way,' Violet added cheekily.

'Mary, Jane and I will do the flinging though, do not be concerned, Mr Astin,' Mrs Shaw teased him.

Julius looked a little sheepish. 'Thank you, Mrs Shaw. That is a great consolation. Do go easy on the customers though,' he added with a small smile.

'The detectives are here,' Mary announced, and Julius glanced at the window.

'I best go then; I have a message for Harland.' He looked at Violet, who shooed him from the store.

'You have seen me now, and I promise you we have not forgotten what you have put in place, dear husband. Make sure you and Ambrose do not suffer heatstroke.'

'We will be fine,' he said and kissed her hand before departing, leaving Mary sighing, Jane in love with the tall, dark, handsome proprietor, and Nellie and Violet exchanging amused looks.

'I wonder what the message is about,' Violet mused. 'A crime afoot, I imagine,' she said casually as if *The Economic Undertaker* worked hand in hand with the detectives, and in many cases, the staff did just that.

Chapter 4

IT WAS NEARING ELEVEN-FORTY, and the viewing of the deceased Miss Charity Buckley at *The Economic Undertaker* was well underway, to be followed by a three o'clock funeral. The many attendees included her acquaintances from church, her charity work and school companions, as well as those paying respect to her brother, Mr Earnest Buckley. The mourners had been well spaced across the hour, with more still arriving.

'Please come in. Our sincere condolences, allow me to show you through.' Debonair frontman Randolph Astin, grandfather to Julius, Ambrose and Phoebe, and business manager, coordinated the comings-and-goings in the calm manner in which he dealt with the distraught customers he sold funeral packages to daily. He was the perfect host in troubled times – mature, dignified and sincere.

'Good morning, please accept our sincere condolences. The room to your right, if you will,' he said, greeting two arrivals and then held the door open for two young ladies departing. 'Thank you, ladies.'

Those attending Miss Charity Buckley's viewing were directed into one of the new viewing rooms, previously part of the mourning wear shop, until Julius leased the neighbouring business and expanded *The Economic Undertaker* to meet the increased demand for earlier collection and out-of-home viewings of the deceased.

'Good morning. No appointment? That is of no consequence. I am very sorry for your loss. Would you care to come this way?' he said, directing a teary young couple into a small meeting room and promising to join them promptly. 'I will fetch a cup of tea for you both,' he said by way of excuse to allow him a few minutes' grace.

'I have them, Mr Astin, I will be right there,' Mrs Dobbs said, nodding towards the meeting room. She passed him with a fresh pot of tea and entered the extension to the viewing room to refresh guests who had finished their viewing and were not too distraught to enjoy a cup of tea and the treats that were now part of the funeral viewing and refreshment package for customers.

At the sound of the back door opening, Randolph turned and signalled to Ambrose, warning his noisiest grandson that clients were in-house. 'Hurry and freshen up, I may need help,' Randolph said quietly. 'Where is Julius?'

'Checking Violet hasn't delivered in his absence,' Ambrose said with a flash of a smile and a roll of his eyes. 'I'll be with you in a moment, Grandpa.'

The front door opened again, and Randolph turned and welcomed the mourners, directing them to Charity Buckley's viewing. Given the number of people in the house, the rooms were surprisingly quiet; a dignified low hum of voices provided a comforting din.

Randolph glanced toward the meeting room and saw Mrs Dobbs taking in tea and cake to the young couple. That would give him a few more minutes. The front door opened again, and before he could offer condolences, the detectives entered, removing their hats. They had visited *The Economic Undertaker* on enough occasions to know to enter silently, and as mourners arrived behind them, Gilbert held the door open.

'Please come in. To your left, ladies and gentlemen, for Miss Buckley's viewing,' Randolph said warmly. He turned to Harland Stone and Gilbert Payne. 'Detectives, how might we assist you this morning?' he said quietly and calmly. 'Phoebe is downstairs if you need her.'

'Thank you, Mr Astin, but no,' Harland said. 'We wish to see Miss Charity Buckley's body before her burial.'

'Oh,' Randolph said, surprised, with a look to the busy room nearby. 'Of course. The viewing will finish in twenty minutes. Can you wait until then?'

'Certainly, but if we believe the coroner needs to view her remains, we may have to cancel the funeral, Mr Astin,' he said apologetically.

Randolph gave Harland a raised eyebrow... an expression his grandsons knew well from their youth, often signaling a need for explanation in relation to their behaviour. Then he smiled. 'You are creating paperwork for me, Detective.'

'We might have her to the coroner and back before the funeral, depending on the timing,' Gilbert suggested, and Harland agreed with a smile to Randolph, and then remembered where he was and quickly sobered.

'It's a three o'clock funeral, so that will put the coroner through his paces,' Randolph said, and several young people walked past, thanked Randolph and departed.

Once the door closed, Harland asked, 'Is it possible to request Miss Buckley's next of kin remain after the viewing so we may have a word with them?'

'I believe her parents are deceased, Detective. It is her brother who is responsible for the viewing and burial. I shall ask Mr Buckley to remain.'

'Thank you, and may we wait downstairs with Phoebe until then?' the senior detective asked.

'Of course.' The door opened. 'Good morning, please enter and to your right for Miss Buckley's viewing,' Randolph said with a glance at the clock.

The rush of air up the hallway told them someone had opened the back door, and then, Julius entered. He did not need to be warned that customers were in-house and soon approached the group quietly.

'Detectives,' he said with a smile and a nod. 'I need to speak with you both, but do you need help, Grandpa?'

'Yes, but Ambrose will be here momentarily. Ah, here he is now,' Randolph said. 'Ambrose, will you finish the viewing, please? I am not expecting too many more now; it finishes in a quarter of an hour. Will you notify the detectives as soon as the mourners have departed and ask Mr Buckley, the deceased's brother, to remain to speak with the detectives? I have unexpected in-house clients.'

'Done,' Ambrose said, moving towards the room where guests milled around, but remaining near the door to greet or farewell mourners. Mrs Dobbs passed with the teapot and empty plates, and Randolph said, knowing Julius was a stickler for routine, 'Lad, go wash up. Detectives, if you will head downstairs, Julius can meet you there.' With that, he took a breath, put his shoulders back and entered the small meeting room ready to sell a package.

Phoebe could hear all the movement upstairs, the opening and closing of the door, her grandfather's well-modulated tones, the footsteps from the kitchen to the viewing room as Mrs Dobbs cared for the bereaved, and the number of feet circling around the body of Miss Charity Buckley resting in her last hours above ground. She was pleased to be downstairs, away from it, although she listened for the small bell on the front desk signalling help was needed upstairs.

The gentleman lying on her table was elderly, but he looked older in death than he did in life. She knew this as Mr Harold Grindley, aged 71, sat beside her as she worked.

'It sounds as if you have had a good life,' Mr Grindley,' Phoebe said, smiling. 'Although I suspect from what you say that you are the type of gent who can make the best of any situation.'

'Ah, thank you, dear heart. It has been a grand life. I've had my trials, but haven't we all? But to get to my age, that's a fine innings.'

Phoebe laughed. 'Indeed. Are you looking forward to the reunion with your loved ones?'

'Oh, I cannot wait to go through the pearly gates. As soon as I am in the ground, I'll have my arms opened wide to hug them all, assuming I'm going in the right direction,' he said with a wink and smile, pointing to heaven.

'I've no doubt. But I shall say a little prayer for you anyway,' Phoebe teased. 'How is that, Mr Grindley? Is that how you like your hair parted?'

He rose to look at himself and smiled. 'You have me looking most handsome. I barely recognise myself. Thank you, Miss Astin.'

'Thank you, Mr Grindley. It has been a pleasure.'

'The pleasure is all mine,' he said, gave a small bow and then quickly disappeared as the sound of footsteps had Phoebe looking to the stairs. She carefully covered Mr Grindley in case some mourners at the viewing had inadvertently made their way downstairs, but on looking up she saw the handsome face of her beau, Detective Harland Stone, and the kind smiling Detective Gilbert Payne in close pursuit.

'Harland! Detective Payne, this is a lovely surprise,' she said, moving to greet them. 'And I didn't even request your presence.'

'I have been missing your summonses,' Harland teased, greeting her with a kiss to the hand, as Gilbert coloured slightly. Harland rarely showed affection in public, and not while on the job.

'He has forgotten himself,' Phoebe said to Gilbert, making both gentlemen laugh. 'Your openness is working wonders with him, Detective Payne.' Harland cleared his throat awkwardly.

'Oh, I cannot take credit for that, Miss Astin,' Gilbert said. 'But I endeavour to remain true to myself, and my mother always says life is short; do not miss the chance to appreciate those we favour.'

'A wise woman,' Phoebe said. 'I believe Emily is quite taken with Mrs Payne,' she said of her dear friend, fellow *Vexed Vixen* and Gilbert's belle.

Julius came down the stairs looking slightly damp from his wash up and greeted his sister and the detectives again.

'I'm glad I caught you, detectives. I have a message for you from Father Taylor of St Mary's Parish, South Brisbane,' he said.

Phoebe laughed. 'A message from Father Taylor? Oh dear, what have you done?' she asked Harland.

'Nothing, I assure you. I don't even know Father Taylor. Perhaps he's decided to pray for my soul.'

'The earlier he starts, the better,' Julius quipped, ribbing his friend as he pulled a note from his suit. 'He asked me to give you this. It was left on his chair in the confessional, and he did not see by whom, nor was there anyone in the church that he believed would have written such a message.'

Harland read it aloud.

'Forgive me, Father, for I have sinned.
She broke the fifth, and I broke the sixth. She was deserving,
and I will do so again.
No one escapes divine retribution.'

The senior detective looked to his partner, Gilbert, a God-fearing young man, and Gilbert responded, 'The sixth commandment, Sir, in Exodus, King James version is "Thou shalt not kill". Most worrying. Although the more accurate translation from the original Hebrew is, "Thou shalt not murder".'

'How intriguing,' Phoebe said.

Harland agreed and stored away Gilbert's distinction of the two. He never knew when his protégé's observations might prove useful, and many had in the past.

'Where is this victim then, I wonder,' Gilbert mused. 'Perhaps one of the other detectives is on the case.'

'Upon our return to headquarters, we will check whether there have been any recent slayings that might fit the description,' Harland concluded, pocketing the note.

Julius nodded. 'Father Taylor doesn't expect there is much you can do with that, but thought it best you have it.'

'If we are near St Mary's, I'll call on the priest,' Harland thanked Julius. 'To the business at hand. I'm afraid we have a witness who believes Miss Charity Buckley might have met foul play.'

Phoebe gasped. 'Miss Buckley, who is currently having her viewing? Oh, how awful!'

'You are going to cancel the funeral this afternoon, aren't you?' Julius asked drily, and Harland gave a huff of laughter.

'I thought you would be happy not to have a funeral in this heat?'

'You are delaying the inevitable,' Julius said, 'and creating paperwork for us. But never let it be said we stood in the way of justice.'

'A fine citizen you are, Julius,' Harland tapped him on the back. 'If we can see Miss Buckley as soon as her viewing is over, Gilbert and I might determine if the wound warrants the coroner having a look.'

'And we promised Mr Astin senior that should we need to remove Miss Buckley, we would try to get the coroner to prioritise his study of the body and return it before the three o'clock funeral,' Gilbert assured Julius.

'We will need to collect it no later than two o'clock in order to get to the cemetery,' Julius glanced at the clock.

'Consider it done, assuming Tavish is there,' Harland said and then turned to Phoebe, speaking quietly. 'You did not have a visitation from Miss Charity Buckley?'

'No, but I cleaned her wound as best I could, and covered it with the cape. I may have ruined your evidence.'

'Miss Astin, you are amazing to be so brave,' Gilbert said in awe.

'Thank you, Detective, but it was not too distressing.'

'Can you describe what you saw before cleaning, Phoebe?' Harland asked, and the lady mortician nodded.

'The injury was on the right side of her head, at the back,' she showed the area, touching her own head. 'It felt slightly caved in, but not shattered as one might expect if the wheels of a carriage or a horse's hoof had made contact.'

Phoebe avoided looking at Julius; their parents' death had been by horse and cart, and Julius had been a witness at fourteen. He did not welcome sympathy.

'In those cases, often a viewing is out of the question,' Julius said.

'I wonder she did not tell you of her death if it were brutal,' Harland said.

Phoebe shook her head and, keeping her voice low, said, 'Not all who have met a terrible end appear to me. Some are pleased to leave their violent death and their former life behind; others remain at the site of their death until their soul is at rest.'

'Is that so?' Gilbert asked, fascinated. 'So there may be some truth in sights being haunted.'

Phoebe nodded.

'If need be, might you accompany us to the site then, Phoebe?' Harland asked, looking between Phoebe and Julius.

Julius held up his hands. 'That is Phoebe's decision; I know my place,' he said with a wink at her, having recently redefined their relationship.

She grabbed his hand and squeezed it before looking back at the detectives. 'If I can be of assistance, I will be happy to do so.'

'We shall be mindful of your safety, Miss Astin,' Gilbert assured her.

'I was never in any doubt, thank you, Detective Payne,' she said, smiling at the kindly detective.

With that, the clock chimed, marking the hour and the end of the viewing session. Phoebe bid the detectives goodbye as Julius offered to escort them upstairs to meet the deceased's brother and see Charity Buckley's body for themselves.

Chapter 5

THE DETECTIVES HAD HITCHED a ride to the morgue in the trap with Claude and the body of Miss Charity Buckley in the back, fresh from its viewing. While there, Claude collected a body for *The Economic Undertaker*, and returned, leaving the detectives to wheel the body to the coroner and beg for his earliest intervention.

To Harland's relief, Tavish was finishing an autopsy and fifteen minutes later, leaving his assistant to tidy up, he promoted their case over his other clients.

'They are not going anywhere,' Tavish said jovially as he retrieved the slim piece of paper—the police report—that recorded the death of Miss Charity Buckley, and allocated it to its own folder.

'What have we here then, young lady?' he said, as Harland and Gilbert stood nearby, hats in hands, patiently waiting.

Ten minutes later, Tavish looked up from inspecting the wound. 'You can let Julius know he may have the body in time for her funeral.'

The detectives exchanged relieved looks, and Harland dispatched his protégé to *The Economic Undertaker* to advise collection in an hour would be possible.

Harland turned his back as Tavish removed the clothing the young lady wore that she was to be buried in that day, and pulled a sheet over her. 'Miss Astin did a lovely job with her presentation.'

'She is the best and very considerate of her subjects,' Harland agreed, not seeing the small smile on Tavish's face at the expected praise.

'You may join me now,' Tavish said, and adjusting the sheet as required, proceeded to study Miss Buckley's head and body and make brief notes; Harland observed Tavish and his reactions. Occasionally, the coroner made a knowing sound or a small humph of surprise and then, in under thirty minutes, announced, 'I shall dress the lady ready for collection and tell you my thoughts.'

'Thank you for this, Tavish. I owe you a favour,' Harland said, turning again, allowing the deceased her modesty. A glance at the large clock on the wall told the detective there were fifteen minutes to spare; Julius should arrive any minute.

'Excellent. I will think of a way to draw on that favour,' Tavish teased. 'You may turn now; she is dressed. Well then, Harland, I believe you have a new case.'

Harland groaned. 'Better we find out now than when she is in the grave and has to be exhumed. What have you got, Tavish?'

'There is no evidence of death by being struck by a horse and cart. There is evidence of a skull injury – a depressed fracture where the skull indents inwards from being struck. A horse and cart would have caused bruising to the neck and arms, swelling, scalp wounds including cuts and grazes, fluid leakage from the nose or ears, and much more damage than the clean wound to the back of her head.'

'Could she have fallen and hit her head, thus her death may still have been an accident?' Harland asked.

'In this case, I don't believe so. The wound that caused her death is a very distinctive shape, and if a fatal fall resulted in her lying dead on the street, there would be more abrasions.'

'It appears then that we have a murderer at large,' Harland concluded, and Tavish nodded.

Gilbert re-entered with Julius to hear Harland's last words and inhaled sharply. 'Mr Walter Lomer, the witness was right!'

'Julius, Detective Payne,' Tavish greeted them. 'It appears the young lady died of a blow to the head with a sharp, heavy object. The shape is of a small square with sharp edges. I cannot think of anything like it, but I will ponder it. You may take her, Julius, and make your funeral on time.'

'Thank you, Julius,' Harland said. 'I'm glad we didn't have to let the family and mourners down.'

'As am I,' Julius said, and in haste, wheeled the covered body to the door. 'I'll leave the trolley with your staff, Tavish. Good day, gentlemen. Oh, by the way, Miss Lewis has just arrived. I suspect she'll be in shortly for her story,' he warned them.

'I expected nothing less. Tonight at the club?' Harland asked before Julius exited with his charge. 'The ladies have their *Vexed Vixen* gathering.'

'See you there,' Julius agreed, hurriedly departing to the hearse where Ambrose awaited.

'The object... how large?' Harland asked, returning to the case at hand.

'Small but with weight and sharp edges. I would surmise similar to the end of a walking cane perhaps, but it is square,' Tavish said, and the two detectives considered this. 'Did you mention to the family at the viewing that her death might have resulted from foul play?'

'There is only a brother,' Gilbert said, 'but we decided if we could get you to see the body, Doctor McGregor, without disrupting the funeral, we would not inflict the trauma of his sister possibly being murdered on him today.'

Harland agreed. 'We had a word with him enquiring about his sister's movements that day, but he was too distraught to assist. It will wait until tomorrow for the poor fellow.' He glanced at the clock. 'We had best go to a funeral then. You never know who might appear to see the young lady into the grave.'

The door swung open. 'Is it murder then, detectives? Can I come to the funeral?'

Tavish laughed, Harland sighed and Gilbert greeted reporter Lilly Lewis, suggesting she come along as he was about to hail a hansom for their journey.

In the five months since he began courting Miss Billie Prout, who refused to answer to Willamina, Ambrose Astin, second-born and middle child, felt as if he were number one, at last. She sought his opinion, cherished his company, and he had someone he could call his own.

Billie's sassy attitude, constant energy and ambition kept him on his toes. He had never experienced a relationship like it before, certainly not with his former belle, Kate. But he imagined that was what life was like with Miss Lilly Lewis – his unrequited love who was now paired with the private investigator, artist, and Julius's close friend, Bennet Martin.

Having hurriedly loaded and secured Miss Buckley into the coffin in the back of the hearse after collecting her from the coroner's rooms at the morgue, the Astin brothers made their way to St Patrick's for the early afternoon funeral. Ambrose marvelled at how Julius could go from rushing to driving the hearse at its customary slow pace, as the pair acknowledged those who stopped to allow the hearse and its passenger to pass.

Julius said, 'It would be nice to have a small break at Christmas, but death has no manners.'

Ambrose gave a low chuckle, knowing better than to smile or laugh out loud while riding in the mourning vehicle. 'I appreciate the days off you offered me, but why did you not take them for yourself?'

Julius gave a shake of his head. 'It is a nice reward for your efforts and those of Will and Claude. Grandpa is happy to work since our aunt is visiting, and Violet does not want to be at home in the heat waiting to deliver, so will provide any required mourning wear with the help of the ladies. They were all reluctant to take time off for their own reasons. Charlie and

I will manage, and Phoebe is happy to work given Harland will do so. Is Miss Prout in the office?'

'Ah, Billie. Prout Monumental Masons will have a sales team working only. Headstone placement can wait until after Christmas, so she will take the same days off as me.' He cleared his throat slightly as if to announce something important. He said seriously, 'We have been speaking about the future.'

'That's promising,' Julius said and glanced at Ambrose. 'Isn't it?'

'Absolutely. One day, Billie will inherit the business as she has no brothers to contend with and she is a formidable part of the business already.' Before Ambrose could elaborate, Julius sighed.

'Of course I knew the day would come, but I always hoped our sons and daughters might run our business together. A silly daydream, but it is a family business. Naturally, you will move into the Prout business if you are wed.'

'No,' Ambrose said with a shake of his head. 'I don't wish to do that.'

'You don't?' Julius exclaimed, surprised. So surprised that he even smiled with relief.

'Do not smile while we are in the hearse, please, Brother. We are professional funeral directors,' Ambrose nudged him, firing back the reprimand he heard often.

'Right you are, Brother,' Julius agreed, pleased. 'Remiss of me. Tell me then, quickly before we arrive, what is your plan.'

'Do I have you curious now?'

'Absolutely. In a matter of minutes, I have gone from losing you to having my dream still a reality.'

'It is a lovely dream,' Ambrose said sincerely. 'Well, Billie and I thought down the track when we wed, which is inevitable,' he boasted, and Julius gave him an encouraging nod, 'that we would absorb Prout Monumental Masons into *The Economic Undertaker*. It would remain Prout by name, but if the office could be next door, for example, and we sold only Prout products, then we would have a dedicated market and all aspects of the funeral business covered.'

'Yes! Viewing, coffins, burial, mourning clothes, headstones,' Julius said. 'Brilliant.'

'Yes, we are,' Ambrose agreed smugly and continued, 'It would eliminate one of our roles too. Currently, Grandpa sells the headstones through catalogues. Now, he need only direct them next door, or call in a Prout Monumental salesperson to the initial meeting, or, as Billie suggested, have a package that includes the funeral, a standard coffin and headstone or several to choose from in that package.'

'That is an excellent idea,' Julius said, inspired. 'Would Prout Monumental Masons still sell to other competitors?'

'We discussed that, and Billie believes there is no reason not to do so, but she thinks business will eventually drop off and won't be worth their while to pursue.'

'Yes, and that may happen as loyalties re-align,' Julius said. 'Once people realise how easy it is to use our services, since we provide everything in one place, the future of the business for our children looks very promising,' Julius stated, relieved and excited.

'That is what Billie said. During grief, the simpler the process, the better for the bereaved. She is like you, brother, with her astute business mind; I fear what the two of you might come up with when put together.'

Julius accepted the compliment, thanking his brother. 'I confess, I thought you might go the way of Uncle Reggie.'

'You have said that before, that I could leave the family for love, but you don't know the depth of my loyalty,' Ambrose said.

Julius steered the horses and hearse toward the cemetery gates, setting aside the emotionally intense discussion between the two brothers, as they approached the gathered mourners.

'Are there any ghosts near the gate?' Ambrose teased his brother and saw Julius's droll expression as they drove through.

'You persist in trying to find out if I see spirits or not; are you not bored by the query yet?'

'No. Because I know you can, and you won't trust me to say so. I will not tell a soul. Not my belle, nor will I discuss it with family members unless you raise it yourself. But you can, can't you, see them?'

They neared the plot that waited for its new inhabitant, with the priest standing nearby to smooth Miss Buckley's entry from this world to the next.

Ambrose never expected Julius to respond in the affirmative; he never had before when Ambrose posed the same question, almost weekly. But whether it was Ambrose's new commitment to the family, his recent maturity, or the prospect of him honouring the business, Julius relented and turned to him.

'Can you see that young lady standing by the graveside in the cream dress with the Christmas bonnet?'

Ambrose looked around. 'No. Where? Near the gravesite we are to arrive at?'

'Yes.'

'There is no one there,' Ambrose said, squinting as the light through the trees temporarily blinded them driving forward.

'Then that should answer your question.'

Ambrose inhaled sharply, smiled and quickly sobered.

'Thank you, Julius.'

'Not a word, Brother,' Julius warned.

And bringing the hearse to a stop, the brothers alighted to bury Miss Charity Buckley, whose spirit stood graveside as if a guest at her own funeral.

Chapter 6

THE INVITING GLOW OF the many evening lanterns added to the picturesque atmosphere of the popular Christmas markets. Despite the warm night, an intrepid fellow paraded as Santa Claus in full costume, carolers sang in harmony, children dodged between the adults in games of chase, and table upon table featured gifts and sweets for purchase.

'I love this time of the year,' Phoebe said, her face aglow with excitement, and her red dress most fitting for the Christmas theme.

'We should come again when we have more time,' Harland said, conscious of the fact Phoebe was due at the *Vexed Vixens* dinner in under an hour. 'On our last visit, we spent little time exploring.'

'And as a consequence spent little money, so that's probably a good thing,' she added with a small laugh. 'Aren't the trees beautiful?' she proclaimed at the perfectly decorated large trees on display. 'One day I shall have my own home, and I will show no restraint when it comes to Christmas decorations.'

'I hope that will be my home too,' Harland said, making her blush. 'I can see myself being bossed around as I haul a tree in through the front door and standing on the ladder a hundred times to put up your decorations.'

She grinned and cocked her head to the side. 'And will you do so willingly?'

'Of course. I'm quite adept at handyman tasks and very good at following orders. I can give you references.'

She hit his arm playfully. 'I will call on those when needed, thank you.' Phoebe took a deep breath and straightened. 'To work then.'

'Best we do. The witness saw Miss Buckley heading down a laneway. We shall walk down it and see if she appears to you. If not, we'll hail a hansom at the end of the lane, and I'll drop you at your dinner and head on to the club.'

Agreeing, Phoebe linked arms with Harland and allowed him to escort her to the laneway between two busy streets. There was reasonable foot traffic in the lane as the market was in full swing; traders were coming and going with their wares, and visitors took a shortcut to the major streets. Several residences above the shops also had their entrances on the smaller streets, and occasionally, what appeared to be a hole in the wall would open and someone would scurry in or out.

'Do you know what time Miss Buckley traversed this lane? It seems very busy. Surely someone saw her beside the one witness,' Phoebe said.

'I believe it was nearing nine o'clock. The market was closing for the night, and the noise and traffic had diminished. Miss Buckley was on her way home, and must have cut down this lane... unless the woman walking with her coerced her along this way.'

Phoebe gave a little shudder. 'How frightening.'

They walked on to the end of the lane, and Phoebe could feel Harland watching her, hoping she could help him, help Miss Buckley. 'Can you see that lady in the green dress?'

'Yes,' Harland said, and Phoebe laughed.

'And the one near the corner in the red gown with the Christmas bauble?'

'Yes,' he said again and grinned.

'Sometimes, I can't tell,' she confessed. 'I've actually spoken with a live person waiting in my room on one occasion, believing them to be dead. Luckily, I found out before I asked whether their body was on the way. Grandpa got into trouble that day for sending her to my room without an introduction.'

Harland laughed heartily at the concept, and Phoebe did not admit that Julius had seen Miss Buckley graveside at the funeral. She had not appeared to Phoebe yet.

They walked on to the end of the lane, and turned, traversing the lane two more times before Phoebe declared, 'I am sorry, Harland. She is not here now. It may be too early or busy, or perhaps she does not want to linger where she died.'

'It was worth a try, thank you, Phoebe. Let's hail a cab, and I shall see you delivered safely to Julius's place. I don't want the *Vexed Vixens* to be vexed at me for making you late.'

As the hansom cab approached, Phoebe said quietly, 'That time has passed now; your loved ones are waiting for you past the white light. Go through and go to your rest.'

Harland snapped to look at her before handing her into the cab. He gave the driver Julius's address.

'What just happened?'

'A young boy looking for his parents. I could tell from his clothing that his parents would be long gone. They may have died from smallpox or dysentery, and he was separated from them. He has gone to the other side now.'

'Then the trip was worthwhile,' Harland said, holding her hand as they sat close to each other.

'Yes,' Phoebe smiled at him, grateful for his understanding. 'Yes, indeed, it was.'

Violet welcomed the *Vexed Vixens* as they kissed each other hello, removed their hats, and moved to the dining room to be seated. Each agreed that Violet should not have taken on hosting duties in her current condition.

'Truly, I have done nothing. Our dear cook prepared the meal, Julius and Tom happily vacated and offered to clear away the dishes on their return, and I am in the comfort of my home. Although I am sure your fat friend could pass for Father Christmas at the moment,' she said, rubbing her large body.

'You look gorgeous,' Phoebe said, sitting beside Violet. 'Julius is beside himself with worry and happiness in equal measure.'

'Understandably,' Lilly said. 'And, as I believe I am the fleetest of foot here tonight, I shall take the seat closest to the door in case I need to run for the midwife.'

'What, pray tell, makes you the fastest?' Emily asked jokingly. 'I have very long legs and would like to challenge that notion.'

'I have pursued stories, detectives, and interview subjects at an undignified pace,' Lilly boasted. 'I have even lifted my skirts to run!'

'Straight to the *Miss Emily Yalden School of Deportment* for you, Lilly Lewis,' Billie Prout declared, sitting beside Emily. She fitted in very well in the company of the other *Vexed Vixens*, having joined the group a few months past.

'I appreciate the vote of confidence, Billie, but even I have my limitations,' Emily sighed, earning another round of laughs.

'Which is as good an opener as any for our vexed stories, thank you, Emily,' Violet said. 'Now, while we all serve ourselves, I shall, if you will permit me as the hostess, start, so you can all have a few bites before it is your turn to vex.'

'Thank you, I'm starving,' Lilly said, needing no invitation to begin. 'My appetite mortifies my mother, and she believes Bennet will leave me if I reveal my true self to him before marriage.' She shook her head.

'Has he seen your appetite?' Phoebe asked.

'Absolutely. When we go to dinner, he has the bill to prove it,' she said, amusing the ladies. 'Violet, do go ahead. I shall be quiet and eat this splendid spread.'

'Thank you, Lilly. You'll be pleased to know that I won't bore you with complaints about the heat and my expansion. I am, however, vexed with Julius.'

'No!' Phoebe proclaimed. 'Is not my brother perfect?' she teased.

'I am glad I am sitting,' Billie said, 'because I might have fallen over with the shock. Ambrose is always quoting his brother as if his words are gospel.'

'Let's brace ourselves then,' Emily said, nudging Violet playfully. 'What has he done?'

Violet took a deep breath. 'I am no stranger to Julius's thoroughness.' She could see the small smiles appearing on the ladies' faces and the exchange of glances. 'It is why the business has been so successful and why the ideas we created on our honeymoon were enacted with great efficiency. Now, I am sure he could do the job of the midwife.'

Phoebe could not hold back her amusement, and the other girls did their best to mask it as Violet continued. 'He has done so much research into what I am going through and what to expect in the first year of our child that there will be nothing left to chance or surprise. I cannot say anything without him quipping in, "I believe that is natural" or "It is to be expected",' she said, imitating his deep voice. Violet could no longer keep a straight face as the ladies laughed with merriment.

'Oh, Julius,' Phoebe said between huffs of laughter.

'Don't get me wrong,' Violet said, 'I am very grateful that he is so concerned and interested, and not one of those husbands who will abandon me to have this child. But I just hope something takes him by surprise, and I do not explode at the display of his knowledge bank when tired or pained.'

'Of course there is still one enormous surprise to come,' Billie declared, 'the sex of your child!'

'True!' Violet said, pleased at the notion. 'After that, I am sure he can answer any questions we have about what to expect.'

'Oh, bless him,' Lilly pronounced. 'From what my mother says about raising the six of us, nothing was ever predictable. I think he is in for a rude shock, Violet.'

'He is adept at managing challenges,' Phoebe said but then smiled, 'I cannot wait to see how he manages his firstborn, and to meet my new niece or nephew. Am I allowed to tease him a little about his preparedness?'

'I think you best please, Phoebe, or I may offend if I berate him,' Violet said with a laugh born of frustration. 'I have tried gently, but it only served to make him more determined, and I am sure it is making him anxious.'

'Most likely, as we business people can be rather focussed on planning,' Emily said. 'But some things are out of our control.'

'Well, thank you, ladies; that is my vexation. As I am large and irritable, and the heat is not my friend, I have many minor vexations and could claim the prize of most vexed this month in our group. I am unbearably nitpicky. I promise it shall pass when I have full possession of my body again and when the weather cools.'

'Oh, do go on, Violet,' Emily encouraged her. 'Share a few of your minor vexations so I don't feel as if I am always complaining needlessly about my students. We are, after all, the *Vexed Vixens* and are entitled to a good whine in each other's company.'

'You will feel better for it,' Billie agreed. 'I have nothing to complain about this month, so you can have my share of vexation space.'

Violet laughed at the thought, as if there were only so much space in the room for each lady's complaints. 'I shall then, but do not think poorly of me,' she agreed with a smile. 'Everything bothers me, like our new dressmaker, the widowed Mrs Jane Moss, who has red hair and freckles, and constantly forgets to wear her hat and then complains of having freckles.' Violet gave a shake of her head.

'She sounds like me,' Lilly said. 'I will do better.'

'Mind you do,' Violet teased. 'Then, every single lady who has given birth must tell me her story and the dreadful long labour she endured. My brother, Tom, has kindly made a beautiful cradle and high chair at his place of business, but my sheer joy at his work seems to have tipped him over the edge; it appears anything that can be made from wood for a child is finding its way home. I have no room left for the baby.'

Again, Violet had to stop until the ladies finished with their laughter and comments.

'To finish,' Violet said, 'I almost booted a customer out of the store just the other day as she wanted her mourning dress nipped in to be more flattering. Good grief, her husband is not yet cold in his grave. Oh, I could go on, but I won't. Thank you, *Vexed Vixens.* I promise to be in better humour next meet.'

'I have enjoyed this new Violet,' Lilly said. 'Very spirited.'

'As have I,' Emily agreed. And the ladies toasted Violet and her current state.

'Have you nothing, Billie?' Violet asked.

Billie grinned. 'I am not vexed at all. Mind you, I have tried to find something to contribute, but fall short; I am a disappointing member of our group this month. I am happy in love, happy at work, and love this time of the year. Phoebe, what about you?'

'I, too, have had a pleasant month. Harland is very attentive, and I have a sneaking suspicion he is considering proposing.'

The girls all gasped.

'How exciting,' Violet said. What makes you think so, Phoebe?'

'I could be completely wrong, but he requested a quiet word with Grandpa and Julius last week.'

'That is very suspicious,' Lilly agreed with a grin.

Emily cleared her throat lightly. 'As did Gilbert, with my father.'

'Goodness gracious!' Phoebe exclaimed. 'What of you, Lilly and Billie? Any quiet words with your fathers?'

'Ambrose and I have spoken of our union, and the business in the years to come,' Billie said, smiling happily. 'I have told him that planning is exciting but do not consider this an agreement. I expect a romantic proposal and will not say "Yes" unless I believe it worthy.'

The ladies praised her. 'Well done, Billie,' Phoebe exclaimed. 'I dare not ask the same of Harland as romance is not his strength; he might never propose with that threat. Lilly, is Bennet keen to wed?'

'He has already asked my father and me.'

The ladies at the table spoke over each other.

'Lilly Lewis! What do you mean?' Phoebe exclaimed.

'Why didn't you say so?' Emily asked.

'When did you get engaged?' Violet leant forward with interest.

Lilly held up her hand. 'I have accepted, but it was a practice run. He has written to his parents that he intends to propose, and on acceptance, to marry within the next six months and that I am in agreement. So, if they wish to be present, they must make haste. They are sailing as we speak. Bennet will ask me formally on their arrival for his mother's sake; they are close, I believe. My father would have agreed to anything,' she added with a roll of her eyes.

Phoebe pressed Lilly's hand. 'How exciting.'

'I cannot believe we will have four weddings in the coming year,' Violet proclaimed. 'I cannot wait. Do hurry up and have children so they may play together.'

The ladies spoke of matters of the heart for a while until Violet remembered that, as the hostess, she was meant to direct the subject matter.

'Oh dear, we are way off track, I am failing as hostess, and I cannot be the only one vexed. Phoebe and Emily, you must contribute.'

'Emily, please say your students vexed you; I love your stories,' Billie said.

'Fortunately, they are the major source of my vexation,' Emily agreed, and on Phoebe's insistence, went first. 'I have one young lady; I shall call her Miss Bookish, who, every time I leave the girls to practice their deportment and walking straight with a book on their head, sits herself down to read it. Three times I have told her that is not the purpose of the exercise; I even gave her the dullest book I could find. It would be different if she were a graceful swan, but she is a dreadful stomper.'

The ladies enjoyed the image and laughed at Emily's descriptions, as the owner of the *Miss Emily Yalden School of Deportment* continued. 'Then there is Miss Lovelorn, who, when corrected, replies, "My beau likes me as I am", and I must remind her that her beau gave her the course for her birthday, so perhaps some self-reflection is in order. But I do have some lovely news. Do you recall my worst student that I was going to expel back in July, Miss Martha Hampstead?'

'The student who helped the police with the vanishing groom case,' Lilly confirmed.

'That is her,' Emily agreed. 'Well, I could not be prouder. She has joined the Queensland Women's Suffrage League and has asked me to come along to their luncheon with her. I shall of course.'

'You are making a difference, Emily,' Phoebe said, delighted.

'As are you, Phoebe,' Emily said but could say no more, as Billie did not know of Phoebe's skills. 'It is your turn to vex.'

Phoebe glanced at Billie. 'Perhaps it is time to bring Billie into the group's confidence as hopefully she will be family before long and is now an official *Vexed Vixen.*'

Billie looked up from the second serving of stew she was enjoying. 'What is this then? Tell me it is not an initiation!'

'No, but it is a matter of trust,' Lilly said.

'I assure you I am very trustworthy and discreet. I do work in the death industry and see many odd things and share people's most vulnerable times.' Billie's eyes widened. 'Oh, Phoebe, are you going to tell me you speak with spirits?'

All heads snapped to look at Billie.

'Why would you say that?' Phoebe asked, surprised and worried. 'Did Ambrose tell you?'

'Does he know? No, he has said nothing to me. I wondered, that's all.' Billie put down her fork and elaborated, 'The first time I met you, you looked at something in the corner when your grandfather, Mr Astin, was speaking with me. I saw you in the mirror, and there was nothing there. Since that day, I have been studying you with great interest. Forgive me for being so nosy.'

'Goodness, how indiscreet of me,' Phoebe exclaimed, biting her lower lip.

'So it is true! You weren't to know the mirror in the meeting room was in my line of view. In the spirit of sharing confidences, may I share one with you all?' Billie looked at each lady, her wide brown eyes appraising them all.

'Please do,' Phoebe said, inviting her to speak. 'Nothing shall leave this room.'

'I have seen ghosts several times in the cemetery. I am not a vessel to the next world. No spirit has ever spoken with me, but I am a believer.'

'Excellent. Then you will tell no one of my gift?' Phoebe asked.

'Never. You have my word.'

'Excellent, then let me tell you about a spirit I am hoping will visit me... that of Miss Charity Buckley.'

Chapter 7

NORA WALDREN GIGGLED WITH two of her friends as they paid and collected their purchases from a stallholder at the Christmas market. She looked back over her shoulder at the young man who served her and gave him another smile; he tipped his hat and grinned.

'He is handsome, and he's still watching you,' her friend, Liz, teased, as she glanced back and the three ladies hurried on.

'I would never go out with someone who works at the market,' Nora scoffed, and Annie looked shocked.

'But I thought you were interested in him, and he was very nice and polite.'

'Then you can have him,' Nora said, and led the way through the gathered shoppers to the next stall that interested her. Liz and Annie followed.

'You are very naughty, Nora,' Annie teased. 'You should not catch the eye of young gentlemen and flirt if you have no interest in them. It's unkind.'

'Oh, you are too nice, Annie. It's just a bit of fun, and I'm sure he tips his hat and offers that charming smile to lots of girls. Besides, everyone does it. Charity was the worst.'

'Let's not speak ill of the dead,' Liz said. 'Poor Miss Buckley. I read about her death in the newspaper and to think it was first believed to be an accident!'

'The murderer almost got away with it,' Annie agreed. 'I would not wish her death on my worst enemy. How awful to be attacked in a lane, and left to die.' She gave a small shudder.

'Don't be out late, ladies,' a constable warned them as he walked by and tipped his hat. 'There are unsavoury types around; get yourselves home safely.'

'We will, Constable, thank you,' Nora said, and the buxom, small blonde woman gave him the same teasing smile she had offered the stallholder minutes before. When the constable was out of hearing range, she added, 'He would be a good husband if you don't want a man around much and can live on next to nothing.'

Liz tutted at her friend. 'You are terrible, Nora. But he is right; we should head home. Poor Miss Buckley. I remember seeing her at church.'

Nora turned up her nose. 'Charity Buckley got what she deserved. She stole the attention of every man that came into the church charity shop, and Mrs Wilson thought she was the sweetest. Oh, I have news.' She leant in close to the two ladies and said, 'Did you hear about Clara Garnham? Her father lost his job, and they are living off her mother's bakery wage.' She scoffed.

'Poor Mr Garnham,' Annie said, mortified at hearing the Garnham's laundry aired. 'I had best get home or my father will worry.'

The girls agreed and hugged goodbye, Liz and Annie departing together in a different direction to Nora, who made her way through the market to the lane leading to the main street where she would take an omnibus home.

'Hello dear, we are walking the same way. Shall we walk together to be safe?' a voice said from behind Nora.

The young woman turned around and took in the dowdy woman, a head taller but stout like herself. She didn't wish to walk with the woman, but saw the sense in doing so, and given the woman's age—she was close to Nora's mother's age—she thought it best to be polite.

'If you like.'

'Have you been doing your Christmas shopping?' the woman asked, moving closer as they started down the laneway to the main street.

'Not really. I was just browsing with my friends.' Nora did not ask after the woman a question; she was not interested in conversation with someone she had no time for and wouldn't see again.

'There's lots of lovely craft goods this year,' the woman continued. 'Some ladies are so clever with their hands.'

'If you like those sorts of things. My mother says you just come home with a lot of rubbish you don't need, and I agree.'

'That's a shame,' the woman said and moved closer, taking Nora's arm.

'What are you doing?' Nora snapped, pulling away.

'I just lost my footing, dear. My legs have served me well, but they aren't as young as they used to be. Perhaps you will let me lean on you for a moment?'

If the woman sought charity from Nora Waldren, then she would be sorely disappointed. Nora sniggered and attempted to pull away.

'Let me go.'

The woman pulled her closer, and Nora saw the nasty sneer on the weathered face, and felt the tight grip on her arm.

'You are a nasty young lady, aren't you, Nora Waldren?'

Nora gasped. 'How do you know my name?'

'You look like an angel, but you are a fallen angel,' the woman growled near Nora's ear as she pulled the young woman so close that there was no light between them. The woman hissed, 'You broke the ninth commandment.'

'What are you talking about? Let me go now!' Nora snapped, angry and fearful. She glanced around. They were alone. The laneway was dark, a place of shadows where she could be struck and no one would know. Not a person was in sight.

Panicked, with her heart racing, breath hitched, Nora saw her life flash before her. She did not want this to be her last day, or how her life ended, in a deserted dark alley, with people talking about her, like she had spoken of Charity deserving her fate.

Nora reached up and struck the woman in the face. With one almighty tug of her arm, Nora wrong-footed her captor, and came free.

'You horrid girl!' the woman swung at the smaller blonde, and missed.

Gasping in surprise and relief to be free, Nora dropped her shopping, lifted her skirt and ran the race of her life toward the end of the alley. Panic flooded her body; she did not look back to see if the woman was in pursuit, and in moments burst onto the main street.

'Wait, wait, please,' she screamed at a passing hansom as she ran up to it.

The driver pulled the horse to a stop, and Nora hurled herself into the carriage, giving him her home address. Only after settling in the back seat did she look back. No one was in sight or in the laneway. Not even a shadowy figure.

'Are you all right, Miss?' the driver asked.

'I was just threatened.'

'I'll take you to the police station right now.'

'No. No, thank you. I want to go home. I'll go there tomorrow morning with my father,' she said, her breathing settling.

'As you wish, Miss,' he said, and Nora looked back once more, but there was no sign of the woman.

'The ninth commandment,' she whispered, and then her emotions broke and Nora cried, gulping for air, hiding her face in her handkerchief with the butterfly sewn into the corner by her mother. She had thought the embroidery a waste of time when presented with the gift. Now she was grateful for its comfort, its connection to home, and knowing she would see her mother again shortly.

Across town, private investigator and artist Bennet Martin put the round of drinks down on the table before him. It was his turn for the shout, and he could not help but think of what an odd group of friends they were. Since arriving on Australian shores to get away from his domineering father, who wished his son to join the police force and rise to the rank of detective in his father's footsteps, Bennet had become inadvertently involved with the law, working as a private investigator. One day soon, he would work full time as an artist; it was only a matter of time.

'So you are here to stay then, are you, Bennet?' Tavish's recently arrived twin brother, Brodie, asked in his thick Scottish accent. 'You are not yearning for home?'

'I can't say I am, Brodie,' Bennet said, as the men had all met enough times now to drop formalities. He raised his beer glass for the toast. 'I have new friends, a lovely young lady who I will wed as soon as my parents arrive in a matter of months, and work I enjoy. Might I say, although it is an unpopular view,' he glanced at Julius, 'it is so wonderful not to have a cold Christmas.'

Julius scoffed. 'Spend a day with me and I will change your mind.'

'The heat is an affront, but the light is different, and there's a raw beauty about the place,' Brodie said.

'I agree,' Bennet said. 'The landscape is strikingly different. I intend to travel to the country in the coming weeks to do some painting. You are welcome to accompany me to the bush, Brodie, if you are still in town.'

Tavish gave a chuckle. 'I have already given my brother a sample of country life, and I think it is safe to say that Brodie is not much of an outdoorsman. He likes his warm fireplace, excellent brandy and his journals.'

'There's a lot to be said for that,' Julius said, and Brodie thanked him.

'For twins, you are not alike physically or by nature, then?' Harland asked.

'No, which is a good thing,' Brodie said, nudging his twin. 'Tavish believes he got the looks, and I got the brains, and our parents had no trouble telling us apart.'

The men chuckled as neither man could truly be described as handsome, especially in the present company.

Brodie continued, 'I am pleased to be here for my twin's pending nuptials, and his lady, Miss Isabelle Yalden, is a fine woman.'

'That she is,' Tavish agreed.

'How she will put up with you though, baffles me,' Brodie continued, teasing his twin. 'Tavish was always the wild one, getting me in trouble and wanting to wander the highlands. He has not changed, but Miss Yalden may tame you. Last weekend we took a hike into your outback, and it was quite perilous. I think Miss Yalden was as pleased to return home as I was that day.'

'The laugh of the kookaburra scared the hell out of my brother. I thought he was going to run back faster than the horse and carriage,' Tavish grinned.

'What a ferocious sound and those cockatoos! I declare that is what a pterodactyl dinosaur would sound like,' Brodie exclaimed, and the men laughed while Bennet sympathised.

'It is not for the faint-hearted.'

They turned their attention to the fight in the ring below, which was over before it started.

'How dull,' Bennet said. 'Well, it will be a year of major life changes for us all. Wives, children, responsibility.'

'What of your protégé, Harland? Will he ask Miss Yalden for her hand soon?' Tavish asked after Emily, the cousin of his fiancée, Isabelle. 'You might need to give him a raise to support a wife. The young fellow is astute.'

'He has already asked Miss Yalden's father for permission and yes, he has been a surprising young man,' Harland agreed. 'When we were first partnered, I thought I had my work cut out for me, but he has excelled.'

'His penchant for facts is astonishing. Although I suspect you could give him a run for his money,' Bennet said to Brodie, a linguist for the Society of Antiquaries in his Scottish homeland.

'The challenge, however, is knowing when to store his gems of knowledge and when to discard them,' Harland said.

'He sounds like a fascinating young man,' Brodie said. 'I would like to meet him. Share one or two of his observations, Detective, if you will.'

Harland told of Gilbert's accurate interpretation of a nursery rhyme that helped solve one of their earlier cases, how he knew a doll's glass eyes dated it thus exposing the culprit's lie, and how the difference in timber made their victim's death by falling through the floor unlikely.

'On our current case, we received a confession of sorts,' Harland told them of the note. 'Gilbert told me the difference between the sixth commandment's interpretation in the King James Bible versus the original Hebrew translation. Time will tell if that is relevant.'

The men smiled at Gilbert's pedantry but not Brodie, who looked fascinated.

'They are markedly different,' Brodie said, and the men sobered so as not to insult Tavish's brother. 'In Exodus, King James Version, it is written as, "Thou shalt not kill". The more accurate translation from the original Hebrew is, "Thou shalt not murder".'

'That is precisely what Gilbert said,' Harland agreed. 'Why is that so markedly different?'

'Because thou shalt not kill has exceptions. To kill in times of war and self-defence is permitted and is not considered a violation of the commandments. The Hebrew version, "Thou shalt not murder," conveys that the deed is the intentional, unlawful taking of a life. An unjust murder.'

'That is interesting,' Bennet said, turning his attention to Harland. 'Which one is it then, and would the killer be aware of the interpretations?'

'I cannot say. The writer left the note in a confessional box, so he is likely aware of doctrine, but from his admission, he appears to think the killing is justified. Regardless, there is a young woman that Julius buried today who needs justice, and given the writer said he is likely to break the sixth commandment again, I suspect we are talking about the Hebrew translation... murder.'

Chapter 8

IN STARK CONTRAST TO *The Courier*'s often irritable and cigar-loving editor, Alex Cowan, Lionel Faherty, the acting editor, preferred to maintain a quiet demeanour during his morning meetings, which he scheduled punctually at 9am, and he would sit in the centre of the newsroom. A neat man, reserved, and well-respected, he said little and still got the results that the bellowing Alex Cowan got from his reporters.

With the editorial meeting well underway, Lilly wasn't sure if she preferred the informal gathering or felt more pressure with everyone having to pitch their projects in front of each other.

'I'll have it for the morning edition, Lionel,' the ever confident, smooth-talking Lawrence Hulmes said of his interview with a well-known actress passing through with her stage play.

'Excellent.' Lionel worked his way around the room, coming at last to the only female reporter on the team, sitting amongst the suited men, wearing a lilac dress and a determined expression. 'Lilly, what has your attention then?'

'A potential murder, Mr Faherty,' she said, pitching by herself given Fergus's absence. She heard the titters of laughter and saw a few of the journalists nudge each other. They might well laugh, yet Lilly and Fergus had proven themselves capable crime writers, and not everyone was amused at her announcement.

The acting editor quietened the group. 'Given Lilly has had more inches of copy space and breaking stories in the last year than most of the seasoned journalists in the room, I think you can wipe the smirks off your faces.'

Lilly was grateful for his support but also uncomfortable with it; she didn't wish to make enemies amongst her colleagues or show them up. She could not afford to antagonise her workmates.

'Thank you, Mr Faherty, but I suspect my esteemed colleagues find my exuberance for a good murder amusing,' she said with a charming smile that gave Lawrence Hulmes a run for his money. 'I'm trying to moderate it,' she said. This time, her comment elicited welcome laughter, as Lilly, with five brothers, was well-practiced at laughing at herself.

Mr Faherty smiled as the men now defended her.

'Don't you change, Lilly; we like you just the way you are,' Lawrence said and gave her a wink.

'You're a bonzer gal, Lilly, keep up the good work,' one of the amused journalists said, and Lilly thanked him.

'Your story then?' Lionel Faherty got the discussion back on track.

'Well, Sir, a young woman in a Christmas bonnet died several days ago after attending the Christmas market. The police believed a horse and cart struck her and she was left to die in the street; they returned her body to her family. But a witness has come forward and claimed that Miss Charity Buckley was being led rather roughly down a side street by a woman and that all might not be as it seems.'

'Not much to go on,' the acting editor said.

'There's more,' Lilly continued quickly. 'As I work closely with Detectives Stone and Payne, they allowed me to accompany them while they investigated the witness's claim. They retrieved Miss Buckley's body after her viewing, and the coroner inspected it before the funeral. Dr McGregor found the wounds were inconsistent with a carriage accident, and that she was probably struck on the head with a heavy, square object and abandoned. They will allow me to report on their investigation, Sir.'

'Excellent, do so. Give me a piece for the afternoon and morning editions. Who was she? Who saw her at the market? Get as many quotes as you can. Talk to that witness; shadow the detectives. Good job, Lilly.'

'Thank you, Sir.'

'Oh, and pick a partner to help you, given Fergus will be away for a few weeks.'

The newsroom stilled, and Lilly could not believe the acting editor was letting her pick a partner and not allocating one to her.

'Thank you, Mr Faherty,' she said in awe and glanced around.

Several of the men put up their hands or voiced that they would be happy to partner with her. The chance to report on an active investigation made a pleasant change for most of them. She heard scattered requests.

'I'm already on police rounds, I could step up.'

'We'd make a good team, Lilly,' Lawrence said, and gave her his most charismatic grin.

'I could use a break from the finance and banking pages.'

But Lilly knew who she wanted to work with... a senior reporter her father admired, who had long since been overlooked but was always the first to congratulate her and

Fergus. He had worked on many stories over the decades, including crime and police news.

'Mr Faherty, if he is willing, I think I could learn a lot from Ted,' she said, looking to the older man at the edge of the newsroom.

All eyes turned to Ted, and his surprised look quickly changed to a large grin. 'I'd be delighted.'

'Lewis and Egan then,' the acting editor said, respecting Lilly's choice. 'I'll get someone to cover racing then, Ted. Get to it, everyone. Don't miss your deadlines, and if you're not going to make it, let me know so I don't have a hole to fill.'

He got up and left the room as Lawrence Hulmes dramatically feigned that Lilly had broken his heart to the laughter of the surrounding journalists.

Ted rose. Since his desk was stuck in the corner as if the newspaper had forgotten him, he said, 'Best I take Fergus's desk then and sit nearby since we'll be swapping notes, if you don't mind the smoking?'

'Not at all,' Lilly said, and cleared some of Fergus's possessions to one side so Ted could inhabit it. She watched as the grey-haired, grandfatherly-looking man of medium height and build, grabbed a handful of items and moved to his new abode and set up his desk.

'Thanks for this, Ted,' she said quietly. 'I hope you don't mind having a break from the racing.'

'Not for a moment, and thank you, young lady. It's been a while since I reported on the beat, but I'm sure my blood is still pumping.'

Lilly laughed. 'Shall we do just that then? Head to the market and see who might recall seeing Miss Buckley?'

'I'll get my hat,' he said, and the new, odd, reporting team departed, excited for the pairing and the mystery unfolding.

The solid young man's hands fisted, his lips thinned, and his anger was quick to rise. Before him, Detective Harland Stone and Detective Payne had arrived early to catch Mr Buckley lest he should depart for work, and he was not impressed with the turn of the conversation.

'I told her she should not go out alone. Men cannot be trusted, and she was a virtuous, beautiful woman,' Earnest Buckley said of his sister as he paced in the kitchen, where he had directed the detectives. The tea he offered went by the wayside as he returned to sit at the table opposite them.

'Was she in a relationship, Mr Buckley, or did she have a close friend, male or female, that we could speak with?' Harland asked.

'She had me. That is all. Our parents are dead. She had me,' he said again. 'Who did it? Do you know?' He ran a hand through thinning fair hair. Like his sister, Earnest had the same dark brown eyes, but the resemblance finished there. She was an attractive woman; Earnest was neither handsome nor did he have an easygoing charm.

'We are going to find that out, Sir,' Gilbert assured him, 'but we are not convinced a man harmed your sister. Miss Buckley was last seen in the company of a woman who seemed to be leading her away from the market. Might you know who that was?'

He exhaled. 'A woman. Why would a woman cause her harm?' He shook his head.

'Did your sister work or volunteer?' Harland continued, trying to gain something useful from the obstinate Earnest Buckley.

'She volunteers three days a week at the church's charity shop. She does not need to earn an income; I will provide for her until she is married.'

'And what line of work are you in, Mr Buckley?' Gilbert asked.

'I am a teacher of Latin, history and natural science at St Joseph's Boys' School. My life's work is to integrate faith into the everyday lives of the boys and to embody the fruit of the Spirit in their thoughts and actions,' he continued

grandstanding. 'I ensure adherence to the school's motto –
Summum Meum pro Gloria Eius.'

Looking pompous and full of his own importance, he
did not translate the Latin for the detectives and appeared
surprised when the senior detective spoke.

'My Utmost for His Glory. I went to one of those schools,
Mr Buckley,' Harland said, his eyes narrowed at the man's
speech, which seemed well-rehearsed. He recognised the type
of teacher Earnest Buckley would be from his own years at a
boys' boarding school – quick to anger, adept with the cane,
and powerful in the only arena in which he had power.

Out of curiosity, Gilbert asked, 'Are you familiar with the
sixth commandment, Mr Buckley?'

'Naturally. Thou shalt not kill. Exodus 20:13.'

'Do you believe there are literal interpretations of this?'
Harland asked.

'Of course. Those who kill in war or self-defence are not
killers. The killing of animals that we consume for meat is not
breaking the sixth commandment. Why? Are you saying my
sister was killed because somebody was acting in self-defence?
She was barely five feet four inches, I don't think she could
inflict an injury that warranted striking her down.'

'No, I am not saying that,' Harland answered bluntly, and
admonished himself for allowing his disdain to get the better
of him.

'You and your sister both have virtuous names, Mr Buckley,' Gilbert said, 'Earnest and Charity. Was your sister God-fearing? Did she study the Bible?'

'Our parents raised us as such. The church remains my salvation.' He glanced at the photo of the Sacred Heart on the wall, and then to a cross in the corner.

'Where is your parish, Mr Buckley?' Harland asked. 'St Joseph's?'

'No, I teach there, but St Mary's is where my family and I have always attended church. After our parents' death, my sister and I continued to attend there.' His breath hitched, realising he would now attend by himself, the last of the Buckley family. 'I shall pray for the soul of her killer. I will pray that you can capture him.'

'That would be helpful,' Harland agreed. 'May we see your sister's room in case there is something that might assist us?'

'She wouldn't like that,' he said, rising, and Harland remained, letting Gilbert follow the school teacher. Harland took the opportunity to study the living room. It was barren except for a photo of a couple whom he presumed were Earnest and Charity's parents. The room had no personality, very much like its inhabitant.

Both men returned within ten minutes, and Harland thanked Earnest Buckley for his time. 'If you think of anything that might assist us, please call at the station, and we are sorry, Mr Buckley, for the loss of your sister.'

Earnest collapsed into the closest seat around the kitchen table as the detectives headed for the door.

'I am all alone in the world now,' he muttered.

Harland held the door for Gilbert, who looked back at the hunched figure at the table. The young detective said, 'You are not alone, Mr Buckley; you have the Lord by your side.'

'Yes. That is true, and it is Christmas,' Earnest Buckley muttered. 'Perhaps there will be a miracle.'

Outside, Harland muttered, 'I don't know what sort of miracle he is hoping for, but I'm pretty sure his sister won't be rising from the dead. Was there anything of interest in Miss Buckley's room?'

'No. She lived frugally, by all appearances.'

'Or her brother has already cleaned out her room.' Harland looked to his protégé. 'Given you asked about the commandments, do you think there is a connection between the note left in the confessional box and Miss Buckley's death?'

'Perhaps, Sir,' Gilbert said as Harland hailed a hansom to take them to the Christmas market. 'Mr Buckley seems devout, and the confession was handed in at St Mary's – the parish the Buckley family attend. I thought there might be a connection and maybe Miss Buckley was the victim.'

'We'll visit their church; I promised Julius I would call in on the priest if we were in the area, so we'll make it our business to do so. Following that, we'll drop into the church charity shop and see if Miss Buckley had any friends or relationships we should know about.'

'Be prepared to buy something, Sir. My mother has volunteered at our local church charity shop, and I warn you, we will not get out without a purchase.'

Harland chuckled. 'I will brace myself, thank you, Gilbert.' Moments later, as the Christmas market came into sight, Harland added, 'Speaking of bracing yourself, there is Miss Lewis. Prepare for an onslaught of questions.'

Chapter 9

IT WAS NOTED BY the lady mortician at *The Economic Undertaker* that her brother, Julius, seemed to spend more time around the office than in the past, hovering, waiting for baby news, or perhaps Phoebe was just imagining it. But as he came downstairs to greet her with his large dog, Rufus, in tow, she could not help but tease him.

'Phoebe, good morning. Did you have an enjoyable gathering?' he asked, looking striking and well-groomed as always, ready in his dark suit for the day's work.

'Hello, brother, hello Rufus. We did, we always do, and thank you for the use of your abode,' she said, giving the much-loved dog the required attention for his show of excitement. 'I must commend your cook; what a marvel!'

'A lifesaver for Tom and me,' Julius agreed. 'Don't tell Violet I said that.'

'I think she knows,' Phoebe said with a smile. 'I thought you had a funeral this morning?'

'Ambrose and I do. But there is no need to rush to it. The dead aren't in a hurry,' he said, taking a seat on the couch before the morning funeral would require him to stand still for the length of the prayers and service. Rufus jumped up beside him, turning twice and settling.

'But what if you encounter a large number of vehicles and have to hurry the hearse along? I know you consider that undignified, and it would mortify Ambrose.' She laughed at her own joke, knowing Ambrose would enjoy it very much and was always getting in trouble for doing just that.

'Ambrose would congratulate me, but I won't leave that late. I have done this before a few times,' he retorted.

'True,' Phoebe continued, teasing him, her purpose unbeknownst to Julius, but she wanted to see his preparedness for herself; it was an endearing aspect of his nature. 'You may have to let Ambrose drive the hearse once you have your little one, in case you fall asleep at the reins. I believe babies are very good at interrupting sleep in the early days.'

'It is to be expected, but I will work to ensure Violet and I are not too taxed. Nor Tom, as he must be rested for his workday. We can get help if needed,' he said.

'Is there anything I can do to be of assistance now that the time is drawing near, Brother?' she asked, putting an apron over her lavender dress and placing her brushes on the table before her, ready for her first client.

'Thank you, Phoebe, but I believe I have matters under control. Unless you have insights into the process that I might not have heard about or researched?' He sat forward now looking concerned, his hand pausing from patting Rufus. 'Do you?'

'No. I am sure, knowing how prepared you are in business, that you have left nothing to chance. Personally, I would stock up on small cutlery, bibs, caps, socks, clothing, a crib, powder-box, summer and winter blankets and flannels, knit socks, which I believe mothers find preferable to crocheted ones as they wear better. I am sure Violet has her own wardrobe prepared and has thought of the little things, like extra pegs for all those nappies.'

'Powder-box,' he mumbled as if noting an item that wasn't already in the baby's room.

Phoebe continued. 'I was speaking with Mrs Dobbs, and she said there were some excellent books that might be most helpful, her favourite being *The Mother's Book* by Lydia Childs... I think that was the author. Mind you, it is forty years since Mrs Dobbs had her firstborn, so the advice might be dated.'

'Thank you, Phoebe. I have found several publications and purchased them for Violet,' he agreed, 'but that was not among them.'

'No cause for concern, Mrs Dobbs assured me you would have a manual now from the midwife,' she said, continuing to test if his feathers could be ruffled.

'Yes, possibly... I am not sure of that.' Her brother now appeared slightly stunned. 'I shall discuss that with Violet and—' Julius stopped suddenly and looked at Phoebe. 'I was Violet's vexed subject last night, wasn't I?'

'You? Goodness, Julius, surely not!'

He rose, walked around with hands behind his back before turning to give her a wry look. 'I am vexing and have made it onto the *Vexed Vixens* agenda. I am unsure whether I should feel honoured or mortified.'

Phoebe laughed. 'You may have been discussed, but only with great affection,' she assured him. 'You are going to be a wonderful father, and you are a wonderful husband and brother, Julius. But if I may suggest something?'

'Go ahead,' he said dryly, making her laugh again.

'Allow for a little spontaneity and a few surprises. Remember, there are memories to be made, mistakes and life lessons that will be part of the journey. Preparing does not always ensure a smooth road, and no one wishes to live life according to a manual.'

He exhaled and nodded. 'I see. I am being too officious.'

'Never that. Prepared certainly, as is your nature. But do not worry. Violet rejoiced that you had gone to great lengths to prepare, but hoped the only surprise would not just be the baby's sex.'

Julius huffed but conceded that was probably true.

Phoebe assured him, 'Violet said you were the best of husbands and loved that you would not abandon her to juggle everything by herself. She was a little worried too, that you might be making yourself anxious.'

'It is hard not to when you think of all that could go wrong,' Julius agreed in a rare show of vulnerability.

'Then we shall think only of all that can go right. After all, our dear mother had three charming children; it is a natural process as old as time itself.'

'Thank you, Phoebe, let us think of it like that. Any other advice from the *Vexed Vixens*?'

'No. To be honest, we were all a little jealous of Violet's state and attentive husband; you have set a high benchmark.'

Julius' expression softened. 'I shall take your advice on board, thank you, Phoebe. And I'd best get to that funeral then. I'd hate to speed in the hearse,' he added with a raised eyebrow, making her laugh.

With a pat for Rufus, who usually spent his mornings in Phoebe's company, Julius took the stairs two at a time. Phoebe smiled after him. He may be pedantic, but her brother was always open to suggestion. Still smiling, she ducked next door to tell Violet about the conversation before customers arrived at both places of business.

The Christmas market drew different crowds depending on the time of the day. The morning was for the household shoppers stocking up on poultry, herbs, fruit and vegetables as needed for the pending feast and invasion of family and friends in the days to come. Lunchtime and mid-afternoon drew those shoppers who sought something in particular or were dedicated to getting a gift or browsing during a lunch break. The early evening was for families with children, and after 8pm, when the children were home in bed, the couples wandered around admiring each other and the Christmas decorations.

It was among the housewives, housekeepers, and market stall holders that reporters Lilly Lewis and Ted Egan strolled to start their interviews.

Lilly brightened. 'Ted, they are here! What perfect timing!'

'Who would that be then, Lilly?' he asked, bumping his hat a little further back on his forehead to peruse the crowd.

'The detectives. Come and I'll introduce you,' she said, waving at the detectives and laughing at Detective Harland Stone's expression as they neared.

'You do not look pleased to see me, Detective Stone, but I won't take it to heart,' she said in jest.

'Whatever gave you that impression, Miss Lewis? I always look this surly,' Harland said with a tip of his hat and a small smile to show he had a sense of humour behind the serious facade.

'Detective Stone, Detective Payne, this is my partner in Fergus's absence, Mr Ted Egan.'

'Good to meet you both,' Ted said, accepting the offered hands and shaking.

'Mr Egan!' Gilbert said. 'My mother loved your "Around Town" column and was bitterly disappointed when you ceased writing it to move to the racing column. She said it has never been as good since.'

'Well, that's most flattering, thank you, Detective and your dear mother,' Ted said in good humour. 'The horses are much easier to interview, however, than some of our businessmen and politicians.'

'Of that I have no doubt,' Harland agreed.

'We are here to seek witnesses,' Lilly said. 'The editor has given us permission to write the story, so can we shadow you, detectives?'

Harland nodded. 'If you wish.'

'I might start at the opposite end, Lilly,' Ted said, 'and then we can compare notes.'

'An excellent idea,' Harland agreed. 'Do share anything of interest, won't you, Mr Egan?'

'Right you are, Detective.'

'If it isn't Ted Egan!' a stallholder said loudly. 'Are you writing the police beat again, Ted?'

'Hello there, Joe. No, I'm partnering with the very talented Miss Lilly Lewis to write about a crime!'

'I wouldn't want to be a criminal then,' Joe said, nudging his wife, and the next stallholders also gave a laugh. 'Ted always had his nose to the ground when it came to a clue or two. Knew more than the police in your police beat column, I reckon.'

Ted thanked him, cleared his throat with a little embarrassment and introduced the detectives and Lilly. He continued, 'Well, maybe you can help us, Joe,' Ted said and mentioned the young woman's death.

'I think we might be best to accompany you, Mr Egan,' Harland said, 'if you have no objections. You clearly have the contacts.' The detectives now stayed put, given Ted appeared to have an easy-going manner and stallholders willingly spoke with him.

'No objections at all, detectives,' Ted said, and Lilly smiled beside him as if she were making the job easier for the detectives.

'I saw her,' Joe said. 'So did the wife.' Joe's wife, who looked similar to her husband in height and appearance, came to stand beside him and nodded most solemnly in agreement.

'Ted Egan! You're back from the dead then; it is good to see you,' a burly man said as he placed a large box down at the next stall, and wiped his hands on a pair of dungarees. He extended his hand to shake Ted's vigorously.

'Yes, still standing, Albert. You haven't changed a bit. Beating age off with a stick, are you?' Ted said and made the man grin with pleasure.

Again, Ted introduced his writing partner and the detectives.

'So you're the reporter, Lilly Lewis,' Albert said, and sized Lilly up. 'You're mighty small with a big pen, young lady. I've read all of your stories. Good reporting, good yarns.'

'Thank you, Sir,' she said, delighted. 'Can you help us then with our next one, please?'

This time, Harland briefed Albert, the newcomer, on the crime afoot, as Joe and his wife nodded along like experts on the subject.

'I was just saying I saw her, so did the wife,' Joe told Albert. 'She was a pretty little thing with a lovely Christmas bonnet, which everyone was commenting on. Decorated it herself, she said.'

'Was she by herself, Sir?' Gilbert asked.

'She was, Detective, and she shopped for quite a while, because she came back here twice,' Joe's wife said, answering for her husband. 'She looked at our nativity scenes—they are excellent workmanship—and then, about half an hour later, she came back to buy one.'

'That wasn't in her basket when it was retrieved,' Harland said to Gilbert, who noted the detail.

'Perhaps it fell out when she had the accident,' Joe said, and then his eyes widened. 'But it was not an accident, was it, or you wouldn't be here?'

'We don't believe so, Sir. Which way did she go after leaving your stand, Mrs...' Harland asked Joe's wife.

'Gertie will do. But if you are quoting me in your story, Miss Lewis and Ted, best to say Mrs Gertie Hurley.'

'Of course, Mrs Hurley,' Lilly said, noting the name.

Gertie, full of self-importance, continued, 'I last saw her over there at the lucky wheel. I only noticed because a loud shout went up when someone won a prize, and I saw her there with the bonnet on.'

'Did she appear to be alone then?' Harland asked.

Gertie thought for a moment. 'I couldn't say, sorry, Detective. She was in a group watching the lucky wheel going around. So, there were people all around her.'

'And you, Albert?' Ted encouraged him. 'Did you see the young woman during the night? Anything you remember will be helpful, I'm sure.'

'I didn't see her at the market, Ted,' he said, folding his large arms across his chest, 'but I saw her when I was leaving the market. I closed my stand a bit early when the crowds thinned. Got a lot of boxes to pack and remove.'

'What do you sell, Sir?' Gilbert asked, looking next door at Albert's stand, which as yet hadn't been set up.

'Pickled goods. All made by the mother and the wife. Anything you can pickle, I will have on sale. The wife will be here shortly to display them. They're heavy jars and bottles, and takes me a while to load and unload.'

'And you saw Miss Charity Buckley on your departure, Sir?' Lilly hurried him along.

'I was just leaving, driving the cart down the laneway,' he said, pointing to the very laneway where Miss Buckley's body was found, 'and she was walking along with another woman, arm in arm, at a good pace.'

Everyone's ears pricked up now, glances were exchanged, and Albert could tell his words had punch. 'What have I said then?'

'We think that lady with Miss Buckley might know more about the young woman's demise,' Ted said, assuring Albert he was in no trouble, quite the opposite, he might save the day. 'What did she look like, this other woman, Albert?'

The large man exhaled and looked around. 'Like anyone of these ladies. A little bulk on her, as most ladies gain after finding a man, settling down and having a family.'

Lilly bit back a retort as Ted nudged her, a small smile playing on his lips.

'Go on, Sir, any minor detail might help,' Gilbert encouraged him.

'Let me see.' He looked around. 'She was about the same build as that lady there,' he said, pointing to a solid lady, well girdled and respectably presented. 'The woman was bigger than the girl with the Christmas bonnet, about half a head taller,' he said and pointed at another lady. 'About her height.'

'Did you see her hair colour or any distinguishing features?' Harland asked.

Albert shook his head. 'I was driving past. I raised my hat to wish them good evening, and the young one looked at me, but the older woman didn't. Her clothes were dowdy, grey skirt and a cream top, I think. Maybe she just looked dull next to the bright young lady.'

'Thank you, Sir, that is most helpful,' Harland said as Gilbert scribbled down the description of the clothes. 'Have any of you seen that lady before?'

They all shook their heads in the negative, and Joe added, 'She might come here often, but there's lots of people coming and going. We only noticed the young lady 'cause of her hat.'

Harland thanked the stallholders again and departed with Gilbert in tow. Leaving Ted to confirm names and enjoy his moment in the sun with his admirers, Lilly hurried behind the detectives as they continued through the market, keen for any insights the detectives might discuss that she could convert to a quote for her article.

Chapter 10

Ambrose Astin had been waiting for the next time he was alone with his brother to drill him, and a trip to the cemetery seated alongside Julius in their formal attire as they proceeded at a measured pace, was an opportune moment for interrogation.

No sooner were they on the road and out of *The Economic Undertaker* grounds, Ambrose asked, 'So have you always seen them?'

'Who?' Julius glanced his way and then returned to looking forward, serious and professional.

'Spirits! Can you see any now?'

'Oh, that. No.'

'Is that not odd? Surely there must be a few ghosts haunting the sidewalks. Victims of accidents or former residents who have not moved on.'

Julius glanced at his brother again. 'Not necessarily. If I am accidentally killed out the front of our shop, I have no intention of lingering.'

'Mm, perhaps not, but that does surprise me,' Ambrose agreed with a chuckle. 'I thought you would be constantly visiting and nagging me from the other side.'

'It has merit,' Julius agreed, 'but hopefully it won't be warranted.'

'It is a terrible idea. I will not have a minute's peace,' Ambrose said and began to mimic his brother. 'Do not stomp with clients in-house, do not drive the hearse so fast, stop smiling on duty, stop...'

'Being dramatic,' Julius cut him off but could not help but smile on hearing the well-worn sayings.

They rode in silence for a brief while before Ambrose began again with his questions. 'With Phoebe, we have always known, but why have you only now chosen to trust me and tell me you see the dead? Unless you are new to it? Might it still come to me?'

'Why would you want to see them? I certainly don't,' Julius said. 'And it is not new to me. Since childhood, they have been there. I have ignored them, and they have left me alone for the most part.'

'Have they? Not always. The more I think about it, the more I realise you appeared distracted at times. Was that because of a troublesome spirit?'

'Unlikely,' Julius said, 'most likely because of you.'

Ambrose chuckled before moaning. 'This heat.' He persisted, 'Then why tell me now? Is it because I spoke of working in the business for life, and Billie's business joining ours? Did I prove my loyalty?'

'You showed me your loyalty to the family, that is more important than the business.'

'You thought I might run away like Uncle Reggie, never to be seen again. I've told you before that would never happen.'

'And then you showed me. Thank you, Ambrose. Please remember, do not tell anyone about the visions. Not even Billie... yet.'

'On my word. But who does know?'

Julius hesitated.

'Everyone but me,' Ambrose said, and looking away hurt, he gave a small shake of his head.

'It is not like that,' Julius hurriedly assured him. 'It was strictly on a need-to-know basis only. I hadn't even told Phoebe until recently.'

'Why did you then?'

'It was accidental. When we had that dastardly debutante in-house for burial, Father Damien Horan appeared to both of us in her room, startling me, and asking us for help. I could hardly deny it after that.'

'And Grandpa and Grandma?'

'Again, only recently. Uncle Reggie tricked me, although he says it was not his intention, but he desperately wanted a message passed to Grandpa and wanted it delivered man to man.'

'How did he trick you?' Ambrose asked, his curiosity overcoming his hurt.

'I didn't know that Grandpa was in the cupboard in Phoebe's room putting shrouds away, Uncle Reggie started talking to me. I thought we were alone...'

'Ah, so you spoke to no-one.'

'So it appeared to Grandpa, who revealed himself most sheepishly. So naturally, Grandma was informed, but she said it had been evident since I was a child, so I was not telling her anything she didn't know.'

Julius turned the hearse down the street toward the cemetery, their final destination.

'And I'm assuming your wife knows.'

'I had no intention of telling Violet either, even though that might be unscrupulous; I was worried it might end our relationship. But I also thought honesty was essential, and she asked me straight out. Once Phoebe revealed she could see spirits to Violet, naturally she wondered about you and me.'

'But she didn't leave you,' Ambrose said and tipped his hat to several mourners walking towards the entrance to the cemetery.

'She didn't like it, and thought about it for 24-hours. The longest day and night of my life. But she accepted me.' Julius looked to Ambrose. 'And now you know.'

'About time then,' Ambrose said, never one to be in ill-humour for long, and the brothers exchanged a brief smile before driving through the cemetery gates where they could see the mourning party and priest waiting graveside.

Content, Ambrose kept the rest of his questions to himself, intending to find out a great deal more about Julius's talent in the days ahead. The Astin men began their funeral duties.

Within the hour, as the funeral came to its conclusion, Ambrose's spirits lifted again. He never thought he could be so excited in a cemetery, but he spotted the Prout Monumental Mason wagon entering the South Brisbane cemetery grounds and his beloved sitting next to the driver; another man sat in the reverse seat.

Julius nudged him. 'Do stop looking so happy, at least until the mourners leave, then you can skip around the headstones to your heart's content.'

'Billie is here,' Ambrose whispered. 'Once the deceased is in the ground, I'll leave you to thank the reverend and pay the gravediggers while I visit her.'

Julius looked over to see the well-signed wagon passing and a very demure Miss Billie Prout looking their way. She gave a small nod and resumed looking forward.

'See, you two are both so strict on the job,' Ambrose said with obvious pride in his voice.

'Miss Prout will be a wonderful asset to the business, and to you. If she can succeed in training you where I have failed, primarily due to exhaustion, I shall be eternally grateful,' Julius stated wryly, and Ambrose responded with a soft chuckle.

The words they knew so well were now falling from the Reverend's lips, the blessing ending, and, on cue, the two Astin men moved forward to lower the dead into their permanent bed.

'Wait!' a lady's voice broke the peaceful ceremony. All eyes turned to a young woman in a mourning dress that Julius recognised as one of *Beyond the Veil*'s designs. It boasted a little lace, for those who wished to flaunt convention. 'I need to put this in his casket,' she said, holding a portrait of herself.

'Outrageous!' a mature woman declared. 'How dare you!'

'The mistress!' Ambrose whispered to his brother. 'How exciting! We haven't had one of those for a while.'

Julius gave a low groan, and the reverend looked at the two men from *The Economic Undertaker* to step up. Ambrose nudged Julius. 'What do you want to do?'

Before Julius could respond, a senior man waving his walking stick came forward. 'My late brother needs none of that. Take your portrait and leave, you young hussey.'

'Disgraceful,' several voices echoed. 'And with his wife present, the hide of her.'

'I was to be his wife, he promised me,' she said, standing taller. 'You, sir, open the casket for me.' She demanded, approaching Ambrose, who looked to his brother for saving.

Julius's lips thinned as he prepared for an unpleasant situation. He stepped forward. 'Madame, I'm afraid that won't be possible now. The Cemeteries Act of 1890 declared that every coffin and grave must be airtight and watertight, and as we conducted the viewing for Mr Nelson earlier, his coffin has been sealed.'

'There you have it. Now take your portrait and depart,' the middle-aged daughter of the deceased snapped at the younger woman. 'How disrespectful to my mother!'

'Leave now, or I will see to it,' a tall young man said, stepping forward. 'My grandmother does not need your sort here.'

'Is that true?' the mistress ignored the family present and asked the priest.

'Mr Astin would know best; my speciality is in prayers, not burials,' the Reverend said with a kindly look.

The young woman huffed, glared at Julius and then the funeral party. She neared the bereaved wife—at least thirty years her senior—and Julius stepped forward prepared to waylay her. But with a dramatic swish of her gown, the mistress turned and departed.

'Did you see that lace?' another woman muttered. 'What next?'

Ambrose exhaled with relief as the mourners thanked them for their counsel, said a few words to the dearly departed and soon departed themselves.

'How did you know that about the 1890 Act? That only came out last year.' Ambrose nudged his brother, who gave him an odd look.

'It is our job to know the act.'

'Oh, right, of course. Is it true what you said about sealing the grave and coffins?' Ambrose asked, ensuring no one but the reverend could hear.

Julius grimaced. 'There's some truth in it.'

The reverend laughed. 'Near enough then, Mr Astin. Let's spare the bereaved any more pain than necessary,' he said, folding his notes and closing his prayer book.

'Which parts were true?' Ambrose asked, grinning.

Julius smiled. 'Well, I was quoting rules for coffins in vaults, not in the earth, and the 1890 Cemetery Act was for the state of Victoria. Our own state hasn't updated the Cemetery Act since 1865.'

Ambrose slapped his brother on the back. 'Well done, it served its purpose.'

'Peace prevailed,' the Reverend agreed. 'Good day to you both until next time.'

The Astin brothers farewelled the reverend, and Julius turned to Ambrose. 'Go say hello to your lady.'

Ambrose grinned. 'I shall.' He departed, leaving Julius smiling as he watched his brother before he turned his attention to the grave-digging father and son, the Redfords, who worked regularly at South Brisbane Cemetery and the three of them shared a small chuckle about the situation averted.

Billie saw Ambrose approaching and excused herself from her colleagues, who were in the process of securing a gravestone placement. She met Ambrose halfway.

'Hello handsome,' she said teasing him. 'Burying the dead?'

'It's what I do best,' he said, taking her hand and kissing it. 'Might I steal a kiss on your cheek?'

'You may not,' she said, giving him a shocked look. 'Your brother might topple into an empty grave from shock, or my colleagues might report back to father that I am canoodling in the cemetery.'

'Canoodling,' Ambrose grinned. 'I wish. Fine then, I shall satisfy myself with just the vision of you.'

'I have some news,' Billie said and lowered her voice. 'Phoebe told me I could tell you.'

'What is it?' he asked, watching the animation on her face with nothing short of adoration.

'Phoebe told me she sees and speaks to spirits! I confess I suspected as much. I saw her once or twice looking sideways in mirrors or giving a brief nod to an empty room. How exciting!'

'It is a well-kept family secret, so now you are family.' As tempted as he was, he did not mention Julius's skills and would keep his promise and the trust invested in him. 'She has assisted quite a few of the dearly departed to rest in peace.'

'How gratifying for her, and very kind,' Billie said. 'Can you? Or will you reveal that if and when you are comfortable to do so?'

'My dear, I can reveal to you right now that I do not have that talent, but I would welcome it. My skills lie in other areas. I am an excellent kisser, I believe.'

'Who told you that?' she feigned disbelief. 'I will not believe that without proof.'

Ambrose laughed. 'Since we are asking questions of each other, tell me, Billie, do you know the Cemetery Act very well?'

She looked surprised. 'Of course, it is our job to do so. Mind you, our act does need updating. It was released in 1865, and the Victorian Act was just updated last year.'

Ambrose rolled his eyes. 'I sometimes think you and Julius would be perfect together.'

'Don't be ridiculous. We are both so pedantic, we would drive each other to distraction. Within a few months he would want to bury me, and I'd be designing a headstone for him.'

Ambrose laughed with abandon. It was the words he needed to hear, the security he sought.

'But your brother and I will be excellent business partners, as witnessed by my pitching my headstone designs to him, and his good sense in taking on our business,' she said, now gesturing towards the two Prout Monumental Mason men waving at her to peruse the gravestone that had just been erected. 'My men have finished their work,' she said, acknowledging them.

Ambrose glanced back. The gravediggers were also finishing, and Julius motioned him over.

'I shall leave you to your inspection then, Billie darling. Julius, too, is ready to depart. I will be at your place of work to walk you home this evening,' he said with a tip of his hat.

'And I shall be waiting for you,' she said, and quickly, rising to her toes, kissed him on the cheek and departed, looking back with a cheeky smile as he stood surprised and grinning, before turning and striding away, confident, happy and in love.

Chapter 11

HAVING COMBED THE CHRISTMAS market, taken as many statements as possible and parted ways with reporters Lilly Lewis and Ted Egan, the detectives made their way to the church charity shop where Miss Charity Buckley had volunteered before her untimely death.

'I shall wander around the market this evening after I walk Phoebe home to see if there is anyone we missed today who might recall Miss Buckely and her companion,' Harland said.

'Do you wish me to meet you there, Sir?' Gilbert asked.

'No need, thank you, Gilbert. I won't dwell. Do you have plans with Miss Yalden tonight?' he asked after Gilbert's belle, Miss Emily Yalden.

'I do, Sir. We are going to dinner. It has become a happy weekly routine we have fallen into, and I am deciding whether proposing there would please Emily or if I should do something more romantic.'

Harland grinned, an unusual sight on the job. 'Well, that is good news indeed, Gilbert. I will hold my congratulations until it is official. I am also pondering the same with Phoebe. Neither of us likes to be the centre of attention, and I suspect you and Miss Yalden are the same.'

'Very much so, Sir.'

They arrived at the charity shop just in time. The sign on the door listed opening hours from 9.30am to 4.30pm, and it was just after 4pm. A small bell announced their arrival as they entered. Behind the counter stood a matronly lady with grey hair tied back tightly into a bun at the nape of her neck. Beside her, dusting figurines with a cloth, was an attractive young woman with light brown hair, blue eyes and pert features, and nearby, a stout young blonde was removing items from a box and laying them out on the table, donations no doubt. Both looked toward the door to assess the new customers.

'Gentlemen, welcome. Might you be looking for some last-minute Christmas gifts?' the senior woman asked.

'No, thank you, Madam,' Harland said and added with a small smile so as not to offend, 'last minute for me is the day prior.'

She gave a hearty laugh, and the young brunette beside her smiled sweetly at the sight of two well-dressed gentlemen of marriageable age and neither wearing a wedding band; she was by nature, observant. The blonde woman ignored them, focussing on the box before her.

'I am Detective Harland Stone, and this is Detective Gilbert Payne.'

Now her head shot up, and she looked at the gentleman. 'You are here to see me? I am Miss Nora Waldren.'

The detectives looked confused, and Harland said, 'Is there a reason we should be seeing you, Miss Waldren?'

Beside Nora, the other young woman gave a small huff of laughter, but Nora Waldren ignored her.

'I came to the police station with my father this morning, and the sergeant on the desk said I had to speak with Detectives Stone and Payne. I left my details.'

'I see. Let us talk privately in a moment,' Harland suggested. 'First, we hoped to ask you all a few questions about Miss Charity Buckley, if we may?'

'Oh, a terrible thing,' the senior lady said. 'Forgive me; where are my manners? I am Mrs Wilson, and this is Miss Clara Garnham. Nora has introduced herself.'

'Ladies,' Detective Payne said. 'You were all acquainted with Miss Buckley?'

'Definitely Detective,' Mrs Wilson confirmed, speaking on behalf of the ladies. 'Charity worked at the store three days a week. She was from a lovely family, very God-fearing and giving to the church and community.'

Harland noticed the ever so small smirk on Miss Clara Garnham's face. Perhaps she was not as enamoured of Charity Buckley as the senior woman. He was not sure of the look on Miss Nora Waldren's face... was it fear?

'Do you know if she had a suitor or a special friend?' Detective Gilbert Payne asked diplomatically. 'Perhaps someone she had not introduced to her brother yet.'

'She had many admirers,' Clara said and was quickly rebuked.

'Clara, if she did, they were respectful and don't imply otherwise.' Mrs Wilson turned to the detectives. 'There was no one in particular who came to the store to see Charity, if that is what you mean, but many admired her.'

'Was there anyone who came to the store regularly or admired her more than most?' Harland persisted.

Clara did not answer but resumed her dusting with her smirk firmly in place, as Mrs Wilson considered the question. 'The Longbourne boy has always liked Charity.'

'He is hardly a boy, Mrs Wilson,' Nora spoke up.

Clara agreed, informing the detectives, 'He runs his father's produce store and has since his father fell ill. Mr Longbourne is supporting his parents.'

'Of course, he is a young man now,' Mrs Wilson conceded. 'I can remember them in Sunday School together at church, but Charity only regarded him as a friend.'

'Longbourne? Do you have a first name, and might you know where he lives, Mrs Wilson?' Gilbert asked, writing implement at the ready.

'Oh, he would never harm Charity. The boy wouldn't hurt a fly.'

'But he might know more about Charity's circle of friends,' Harland said. 'If he can assist us, then we can ensure Miss Buckley's family receive justice.'

'Her brother, that's all that's left,' Clara spoke up. 'Sidney Longburne lives three houses up from the church, on the left as you stand looking at it. His family's produce store is across the road from where the Christmas market is set up in the square.'

'Thank you, Miss Garnham,' Gilbert said, jotting down the information.

'I am finished, Mrs Wilson,' Nora said. 'I will wait outside to speak with the detectives and head home afterwards if that is suitable?'

'Yes, of course, dear. I will see you on your next shift. Thank you, Nora.'

Nora nodded to Clara and indicated to the detectives where she would wait, departing the small shop. Harland caught the eye of his protégé, and giving him a sideways glance towards Mrs Wilson, hoped Gilbert would understand. The younger detective gave a quick nod and moved to the senior woman.

'Actually, Mrs Wilson, my mother loves a good cup of tea. I see you have some hand-knitted tea cosies. I should include one in her Christmas box.'

'She will love one of these, Detective. Now, we have four to choose from.'

As Gilbert viewed the teapot covers, Harland moved closer to Miss Clara Garnham. 'May I have a word in private?'

She nodded, and they moved to the other end of the counter. Fortunately, Gilbert was maintaining an energetic conversation with the senior woman, and Harland spoke quickly and quietly.

'I gather, Miss Garnham, that you knew Miss Buckley a little better than Mrs Wilson did?'

'I did, and I don't like to speak ill of the dead, Detective, but...' she hesitated.

'Being honest may help us, so please speak ill if you must, Miss Garnham. I will not sit in judgement but appreciate you being candid.'

Harland could tell a little flattery went a long way with the coy Miss Garnham.

'Well, Detective,' she said with a flutter of eyelashes and a demure look, 'Charity was not God-fearing, nor was she sweet.

Anytime a handsome man came into the store, she would literally push me out of the way to serve him. Then she would do her best to charm the gentleman, flirting outrageously. Her brother and Mrs Wilson never saw that side of her.' Clara glanced at Mrs Wilson before adding, 'She was very two-faced.'

'Then there were other suitors we should question?' Harland asked.

'Half the town of marriageable age, I'd say, Detective,' she said sourly. 'And Mrs Wilson was right about one thing... Sidney loved her, but she brushed him off as if he were nothing. He is going to own the fruit and vegetable store one day and deserves her respect.'

'Did you see anyone loitering around your shop or the church watching Miss Buckley or other ladies, like yourself?' Harland asked quickly, seeing Gilbert make his purchase.

'No one we didn't know, Detective. My mother always quotes a proverb – "Charm is deceitful and beauty is vain, but a woman who fears the Lord is to be praised." Charity was all three.'

'Your mother is strong in her faith too?'

'Only when it suits her,' Clara huffed. 'But I warned Charity once. I told her if she was going to put her charms out there, she'll attract the wrong attention.'

'What did she say to that?'

'That I was just jealous. Jealous of her.' Clara rolled her eyes. 'Well, look who got her comeuppance.' She softened. 'I did try to help her.'

Harland could not ask any further questions on that subject as Mrs Wilson joined them, and the manageress dismissed Clara for the day. The young lady needed no encouragement to depart and left with farewells and haste.

'Detectives, the ladies are young and competitive. Despite what Clara might have told you, Charity was a good girl.'

The men thanked Mrs Wilson, departing the store. Harland glanced at the brightly coloured knitted tea cosy. 'A Christmas gift for your mother?'

'No, Sir. My mother detests flouncy things such as this.'

Harland chuckled. 'Get the sergeant to reimburse you, call it research, and he can put it in the kitchen at the station. It will brighten the tea lady's day.'

'Thank you, Sir. Did Miss Garnham reveal anything of value?'

'Yes, Miss Charity Buckley was no saint. Best not to tell her brother though. Let us speak with Miss Waldren then.'

Miss Phoebe Astin hurriedly entered the post office and breathed a sigh of relief that there were only three people in front of her in the queue. She took a few moments to settle herself while waiting as the queue moved forward.

'Busy day, Miss Astin?' the postmaster asked when it became her turn and she handed over the day's letters, invoices and receipts on time to make the late post.

'Certainly was, Sir, but not as busy as yours at this time of the year, I imagine. You must be weary by the end of the day.'

'You are right about that, but it is a cheery time of the year too and everyone is in good humour,' he said, grateful for her acknowledgement.

With the task done, Phoebe exited and took a deep breath on the stairs of the post office. She offered to do the post run while her grandfather tended a client without an appointment, which happened more times than not, and it was pleasant to be out in the afternoon light.

But there was no time to dwell. Harland was meeting her at the office in under an hour to walk her home, so Phoebe hurried her steps to get back in time and freshen up. As she turned the corner near the market, which was tempting with its Christmas delights, but Harland was more so, Phoebe saw a small crowd gathering.

Approaching the people who were obstructing her path, she pondered with curiosity what could be occurring. She circled them, peering over heads where possible and through gaps, but with no time to waste, the lady mortician continued on. Moving away from the crowd, Phoebe almost ran headlong into a young lady.

'Oh, I do beg your pardon,' Phoebe said. 'Entirely my fault. I was trying to see what the fuss was about.'

'It is about me, I believe,' the pert, attractive brunette with the large blue eyes said. 'I am Miss Clara Garnham and I am...'

'Oh, you are a spirit,' Phoebe's voice faded. She looked around to ensure she could not be heard and said, 'I am Miss Phoebe Astin. What has happened, Miss Garnham?'

'Well, I had just finished my shift at the church charity shop and was walking home through the market when suddenly this woman was beside me. She whispered she knew what I had done and then I felt a sharp pain.' Clara touched the side of her head where she had been struck a blow.

'May I ask what you have done?' Phoebe said hesitantly.

'I... I didn't mean to. Am I really dead? I don't want to be—' Miss Clara Garnham was gone.

Phoebe looked around and drew closer. Through a break in the crowd, she saw the crumpled figure on the ground and a police officer and a doctor with his medical bag beside the deceased. Miss Garnham leant over her body as the doctor felt for a pulse. He shook his head, and Miss Garnham disappeared.

'Oh dear,' Phoebe whispered.

'Terrible,' an elderly lady said beside her. 'That's the second lady to be attacked now in a matter of weeks in this area. It is getting too rough for my liking.'

'I couldn't agree more, Myrtle,' a lady of the same vintage said. 'And in broad daylight.'

Perhaps Harland would not arrive this evening, Phoebe realised. He may be called to the site of Miss Clara Garnham's death. Phoebe bid the ladies good day and continued on her way, hurrying back to the office. A crime was afoot.

Chapter 12

Miss Nora Waldren was shaking as the detectives approached her, and Gilbert removed his jacket, wrapping it around her shoulders. It was nearing dusk. The day had been hot and humid, and the only relief was the setting of the sun on what would also be a hot night.

'Thank you, Detective. I am usually much stronger but...' her voice trailed off as she accepted the jacket.

'Let us sit,' Harland said, indicating an empty bench seat near the omnibus stop. Detective Payne remained standing. 'Why did you drop into the station, Miss Waldren?'

Nora gathered herself. 'I met the woman last night... the woman in the laneway, and I think it was the same woman who killed Charity.' She started crying and sobbing between each broken sentence. 'She said my name... and that I was a fallen angel... and that I broke the ninth commandment.'

Harland frowned as he tried to recall it, but Nora blurted out, 'that I was bearing false witness against my neighbours. She held my arm so tight, but I got away and ran and didn't look back.'

'So she knew you, and would you say you broke the ninth commandment?' Gilbert asked.

A flash of the old Nora appeared. 'Why is that important? She attacked me. She was dowdy and horrible, and everything I said to my friends was the truth. Charity wasn't honourable, and Clara's family is struggling because her father lost his job. That's not worth killing someone over.'

Harland cut to the chase. 'Can you describe the woman?'

'Dowdy, a head taller than me, strong, nasty—'

'Had you ever seen her before?' Gilbert cut her off.

'No. A fallen angel... what does that mean?'

'We don't know yet, Miss Waldren, but you need to take care now,' Harland said, and Nora gasped.

'Do you think she might come back for me?'

'We know nothing about this woman yet, Miss Waldren,' Gilbert said, 'and thus, every precaution must be taken.'

With that, Miss Waldren stood, hurriedly handed back the jacket to Gilbert and said, 'I have to go home.' She was heading towards the omnibus before the detectives could say good night.

At closing hour at *The Economic Undertaker*'s place of business, the door opened and Randolph Astin looked up in professional mode, ready to welcome the customer with poor timing.

'Detective Stone, well you won't be after a burial package,' Randolph relaxed and offered a welcoming smile.

'Not today, fortunately, Mr Astin. I am here to walk Phoebe home and see if I was included in her list of vexations last night at the *Vexed Vixen* dinner,' he joked, removing his hat and running a hand through his short dark brown hair.

Randolph chuckled. 'I heard through the grapevine that Julius featured. I believe he is being a most exacting father-to-be with his research and preparations.'

'That does shock me,' Harland said, making Randolph laugh again, and then Phoebe appeared at the top of the stairs.

'Ah, here you are, and looking lovely as always,' Harland said. 'Forgive me for not bringing flowers, but I came straight from an interview.'

'Thank you, Harland,' she said, smiling, 'and you need not bring me flowers. I am always impressed that you arrive here on time, given the pressures of your day. I was worried that I would not be here... a late mail run,' she explained.

'I am delighted you will join us for Christmas lunch, Detective?' Randolph said. 'Let's hope you get the day off.'

'The pleasure is mine, thank you, Mr Astin. I just hope the criminals rest and go home to their mothers' place for lunch.'

Randolph and Phoebe laughed at the image before Phoebe sobered. 'I am afraid I must derail our walk home.'

'Oh, you need to work late? Of course,' Harland said, his disappointment evident.

'No,' Phoebe said and looked around.

'We are here alone, my dear,' Randolph said. 'Julius and Ambrose are due back any moment, Mrs Dobbs has left for the day and there are no customers in the house.'

'Thank you, Grandpa,' she said and returned her attention to Harland. 'On my return from the post office, I ran into a spirit, literally. She was standing, looking across the way at her prone body. She had been struck on the head on the way home from work, and appeared not to understand what was happening.'

'Where was this?' Harland asked, concerned.

'Near where the last attack happened. I didn't realise she was a spirit. There were many people gathered around her body, and the police and a doctor arrived while I was there. She spoke to me briefly, and then when the doctor felt for her pulse, she returned to her body and soon disappeared.'

'Was it the coroner, do you know? Tavish?'

'No,' Phoebe said. 'I believe it was a passing doctor who stepped forward to assist at the behest of a constable.'

'Good. Her body may remain there a little longer so the attending detective can examine it. Did she say what happened?'

Phoebe nodded and relayed the conversation.

'I am concerned that she approached you in public, Phoebe,' Randolph said, frowning. 'In most cases, spirits have appeared to you when you are preparing them. The jilted bride, Miss Alma Thornton, appeared in your bedroom, and now this young lady has done so without her body. This does not bode well for your peace.'

'Do not worry, Grandpa, I am not inundated, I promise, and she did not ask for my help or know who I was. I literally bumped into her not realising she was the deceased, and we spoke for but a moment.'

'Did she say her name?' Harland asked.

'Yes, Miss Clara Garnham.'

Harland stepped back, surprised, bumping against the door. 'But... Gilbert and I just left her less than an hour ago, at the church charity shop. This must be related to my case.'

'I am afraid she is dead, Harland. Shall we go to her?'

The back door opened, and Julius entered, calling out last-minute instructions to Claude and Will. He removed his hat and strode up the hall.

'Ah, Harland, you made it again, impressive,' he joked, and the men shook hands. 'Grandpa, I have told the boys to leave the cleaning of the hearse until the morning. Our first funeral is not until 10am. They will see to the horses now and depart.'

'Good idea. Violet has departed and taken Rufus with her. Did you leave Ambrose at the cemetery?' Randolph asked. 'I knew the day would come.'

Julius laughed and, as always, the transformation was worthy of a moment's fascination for those who loved or befriended the most serious of the Astin family. 'He is walking Miss Prout home, and as there was some commotion around South Brisbane that held us up, we detoured and I dropped him at Prout Monumental Masons on time.'

'That is Miss Clara Garnham, another murder, brother,' Phoebe said. 'I met her on the way back from the post office, her spirit that is. We are on our way now.'

'Another detective may have already been called to the scene,' Harland said, 'but if there is a link to our case, and it sounds similar, the sooner I get there the better.'

'I will take you there in the trap now on my way home, if Grandpa is ready to leave? We'll take the four-seater and drop the two of you off first.'

'Thank you, yes,' Harland said.

'I will lock up,' Randolph agreed.

'I shall get my hat,' Phoebe said, heading for the stairs.

'Harland, help me ready the trap,' Julius said, and everyone sprung into action but halted at the sound of an insistent knock on the door. Randolph, being closest, opened it.

'Detective Payne,' he announced, 'come in.'

'Good afternoon, Mr Astin, I was looking for... Sir!' he said, seeing Harland. 'I am sorry to ruin your walk home, but when I entered the office, we were dispatched to a murder near the market. Hello Miss Astin, Mr Astin,' he said to Phoebe and Julius further inside the reception area.

'Detective, come in,' Julius said.

'We are on our way now,' Harland said. 'Did you keep your hansom?'

'I did, Sir, but how did you know about... oh, of course,' he glanced at Phoebe.

Harland glanced out at the hansom and turning said, 'Thank you, Julius, Mr Astin, we shall go with Detective Payne then and you can depart at leisure.'

'I will ride with the driver, Miss Astin,' Gilbert said, and the party hurriedly departed out the front, leaving Julius to lock up. He watched them board and with a wave returned inside.

'Well, shall we depart at our leisure?' Julius said in jest to his grandfather.

'I'm feeling at leisure, so let's do so,' the senior Astin said with a chuckle, and they headed down the hallway, work done for the day.

Chapter 13

THE CONSTABLE LOOKED UP at the sight of the two detectives approaching with a pretty young lady and smiled with relief. 'We were hoping someone would arrive soon,' he said with a nod to the other constable keeping the public at bay.

'Has the coroner been notified?' Harland asked.

'He has, Sir. The sergeant who sent for you was fetching him.'

'Good job, thank you, Constable. What have we then?' Harland asked as Gilbert reached for his notebook and Phoebe moved to the edge of the crowd as they agreed, in the hope Miss Clara Garnham might appear again and to not draw curious eyes her way.

'The woman has nothing on her to identify—'

'Miss Clara Garnham,' Gilbert said. 'She works at the church charity shop.'

'Oh right. Well, she's got a large wound at the back of her head,' he stated the obvious.

'Did any witnesses come forward who saw what happened?' Harland asked, seeking something useful.

The constable nodded. 'Two, Sir. They saw the woman walking along with another lady. I have their names and addresses.'

'Excellent,' Harland said with a nod to Gilbert, who wrote the information.

'He's the coroner now, Sir,' Gilbert said, and Harland thanked him while he observed the scene. He glanced at Phoebe, who gave a small shake of her head. Miss Clara Garnham had not reappeared as yet.

Phoebe saw Harland coming her way. She had told him not to hurry on her behalf; she was happy to loiter and look at the Christmas market while he waited for the body of the young lady to be removed. Her grandparents knew where she was and that the walk had been diverted to a police crime scene; they would not be worried if Phoebe was late for dinner.

'Please remain where I can see you,' Harland asked, and hurriedly added, 'not that I wish to restrict you, but there is a killer on the loose.'

'I do not feel restricted,' she said, grateful for his thoughtfulness. 'I shall look at the ornaments on these tables. You return to your crime scene, and I'll keep my eyes out for anyone wishing to bare their soul.' They both knew Phoebe was referring to the spirit of Miss Clara Garnham.

'He is handsome,' a young woman said and sighed. 'Well, I am most disappointed.'

Phoebe jumped at the unexpected voice beside her and turned to find Miss Garnham. She moved closer to the large display Christmas tree and out of the thoroughfare of customers where she could talk with Miss Garnham without looking odd. Fortunately, the spirit followed her.

The deceased young lady continued. 'Had I known I was going to die today, I would have taken some risks.'

'Miss Garnham, I am pleased to see you again. What sort of risks?' Phoebe asked.

'I would have kissed the man I so admire,' she said coyly. 'I would have had a whole slice of cake this morning instead of daintily having a sliver, and I would have told that old biddy at the shop where I work what I thought of her.'

Phoebe ignored her tirade, keen to get information should Clara Garnham disappear again like last time. 'Miss Garnham, what happened? Who harmed you?'

Clara shook her head. 'I was walking through the market and heading home when this bossy woman came very close to me.'

'She said she knew what you did.'

'How did you know that?' Clara demanded.

'You told me earlier before the detectives arrived.'

Clara studied her. 'Oh, that was you. Yes, that's what she said, and then she would not let go of my arm and pulled me along the street. I thought she was taking me to confess. She kept saying I had to pay for my sins, and then I felt a sharp pain at the back of my head, and that is all I remember.'

'Your sins? I am very sorry. Do you know who it was?'

'I have never seen her before.'

'Can you describe her? Can you see her now?' Phoebe pushed the deceased Miss Garnham for information, and waved to Harland to indicate she was all right when he looked her way again.

Clara looked around. 'She is not here, but the woman was taller and wider than me, with an ugly hat and very bossy.'

Phoebe refrained from sighing. Recognising that she was unlikely to get much more, she risked asking, 'What did you do, Clara? What might she have found out? You can tell me now that you have left this life.'

Clara hesitated. 'I did it only out of necessity. My father has lost his job, and there were bills we could not pay, and I needed money for a friend. I borrowed a small sum for both of them from the church charity shop box where I work. I fully intended to pay it back of course.'

'Of course,' Phoebe said and then, seeing the body loaded into the wagon, and Harland bidding Gilbert good night, she turned to find Clara had departed with her body and the detective was striding towards her.

'I am sorry that was not the lovely walk I had planned,' Harland said, and Phoebe chuckled.

'It was an odd diversion indeed,' she agreed, accepting his arm. 'I spoke with the spirit of Miss Garnham.'

'You did? Wonderful. I had best get you home. You can tell me on the drive.' Harland hailed a hansom and after settling within, Phoebe quietly filled him in. Shortly after, they pulled up at the Astin family home.

'Will you come in?' Phoebe asked.

'No, but thank you,' he said and then pulled an envelope from his pocket before Phoebe departed the hansom. 'Will you accept this letter and read it this evening?'

Phoebe's heart stopped in her chest. Was he intending to end their relationship? She looked up at him, startled.

Harland hurried to assure her. 'It is a love letter of sorts. The best I could do,' he admitted and looked sheepish.

Phoebe exhaled with relief and then smiled with delight as she accepted the letter. 'Thank you, Harland.'

'Tomorrow evening, work permitting, I was hoping you might visit my home, see if you could imagine yourself there, and of course, if you wish to bring a chaperone – your grandma or a friend, I will understand. But I assure you, nothing dishonourable will happen. I would just like to—'

'I would love to, thank you, Harland,' Phoebe cut him off. 'And I shall read your love letter this very evening.'

Again, she refrained from chuckling at his uncomfortable expression. 'Thank you for the eventful walk home.'

He laughed. 'Quite a diversion. But thank you, Phoebe, for the company and information.' He leapt down from the hansom and assisted her to alight. 'Good night.' He kissed her hand.

Phoebe went up the stairs of her family home and opened the door, turning to wave as he departed for his club in the waiting hansom. Phoebe looked at the letter and hurried upstairs to hide it, to read later in the evening. Her heart was singing with happiness, and then she remembered the spirit of a young lady who had just left this life, and Phoebe was so grateful to have her chance at love.

Chapter 14

Across town, at closing time, private investigator and part-time artist Bennet Martin and his clerk were finishing for the day. Bennet had been too busy heading into the Christmas season to accept any investigation work. Add to this, none of the potential cases that his clerk, Daniel Dutton, presented, interested him enough to change his mind. Thus, absorbed in his studio, the handsome Englishman was unaware his belle, Miss Lilly Lewis, had met Daniel Dutton near the post office recently, and discovered what Bennet would like for Christmas and discussed the future of the agency. Plans were hatched, of which Bennet Martin would soon be the target as the men closed the business for the evening.

'It is so difficult turning down work,' Daniel sighed as he packed up to depart. 'I think we should put on a junior private investigator who could accept and work some of these cases under your banner, and keep the cash flowing in when you are preoccupied elsewhere.'

'You mean preoccupied working on my art commissions that also keep the cash flowing,' Bennet clarified, as he fixed his tie in the downstairs mirror before heading out to dine with Miss Lilly Lewis. 'Everyone wants a portrait before Christmas to give to a loved one. I have only agreed to do a small number, and fear not, I am charging a ridiculous price that will compensate for the lack of investigative work.'

'Are you selecting only the most beautiful subjects?' Daniel teased.

'On the contrary. The ones with the most interesting faces.'

'Ah,' Daniel nodded. 'That explains that horsey-looking woman last week. A most interesting face indeed.'

'Her husband does not mind her being horsey,' Bennet said with a chuckle. 'I believe she is quite wealthy as well.'

'That would make her more attractive to some,' Daniel agreed. 'Here's Miss Lewis now.'

'And right on time,' Bennet said, surprised. 'She expected to be late with her unpredictable deadline. I could have collected her after all,' he said with a last look at his appearance before going to the door to greet her. 'Hello most beautiful lady, story filed then?'

'Ted and I are done and dusted. Oh my, you are handsome,' Lilly teased as Bennet reached for her hand and kissed it.

'It's true,' Bennet agreed, earning a laugh.

Entering the office, Lilly said, 'It is amazing working with a seasoned journalist. He knows everyone and can turn a phrase in the blink of an eye. Hello, Mr Dutton.'

'Miss Lewis, lovely to see you,' Daniel said with a grin.

'Why are you still here? Has Bennet not given you annual leave at this time when you have no clients?' she said, looking from the bespectacled clerk her own age to her beau, Bennet.

'I am a heartless boss,' Bennet agreed, and Daniel laughed.

'I don't like to holiday at the hottest time of the year, Miss Lewis, and the quiet period allows me to catch up, clean out files and do the accounts before the new year begins,' Daniel explained. 'Besides, we are still getting requests for work, which I must decline.' He said the latter with a small sigh, and Bennet rolled his eyes.

'Why don't you take on another investigator to do this work rather than turn it down?' Lilly asked, making herself comfortable on the edge of Bennet's desk and looking most alluring in her mint green dress.

'Miss Lewis, I just suggested the same thing. Your mind is as sharp as mine,' Daniel teased.

'It does have merit,' Bennet agreed, collecting his hat.

Lilly persisted, 'Why not you, Mr Dutton? You have been working with Bennet long enough to have learnt the tricks of the trade. Does the work interest you? And then you could train a new clerk as you know that job well.'

Bennet laughed but sobered seeing the serious expression of his clerk. 'Does it interest you, Daniel?'

'It has interested me since I began working with you two years ago now,' Daniel confessed, the colour high in his cheeks as he expected to be ridiculed.

'Two years! That serves as an apprenticeship, surely?' Lilly said. 'And Mr Dutton accompanied you when you did your undercover research to find the vanishing groom.'

Daniel chuckled, 'I played myself, a clerk.'

'And most admirably,' Bennet conceded.' You have a good eye for detail, and you look most unassuming; that can work in your favour.'

'If Mr Dutton can select the best cases and work those, with the assistance of a clerk, you might find yourself able to work as an artist full-time, Bennet!' Lilly said enthusiastically. 'Unless you get a case that excites you.'

'That would be a case you are reporting on,' Bennet said and then narrowed his eyes and looked from Lilly to Daniel. 'Did you two plan this? Am I being ambushed?'

Lilly huffed. 'If you are complaining because your lovely belle and your loyal employee are trying to make you more money and allow you to do what you love, then you have very little to complain about.'

'You are right, my love,' Bennet said, kissing her on the cheek. 'Daniel, let's do it.'

'Really?' Daniel asked, so surprised he knocked over the stand holding his writing implements. He scurried to collect them and reinstate them on his desk.

'I am a man of action. Select your first case, but I expect daily consultation to ensure you are on the right track. It is my name on the agency door after all.'

'I agree and would be happy with those terms. This is exciting,' he said with a grin. 'I have prepared a financial plan for my new salary and for that of a junior clerk. Shall we discuss it in the morning?'

Bennet shook his head but could not help smiling. 'Very well, my colleague. Who knows, perhaps one day we will be partners or you can take over the agency!'

'Grand ambitions indeed,' Daniel smiled, looking the most delighted that Bennet could ever recall. 'Enjoy your dinner then; I shall lock up.'

They bid the clerk goodnight, and as they passed by the windows, Bennet did not see Lilly glance back long enough to share a conspiratorial smile with Daniel. A good afternoon's work all round.

The sun had set not long after 7pm, and Julius, Violet and Tom finished dinner early, which seemed to help Violet's digestion and allow her to sleep better this late in her pregnancy. An unexpected knock on the door roused them; Julius was rarely called on at night as the deceased were kept in the home, the morgue or hospital until the next morning and the family met with in the office.

Julius opened the door to find a young man bearing a letter.

'I'm Jacob and I have a note from Father Taylor from St Mary's Church at South Brisbane,' the stringy boy said.

'I know both well,' Julius assured him.

'Right. Father said if it was convenient, could you call on him this evening or tomorrow?'

'Did you come from there on foot?' Julius asked, looking behind the boy for evidence of a ride.

'It wasn't far.' The boy looked toward the kitchen, and Violet appeared beside Julius. Both noticed the young man's thinness.

'Go now if you wish, Julius. I am fine, and Tom will be home with me.'

'It might be best if I leave it until the morning,' Julius said, reluctant to leave, and then, on seeing his wife's expression, added. 'I will go now then.'

Tom appeared at the door with them and greeted the young man, a year or two younger than himself, but as tall.

'I will hail a hansom in case you need the horse and trap, Tom—' Julius started but Violet cut him off.

'You will take the horse and trap, and Tom will run to the midwife up the road should I need help,' Violet bossed him.

'I will,' Tom agreed. 'Promise.'

Julius sighed, beaten. 'All right then, I am outnumbered.' He turned to the young man. 'Have you eaten, Jacob?'

'I'm not that hungry,' the boy lied.

'Why don't you come in and help my brother eat some leftovers while my husband saddles the horse and secures the trap? You can both return to the church together.'

Jacob looked to the kitchen again as if entering might cost him, and then Tom began walking toward it, calling over his shoulder, 'It's a roast,' and Jacob stepped inside.

Julius closed the front door, gave Violet a small smile and departed down the hallway to the backyard while Violet took Jacob through to the kitchen to serve him a generous plate of food, which was devoured within fifteen minutes.

Once prepared, Julius issued Tom instructions until Violet shooed him out of the house; Jacob waited by the horse and trap, and Julius found him gently stroking and talking to the horse.

'He's my favourite. His name is Shadow because I knew he would cast a long shadow and I would have him for the term of his natural life. Do you like horses?'

'Yep.'

Julius took his seat in the trap and held the reins while Jacob got in and settled beside him. They departed in the dark for St Mary's, saying little for most of the journey.

Julius subtly studied the dishevelled young man beside him with tattered clothes, long hair overdue for a haircut and dirt that suggested bathing had not been conducted recently. Beside him, Julius felt preened, and he was not the preening type.

As they neared the church, he asked the sullen young man, 'Do you often run errands for Father Taylor?'

'Yep.'

He waited. The boy did not elaborate. His manners needed some work, but not one for small talk either, Julius asked directly, 'Are you sleeping in the church?'

Jacob snapped to look at Julius. 'Why would you ask that?'

He answered bluntly. 'Because you look like you need a good feed, a wash, and a good night's rest.'

'I don't need anything,' Jacob said and looked away.

'You look familiar, Jacob.'

The boy said nothing, and then Julius realised why he recognised the young man, who was much healthier the last time he had seen him standing away from a gathering of people at a funeral that Julius and Ambrose had delivered. From memory, the church community helped with the funeral costs, and it was *The Economic Undertaker*'s bottom package for paupers and those that became the responsibility of the state.

'The *Economic Undertaker*—my business—buried your parents, didn't we? About six months ago.'

'Yep.'

Julius steered the horse onto the church grounds and stopped at the side of the church.

'Do you want me to mind Shadow while you talk to Father Taylor?' Jacob asked. That was the most he had said for the entire journey.

Julius hesitated and decided if Father Taylor found the boy trustworthy, then he most likely was, and he responded in the manner that Jacob had to all of his questions. 'Yep.'

He saw the small smile twitch on the boy's lips and reminded himself he was once that age and had gone through a tragedy; he wasn't the best company or a credit to his family then either.

Julius entered the church and glanced around. A few parishioners had lingered after the midweek mass, and the candles were still lit around the altar. He approached the small

148

room at the back of the altar and called softly, 'Father, are you there?'

'Ah, Julius, you came. I'm very grateful,' Father Taylor said, appearing from the backroom with a book in his hand. 'I hope I didn't disrupt your evening too much.'

'Not at all. How can I be of assistance, Father? Is it Jacob?'

'Jacob? Oh yes, partly. He is a concern that I must deal with shortly, but not the main reason for my request to speak with you. I was wondering who you gave the note to last time, as I've now received another and thought it might be time to speak with the police.'

'Another? In the same place?' Julius asked, concerned. 'There was another murder this very afternoon. I gave your note to Detective Harland Stone, as you requested. He intended to call on you.'

'I am sure he has his hands full, but now I have a second note, and yes, it was left on my chair in the confessional box... and you say there is a second crime?'

'Yes, another young lady. It might be more significant than first thought. Do you have it on you?'

'Of course.' Father Taylor produced the note from the pocket of his cassock and gave it to Julius, inviting him to read it.

'Forgive me, Father, for I have sinned.

She broke the fifth, and to punish her, I broke the sixth.
My vigil continues.
No one escapes the reckoning.'

Julius looked at the priest. 'The sixth?'

'Thou shalt not steal,' Father Taylor responded.

'Hefty price to pay if she lost her life for that. I will see that Detective Stone calls on you tomorrow, Father. Now tell me about Jacob. He is not forthcoming. We buried his parents, if memory serves.'

Father Taylor sighed and glanced through the open door where they could see the young man with Julius's horse and trap. 'You did. He has never really recovered. He was such a lovely young lad, but has dropped out of school, takes work where he can get it, and sleeps in here when he can get away with it. I don't mind, but I have accompanied him to the men's shelter where he can have a wash and a hot meal, but he is at that awkward age – not a boy and not comfortable with men, and he always returns here.'

'Is he interested in the priesthood?' Julius asked.

'Oh, I wish, Julius,' Father Taylor said dramatically, making Julius chuckle. 'I tried to recruit him. But no, he appears to prefer labour of sorts. He loves animals; feeds the pigeons, which I try to move on, and he seems to have an affinity with dogs and horses.'

'Hmm,' Julius mused. 'I will need a junior stable lad after Christmas.'

'Will you? God moves in mysterious ways. I have been praying for Jacob to find a champion, a man with several businesses who employs widely, and here you are.'

'Well, you summoned me,' Julius said drily. 'Two birds with one stone?'

'You might say that,' Father Taylor grinned. 'Is one of your staff leaving?'

'No, Charlie has shown an affinity for the mortician work and has been studying the trade with Phoebe for some time now. We need him to move into the role permanently. A lot more customers are choosing not to have viewings in their own homes.'

'A good idea, especially in this heat. So, would you consider employing Jacob?'

'Why not if he has a good work ethic? He could start now, as Claude and Will are having the holidays with their families, and Charlie could teach him the ropes.'

'Julius, that would be wonderful. It is a tragedy losing his kin.'

'What about the rest of his family – aunts, uncles, grandparents?' Julius asked, and Father Taylor shook his head.

'His grandmother is still alive but had fallen out with her daughter over the choice of husband, Jacob's father. She won't take in his offspring—her words—but she comes to mass.'

Julius gave a shake of his head at the hypocrisy.

'There's an aunt and uncle, but they don't like the looks of him; a bit wild, apparently.' Father Taylor sighed, thinking out loud while glancing at the boy. 'Well, he'll have a job, thank you. Once he is earning, he can afford a boarding house.'

'There is a cot and washstand in the stables if he wishes to stay there until he finds something suitable. I will mention the job to him.'

'Thank you, Julius, but be patient. He may not be appreciative, or it might take a while for him to come around. Please don't give up on him if he appears ungrateful.'

'It's all right, Father. I remember being a most disagreeable young man myself. Hard to believe, I know,' he said in jest, challenging the priest to agree and got the expected laugh.

'You turned out all right in the end,' Father Taylor said. 'Bless you, son. I shall expect a visit in due course from Detective Stone. Oh, and the christening of your pending arrival... I would be honoured to do so when the time comes.'

'Thank you, Father. I will advise Violet as she will organise it; it has been suggested that I should step back from trying to organise the birth and arrival.'

Father Taylor hid his smile as best he could, and with that, Julius departed with the note, to have a word with a sullen young man and Detective Harland Stone. He was sure he had heard the priest chuckling on his departure.

Chapter 15

PHOEBE ENDEAVOURED TO MAINTAIN her usual demeanour while in the presence of her grandparents throughout the evening. Ambrose, having walked Miss Prout home, had long since headed out with cousin, Lucian, and upstairs, under her pillow, a letter hummed.

It felt like it was calling her. It had a pulse, a lifeline to the future. But Phoebe did not want to rush it or share it; she wanted to savour it later when her time was her own. So, the dutiful granddaughter played a round of cards with her grandmother as her grandfather enjoyed a book on the verandah on the warm summer night, and finally when it was time to retire, she did so happily.

Dressed for bed, Phoebe settled comfortably under the light cotton bedding. Leaning against her pillows, she adjusted her bedside lamp and opened the letter with the single word on the front, her name written in his handwriting.

The content revealed several pages of beautiful handwriting, no doubt drummed into him at his private boarding school. Phoebe took a breath and began to read.

Dearest Phoebe

Thank you for agreeing to read this letter, which I will do my best to keep shorter than a novel. I am a man of facts, more used to report writing, and I have never written a letter of this nature. I hope you will not be disappointed. As I have introduced Gilbert to the expectations of the detective ranks, he has done his best to draw out some romantic notions from me, but I believe I am a poorer student of poetic thought than he is of policing.

Phoebe stopped to appreciate those few powerful words that caught her attention: 'I have never written a letter of this nature.' She was not naïve enough to believe Harland had not loved before; she had learnt there was a lady he might have married up north had she not become too insistent. But this was the first love letter he had written. With a small smile, she continued to read.

From the day I met you in the company of your family over police business, I could only admire you from afar as it appeared

Phoebe could not help but chuckle at this, even if she did
now feel a small tremor of trepidation. She could hear his voice
in the written words as if he sat beside her, talking of their
future. But she disagreed most vehemently with him. He was
the handsomest man she had ever met. He had a presence that
turned heads when he entered a room, especially hers, and he
was a detective, a man with a suitable career. As for charm, she
did not seek a man who could charm her; love and loyalty were
top of her list, if she had a list, that is. Phoebe continued.

support you in all your endeavours, but I cannot promise I won't be overprotective or insist you rest and chase away those spirits (I would do so if I could see them).

I promise never to dishonour you. You have my loyalty until the grave.

I promise to provide a home for you, and I hope you will consider my house worthy of our future together. I loved it from the moment I saw it, but then, I had no plans to stay long term. My career would determine that, or so I thought, but in fact, you will determine it, Phoebe, in all respects – heart, home, and place. I wish to be where you are. By your side, in the heart of your family and our family.

I hope we will have a family of our own, more than one child so our offspring will have the friendship and affection of siblings as you have with Julius and Ambrose. I hope that is agreeable if you accept me.

It was very agreeable to Phoebe, but again, she could not help but smile at his laying out of facts. She was sure they could have discussed these matters in time, and had already done so on several issues, but perhaps Harland thought now that a serious offer was pending, he needed to be official. She continued to read.

I must now declare my deficiency in understanding a lady's needs aside from the material. I was raised as an only child and knew only the company of boys at the boarding school. I am not well attuned to female emotions and not likely to realise if you are upset unless you are openly weeping before me or hurling items at me. Without those signs, if you would do me the courtesy of informing me in plain speak, I will do what I can to resolve your distress. No doubt I will be the cause of it, or so my married acquaintances tell me that is often the case with husbands.

Phoebe laughed out loud at this. Dear sweet Harland. He certainly was giving some thought to this, overthinking some might say. She understood now Violet's frustration with Julius's need to plan for all possibilities. But Phoebe could not help being flattered, and a little amused.

I am bound to forget important dates, and to be late home or have to depart again soon after arriving. I know this will put a strain on our marriage. I hope you will be comfortable with this, Phoebe, but sadly, I foresee no way around this in my current position.

I can assure you I am tidy and well trained in domestic matters, having had discipline drilled into me at school and from living alone for sometime. But of course you could argue that Rufus could be trained to be as compliant, and that is not to my advantage.

I am sure I have many more faults to lay before you, but I don't wish to deprive you of discovering those in your own good time.

The idea made Phoebe laugh again, and while she loved that big hairy dog, she thought she might prefer the company of Harland. Turning the page, only a few lines remained.

The fact is, Phoebe, I love you. More than I thought ever possible in an earthly union. Enough to make me fearful of this life without you.

The letters I've written but never sent, the future I've imagined but am yet to realise, and the loss I feel every evening I leave you at your gate and walk away – these have no measure.

I hope when I ask for your hand, you will honour me by accepting, and while I am no poet, please know you are my first thought in the morning, my distraction during the day, and my last thought at night. You have given me reason and purpose, and I will lay down my life for you any day, every day.

I am yours if you will have me.

Harland.

Phoebe read the last lines over and over, her eyes welling with tears.

'Yes, Harland. The answer is yes,' she whispered.

Chapter 16

THE NEXT MORNING, THE coroner's office was busy at 10am with both the deceased and the living, just how Dr Tavish McGregor liked it. He had several bodies waiting for his attention and had prioritised the victim of last night's murder for Detectives Harland Stone and Gilbert Payne.

The two detectives had just arrived, keen to know if another murder, possibly linked to the first, was on their hands. Also in attendance, wanting to observe his brother at work, was Tavish's twin, Brodie, visiting from Scottish shores, and reporter Lilly Lewis, looking for today's story, had timed her visit well.

'Shall I proceed, Harland?' Tavish asked and, giving Lilly a wink, asked, 'Can Miss Lewis hear my findings?'

'Yes, I have no objections,' Harland said. 'Where is your fellow reporter, Mr Egan, Miss Lewis?'

'He has gone to seek the constables on duty last night to see what they might have noticed or heard from the witnesses on hand,' Lilly said and turning to Brodie added, 'He is a senior journalist I have partnered with and is so very good at what he does, Mr McGregor. I hope to be as capable one day.'

'From what Tavish tells me, Miss Lewis, you are well on your way,' Brodie said charmingly.

'Very true,' Tavish confirmed. 'Right then. Miss Clara Garnham died from a blow to the back of the skull,' he said, indicating the area. 'She has not been assaulted in any other manner, and the blow was sufficient to kill her.'

'Is it—' Gilbert started to ask, and Tavish cut him off.

'Yes indeed, I would say the type of instrument used is similar, if not the same as that which felled Miss Charity Buckley. A very sharp object with a square blunt base. Small though it is,' he said and drew the pattern on a piece of paper.

'Oh! A second murder and most likely by the same killer,' Lilly said, sounding way too excited and clearing her throat, added, 'How awful.'

Tavish put his head back and laughed. 'You are fooling no one, Miss Lewis. We know a good story excites you.'

The detectives grinned, and as Tavish was about to send the detectives and Miss Lewis on their way, Julius Astin entered.

'Goodness, we just need Bennet and all the gang would be here,' Tavish said.

Julius greeted everyone, shaking hands with the men. 'Just a quick visit. I was looking for the detectives; I have a message from Father Taylor at St Mary's which might relate to your case,' he said to Harland and Gilbert.

Harland looked surprised. 'Another? Should we step outside and let you keep working, Tavish?'

'Not for a moment. I want to know what is going on,' Tavish assured them. 'So, you have already received a note from the priest at St Mary's Parish? Is he sending you penance to do now?'

The men laughed at the thought as Gilbert flipped through his notebook to find where he had recorded the details.

'Thankfully, no.' Harland addressed Julius. 'We haven't visited Father Taylor yet. It was an ambiguous note.'

Gilbert read its contents for the benefit of those present. 'The note read, "*Forgive me, Father, for I have sinned. She broke the fifth, and I broke the sixth. She was deserving, and I will do so again. No one escapes divine retribution.*" It was left in the confessional box at the church.'

'How interesting. What are the fifth and sixth?' Lilly asked.

'Oh, Miss Lewis, shame on you,' Tavish teased her. 'The fifth and sixth commandments!'

'Oh, the commandments,' she declared. 'So the fifth means the victim disrespected her parents, and the sixth reveals the killer took her life. That is a hefty price to pay, is it not? Is this note writer our killer, Detectives?'

Harland gave a small shrug. 'Impossible to say at this stage. What do you have now, Julius?'

'The second note was found last night in the same location as last time.' He retrieved it from his pocket. 'It reads, *"Forgive me, Father, for I have sinned. She broke the eighth, and to punish her, I broke the sixth. My vigil continues. No one escapes divine retribution."* The eighth being, Thou shalt not steal.' He handed Harland the note, who in turn, handed it to Gilbert.

'He chooses to administer punishment,' Gilbert said with disgust. 'He must think he is the Lord's vessel.'

'A vigilante more like it,' Harland agreed. 'The writer is God-fearing, but has no problem acting as God. We also discovered yesterday that the young lady stole because her father lost his job and the bills were mounting.'

'That is a difficult situation,' Lilly agreed. 'How did you find out?' she asked, her news nose twitching.

Harland gave her a small smile. 'Miss Lewis, as always, you have a remarkable ability to sniff out a story. There was another attack, but fortunately it failed.' He protected his source—Phoebe—diverting the subject to Miss Nora Waldren's attack and her gossiping.

'Another young lady? So might they all be connected – the murders of Charity Buckley and Clara Garnham and the woman in the failed attack?' Lilly exclaimed.

'It is looking that way, and we have two crimes the writer has confessed to committing, if the notes relate to the murders, of which we might now assume they do,' Gilbert said with a glance to his superior, who nodded his agreement.

'I am sorry to interrupt,' Julius said and looked at Tavish. 'First thing this morning, the family were on the doorstep to book the victim's funeral and viewing with us. I am to deliver Miss Garnham's body to Phoebe. Are you finished, Tavish, or will you need to do further examination?'

'I am finished if the detectives are?' Tavish agreed, and with Harland's sign off, Tavish covered Clara Garnham.

'Gentlemen, Miss Lewis, I am on the clock,' Julius said, accepting the trolley. 'I promised Father Taylor I would give the note to you, and you would call in, Harland. He is concerned about the safety of his parishioners. Are you able to do so?'

Today, I assure you,' Harland said.

With that, Julius departed with the victim and bade the living good day.

'Well, detectives, Miss Lewis, you have plenty of work to do,' Tavish said. 'Will you be at the club this evening, Harland?'

'I hope to be,' Harland said of the regular weekly catch-up. 'Will you join us, Brodie?'

'Thank you, Harland, but I am attending a literary event with Detective Payne. Not that I don't appreciate the offer to attend the club and watch the boxing again.'

Tavish hit his twin on the back. 'You and Detective Payne will enjoy the literary circle; you are both men of words. I thank you for looking after my brother.'

'The pleasure is mine, Doctor,' Gilbert said, smiling.

'Can I report on this story, Detective Stone? Will you tell me more about the attack?' Lilly asked, cutting to the chase, and the gentlemen turned to her.

'Thank you, Miss Lewis, for keeping us on track,' Harland said. As he always did, he hesitated, thinking about the consequences of releasing the information to the public. 'I can't see any harm in doing so, Miss Lewis, and it might remind the ladies of our community to be careful in their comings and goings. Do you wish to come and see the priest with us? We shall go now.'

'Yes, good Lord! You invited me without my having to ask. I may need a moment to recover,' she teased.

'We are leaving right now,' Harland joked.

'I feel better,' she said in jest and, thanking the coroner, Miss Lewis and the detectives departed.

'You have good friends, Tavish,' Brodie said, observing his twin.

'I have made a home for myself here, brother. I hope you will stay for as long as you can. Perhaps if you lose your heart to a local girl...'

'Perhaps,' Brodie said with a grin as the doors opened, and another body was wheeled in.

Father Taylor was returning to the parish, having delivered the last rites to a parishioner in their home, when, from across the way, he saw two men in suits entering the church with a young lady he recognised as Miss Lilly Lewis. The priest assumed it might be the detectives and hurried to catch up with them.

'Oh, he is giving the last rites,' one of the senior ladies advised them as she refreshed the church flower decorations.

'I am here,' he said with a light pant, and instantly felt the relief of entering the cool church on what was already a scorching morning.

The detectives and Lilly turned to find Father Taylor behind them.

'Ah, Father, do not rush on our behalf,' Gilbert said. 'Detective Harland Stone, Miss Lilly Lewis from *The Courier*, and I am Detective Gilbert Payne.'

'Good morning to you all, and I know Lilly, of course,' he said with a smile and a small bow of the head. 'Come through to the office.'

Father Taylor thanked the parishioner as he moved his guest to a side room, which was deceptively large and included a meeting table with half a dozen chairs. A jug of water and glasses sat in the middle of the table.

'My apologies for taking some time to call on you, Father Taylor,' Harland said, as the priest removed the vestments he wore to give the last rites and joined them at the table in his black suit and white collar. Lilly poured water for the attendees.

'Not at all. You are a busy man, Detective, and, like me, you are at the mercy of irregularities in our job except for paperwork. The gentleman I was just administering last rites to has been lingering for days, but his family thought it best to get the job done just in case he slipped away,' he said with a chuckle. 'Tomorrow, I have a christening. The cycle of life.' He took a gulp of water from the offered glass and said, 'And how are you, young lady?'

Lilly smiled. 'Very well, thank you, Father.' She explained for the detectives' benefit, 'Father Taylor has christened

all the Lewis children and put up with my five brothers'
misbehaviour in church.' She saw his look. 'Oh, fine then,
mine as well.'

The three men chuckled.

'That is more like it,' Father Taylor said. 'I have read your
columns. You have a great talent for delivering the truth.'

'Thank you, Father, and it is good to see you again.'

'So you have no objection to Miss Lewis being present?'
Harland confirmed. 'We will clarify what she can quote
from the meeting.'

'That arrangement suits me well,' Father Taylor said.
'I am not familiar with either of you gentlemen. Are you
practicing?'

Gilbert cleared his throat. 'I am with the other lot,
Father,' he said and earned a laugh.

'We are all God's children. And you, Detective Stone, are
up for recruitment?' the priest asked with a grin.

'Do your best, Father,' Harland joked.

'A challenge! Well, to business,' the priest said with
a nod. 'Both of those notes were delivered a week apart
on different days. They were left on the chair of my
confessional box. I take confessions daily, so they were there
no longer than a day. I scanned the church both times
after finding the note, but I recognised all the faces on the
premises, and I can give you those names.'

'Excellent,' Harland said. 'Thank you. We have two ladies murdered, and another attacked. She survived, and her account matches the witnesses who saw the two murdered ladies being led down a lane near the Christmas market by a solid lady gripping their arm. The deceased were both found dead near or in the lane. Now that you have received a second note, Father, we believe they are connected given the culprit told the surviving young lady she had broken a commandment.'

'Well, there you have it,' Father Taylor said, wide-eyed. 'Dreadful. Were there any witnesses to the actual murders?'

Gilbert shook his head. 'No one saw the felling of the ladies, but it was done with a blow to the back of the head using a small, sharp, square-shaped object, strong enough to penetrate the skull,' he said and hurriedly added, 'My apologies Miss Lewis,' and indicated the area on the scalp.

'Not at all, Detective Payne,' she said, having previously noted the detail in the coroner's office.

'A source believed there were references to the second victim, Miss Clara Garnham, committing theft – the eighth commandment,' Harland said.

Father Taylor nodded. 'It is a delicate matter, and I hate to speak ill of the dead, but if it will help your investigation... Miss Garnham was found to be stealing money from the church charity shop box. She said she would repay it, and it was only a loan while her father was out of work. An unfortunate situation. But charity begins at home.'

'Yes,' Harland said, amazed yet again by Phoebe, who had told him as much directly from the source. 'We heard that as well. The surviving victim was told she was a sinner and broke the ninth commandment.' He did not name Miss Nora Waldren to protect her privacy, but Harland imagined the news would soon come out as she also volunteered in the church charity shop.

'Hmm, the ninth,' Father Taylor said, surprised, 'bearing false witness. Sadly, we have all been guilty of that, I imagine.'

'Too true, Father,' Gilbert agreed. 'We dropped in and spoke with Mrs Wilson and her volunteers from the church charity shop, given our first victim, Miss Charity Buckley, also volunteered there. It was before Miss Garnham's death, but they did not know of any threats to Miss Buckley.'

'Would Mrs Wilson fit the bill?' Lilly asked.

Father Taylor looked surprised. 'She was very angry at the theft, but is a God-fearing woman. Hmm, but whoever is doing your murders believes they are doing God's work too, by the looks of it.'

Harland agreed. 'However, Mrs Wilson does not physically fit the profile, and no doubt someone at the market would have recognised her if she were with the ladies.'

'I agree,' Father Taylor said. 'She had been working in the community for many years, and her husband is well known – he works at the fishery. Very popular at Lent,' he said with a huff of laughter, as the parishioners all ate fish on Good Friday and during the period of Lent.

'Can you think of a parishioner who might match the description, Father?' Gilbert asked and read out the details of the stout woman seen with the two victims.

'Yes,' he said and gave a small shrug. 'Half the parish.' He looked at Lilly. 'Do you recall the two victims, Miss Lewis, or have any idea who in our parish might do such a thing?'

Lilly shook her head. 'I thought Miss Buckley looked familiar, but you might recall, Father, that my mother insists on sitting in the third row from the front on the left every mass, and anyone sitting behind us is a stranger to me.'

The priest chuckled. 'Yes, people tend to have their favourite pews.'

'It is interesting that the killer has not come to you in the confessional, only left a note,' Harland said.

'I've thought about that too,' Father Taylor said. 'Every time I push back the confessional screen, I wonder if it will be them. It makes me think that, from the tone of his or her note and the fact the killer is not asking for forgiveness, that they believe they are doing God's work. If that is the case, gentlemen, you have a very dangerous individual on the loose.'

Chapter 17

PHOEBE HAD LITTLE TIME to appreciate the coolness of her room on this humid December morning, four days before Christmas, or enjoy the rays of light through the window. She was finishing preparation on a body for the 11am viewing, and her brothers had gone to collect another, that of Miss Clara Garnham's. Rufus, on the other hand, stretched as he turned on the couch, not a trouble in the world since he had come across Julius in the cemetery and joined the Astin family.

In the new year, Phoebe would have permanent help; Charlie would begin with her full-time. He would have his own small room separate from Phoebe for when they were not preparing bodies. Here, he could continue his studies or prepare his equipment. It was formerly the walk-in cupboard with a small window up high and enough room to put a desk and bookcase. The shrouds and linen were now closeted upstairs in the new viewing rooms.

What to do about spirits appearing? Inevitably, she would slip up in front of him, but could Phoebe tell Charlie? Could she trust him? It would make life easier if he knew her secret, especially when the detectives visited for information. She would consult with Julius and get his opinion.

No sooner did she have the thought, then the sound of footsteps above and the whirring of the pulley system in the wall told her the body was on its way downstairs via the contraption that cousin Lucian had installed.

Julius hurried down the stairs. 'Morning, Phoebe, is all well? I have Miss Clara Garnham for you.' He reached the bottom of the stairs and gave Rufus a pat in passing, then opened the doors to the pulley system, sidled the trolley into position and pulled out the body.

'Hello brother, so Dr McGregor released her already. Does he believe it is the same culprit?'

'Yes, it appears to be the same weapon. Has she...?' he glanced around.

'Not yet. I had hoped to speak with you about that. I envisage it is only a matter of time until Charlie finds out. Look how Grandpa accidentally discovered your secret while he was putting clean linen in the cupboard and heard you speaking with Uncle Reggie.'

'I have been thinking the same. You say Charlie is quite intuitive and open to the idea of spirits?'

'He senses them, which is quite amazing, and has no fear of the afterlife but cannot see them. Charlie said his mother was the same. I wonder if I should tell him.' Phoebe bit her lower lip as she studied Julius.

'I think it is inevitable, but bide your time until you think he is ready. Speaking of Charlie, I offered his job in the stable to a young man; Father Taylor introduced us. We buried the boy's parents several months ago, and he's been sleeping in the church since.'

'The poor lad, but that's wonderful, Julius, that he'll now have the wage to find board.'

'He turned it down.'

'Oh,' Phoebe said and sighed. 'Maybe he will change his mind. No one likes to think they are receiving charity.'

'I stressed I needed to fill the position, and if he didn't take it, someone would. But of course, he might have grander ambitions than to work in a funeral home. I understand that.'

'Yes. But it is a reliable job, with the opportunity to work in different roles, and the boss is kind enough,' Phoebe teased.

Julius smiled. 'I heard he can be vexatious.'

Phoebe laughed. 'I fear we have mortally wounded you, and you will never forgive the *Vexed Vixens* for that.'

'I shall recover, and there is truth in Violet's vexation,' he conceded. 'As for the young man, if I am not here, and he changes his mind, his name is Jacob Henley. I've let Grandpa and Ambrose know. Charlie will need to show him the ropes given Claude and Will are away.'

He wheeled Miss Garnham's body into place for Phoebe. 'Are you finished with this other gentleman if I take him to the viewing room?'

'Yes, thank you. I'll start on Miss Garnham now.'

'It is not too much?'

'No,' Phoebe said with a laugh. 'I am working at a comfortable pace, and soon, Charlie will join me, and we will be full staff again. Plus the next generation,' she said teasing him.

'True,' Julius smiled. 'I wonder how young they can be to start their apprenticeship.'

She playfully hit his arm and, wishing her client a restful after life, Phoebe covered the first body and Julius departed to raise it in the upstairs viewing room. Pulling back the sheet, she saw Miss Clara Garnham up close in the flesh for the first time.

'Hello again, Miss Garnham. Rest assured, I will do my best to make you as beautiful as you were in real life.'

'Thank you,' a voice said, and Phoebe wheeled around to see the lady in spirit form standing nearby. 'How come you could see me then and again now?'

'I've always been able to,' Phoebe said with a quick glance up the stairwell to make sure Charlie was not in sight and no one was approaching. 'We have not exchanged names. I am Miss Phoebe Astin.'

'I am Miss Clara Garnham. So, I am really dead. What a terrible state of affairs!'

'Sadly, yes. Miss Garnham, is there anything you can tell me that might help the detectives to find the person who harmed you?'

The young woman walked around her body, staring at it as if fascinated by seeing herself lying in state. 'I was pretty, wasn't I?'

'Very pretty,' Phoebe said gently and began her work under the watchful eye of Clara.

'That's what the lady said, the one who was dragging me away. She said I was an angel. But then she ruined it.'

'What do you mean?'

'She said I was an angel. A fallen angel.'

'Mr Astin is coming,' Mary announced from her usual seat near the window. 'Mr Astin, your husband, Violet,' she clarified.

'Brace yourselves, ladies,' Violet teased, and they exchanged small smiles as the door opened and Julius entered, removing his hat.

'Good timing, husband, you have just missed a client, and the next appointment is in fifteen minutes,' Violet welcomed him.

Julius smiled, pleased. 'Excellent. Good morning, Miss Pollard, Mrs Shaw, Mrs Moss. Hello again, dear,' he said to Violet.

The ladies greeted him in the usual fashion; Mary blushed profusely, mumbled a greeting and returned to her work; the widowed Jane Moss looked at Julius with blatant admiration – bold as brass is what her mother would have called it. Violet, as always, was taken by his handsomeness, and Nellie Shaw clapped her hands together and reached for a box near her desk.

'Mr Astin, what timing. I have a small gift for you and Violet. I know it is premature, but you can open it together now and then ensure it gets home safely,' Nellie said, rising and presenting the pair with a beautiful gift-wrapped box.

'How thoughtful, Mrs Shaw, thank you,' Julius said, accepting it and placing it on the table for Violet to open. She did quick work of the wrapping with her scissors and gasped in delight at the contents. Beautiful knitted baby wear, which Violet displayed one after the other, six garments in all.

'Did you make all these, Mrs Shaw?' Julius said, holding a small pair of white knitted booties. 'You must have started months ago.'

'I have had a good nine months,' she said, smiling, delighted with their reaction as the other ladies joined in admiring the pieces. 'I chose a neutral colour as we don't wish to confuse people with a boy wearing pink or a little girl dressed in blue. It is a shame there is no way to know.'

'Oh, if there were, Julius would have discovered it,' Violet assured her, and while the ladies smiled and Mary giggled, Julius gave his wife a wry look.

Then, his embarrassment and delight were evident as Violet leant sideways—as it was impossible to hug front on in her current condition—and wrapped her arms around him, holding Julius tight before releasing him.

'You are a wonderful husband,' she teased.

He cleared his throat, clearly uncomfortable. 'Well, I had best go then. Thank you, Mrs Shaw, they are beautiful.' He stepped back to depart but not without a smile lingering on his lips when Ambrose entered through the back door.

'It is safe to enter, Mr Astin,' Nellie called, and the younger Astin brother entered, beaming.

'Good morning, ladies,' he gave a small bow. 'Ah, here you are, Julius. I visited Phoebe, who said you had just left; I was on your trail.'

'Why? Is something wrong?' Julius asked, concerned.

'No. I was just curious and bored,' he said, and the ladies all smiled, charmed.

'You could have offered to get the mail, or see if Charlie needs help given Will and Claude are away, or—'

'Yes, yes, we get the point. How droll,' Ambrose said and saw the baby clothes. 'Have you been knitting?' he asked his brother, who gave a small shake of his head and ignored the laughs, well used to Ambrose's sense of humour.

'A beautiful gift from Mrs Shaw for your niece or nephew,' Violet said delighted.

'How adorable,' he laughed, holding up a small outfit.

'We had best go then; we have a funeral,' Julius said, keen now to leave before Violet or Ambrose caused him any further embarrassment.

'In two hours,' Ambrose stated.

'Yes, but I'm very busy even if you are not.'

'Then what are you doing in here? You only saw Violet a few hours ago, and look, she is fine,' he said waving his hand near his sister-in-law.

'Good day, ladies, and thank you again, Mrs Shaw,' Julius said, ushering Ambrose to the back door.

'Oh, the pleasure was mine, Mr Astin,' she called after him. 'I look forward to meeting the little one when he or she is wearing them.'

But before departing, Julius returned alone, a serious look on his face, and prepared to wear the teasing, but none came and Violet sobered seeing his concern.

'You will not overtax yourself, will you?' he asked softly, and all the ladies quietly returned to their work.

'No,' Violet promised him. 'I am going to sit right now,' she said and allowed him to lead her to her chair. He kissed the top of her head before departing.

After the back door closed, Mary uttered, 'Oh, he is the best husband in the world.'

'Poor darling, he has experienced some loss and is naturally worried when you are his world,' Mrs Shaw said.

The widowed Mrs Jane Moss agreed. 'Life can change like that,' she said, snapping her fingers.

'That is why I try to keep him smiling and tease him out of his concerns. All will be well,' Violet said, as worried for her husband as he was for her.

Chapter 18

Reporter Lilly Lewis hurried down the stairs to her desk in the smoky den that was the newsroom. She smiled with relief to see her writing partner, Ted Egan, hard at work, as the deadline loomed.

'Miss Lewis, you and Ted will have a story for the afternoon deadline, won't you?' Lionel Faherty, the acting editor, called as Lilly passed his office.

'Absolutely, Mr Faherty,' she responded and hurried to the desk next to Ted.

'Lilly, my girl,' the seasoned reporter said calmly, looking up on hearing someone drop beside him. 'Got a yarn?'

'You bet, Ted. I've been with the detectives and with Father Taylor from St Mary's. He's got a second confession note.' She removed her hat and set herself up ready to write.

Ted grinned. 'Excellent. I have spoken with Miss Garnham's mother, as well as Mrs Wilson, the woman in charge at the charity shop, and found a few witnesses at the market who saw Miss Garnham going off with that woman. I also have the illustrator drawing up a map of the Christmas market and marking on it where both ladies were found dead.'

'Oh, that's perfect! I never thought of that! We have a story,' Lilly said, her eyes wide with excitement. She looked at the large clock in the corner. 'I will hurry.'

'I'm almost done. Write up the bones of your yarn, give it to me as you go and we'll work them together and give it a polish.'

'Right you are, Ted,' Lilly said enthusiastically and hurriedly began her story while Ted re-read his copy and checked facts in his notebook. As she finished one page, she slipped it to Ted, who hurriedly read it.

'Good work, Lilly. How about we lead with the connection between the girls, the futility of their death, and then alarm the reader with the confession made to Father Taylor? What say you?' Ted asked, preparing to rewrite the copy.

'My thoughts exactly!' Lilly said.

Ted began with the headlines and opening paragraphs, and Lilly finished her copy and checked her quotes and names against her notes. Fifty minutes later, they filed their story to Mr Faherty and stood by as he read the copy, should he have questions.

TERRIBLE TRAGEDY AT CHRISTMAS MARKET
TWO YOUNG WOMEN BRUTALLY MURDERED
CONFESSION OF A GOD-FEARING MURDERER
An exclusive report by Lilly Lewis and Ted Egan

It is now possible to give readers more details of the terrible tragedy – the most terrible in the history of the South Brisbane Christmas market of which was the scene of another murder this week.

The two chief actors in the ghastly drama, the murder victims, Miss Charity Buckley and Miss Clara Garnham, were known to each other from their volunteer work at St Mary's Church Charity Shop. Both young ladies were shopping at the Christmas market in South Brisbane on different evenings, and were seen being led away by a robust lady of mature years. This was the last time the unfortunate girls were seen alive by any eye save that of the murderer.

The detectives on the case, Harland Stone and Gilbert Payne from the Roma Street Police Headquarters, confirm the choice of murder weapon is the same. But is the woman seen leading the girls away the murderer?

In a strange twist, which the detectives now believe is linked to the deaths, Father Taylor of St Mary's Catholic Parish received two written confessions around the times of both deaths. The notes were left on his confessional seat and not offered in person by the guilty party. The writer was not seen by the good father or the parishioners.

The motive for the crime is inexplicable, but not so to the confessor, who claims both victims sinned and thus forced the killer to break the sixth commandment—thou shalt not kill—and punish them. The writer of the confession bore little guilt for what he or she claimed to be retribution for the two women.

Around almost every murder there are circumstances that at least indicate motive – greed, revenge, jealousy or passion. But in this case, every such element appears to be absent. The killer appears to believe they are doing God's work.

The question then arises, were the murders the action of a madman or a madwoman, so lost to moral control as to be practically insane?

Those who have known the young ladies for years cannot recall any single incident that would lend any explanation to why they might be chosen.

The editor looked up before reading through the quotes. 'Excellent. Kindly chase up the illustration, and I shall see you both in the morning,' he said and resumed his reading as he waved them away.

Outside the editor's office, Lilly exhaled with relief. 'Thank you, Ted, I am learning so much from you in the way of gathering facts and writing up the story.'

'Are you Lilly, my girl? Well, it warms my heart that you say so.'

'I shall chase up the illustration and leave you to have a drink with the boys,' she said with a nod to the male reporters gathering their hats and preparing to finish the day with a quiet ale or two.

'Do you wish to come?'

Lilly looked surprised and gave a little laugh. 'I've never been asked before, but thank you, I will decline. I wish to catch my breath and organise myself before we start again in the morning.'

'Well done,' Ted nodded approvingly. 'Tomorrow then, we shall see what has turned up. Hopefully not another young lady. Careful as you go now, Lilly.'

'I will. I have no desire to be the headline,' Lilly agreed and bid Ted goodnight as she happily hurried to the illustrator's office to chase up the Christmas Square scene, delighted with the day's work.

Late afternoon in an office at the far end of the hallway of the Roma Street Police Headquarters, Detective Harland Stone paced, as his protégé finished writing up the information gleaned from their day's enquiries.

'We know from the second note there will be more killings, and had Miss Nora Waldren not escaped, we would now have three deaths. I hope she—assuming the woman is our killer—is not intending to work through all ten of the commandments,' Harland said.

'It would not be hard to find sinners to fit,' Gilbert said.

Harland stopped to study the board before pronouncing with a note of surprise in his voice, 'We have nothing solid whatsoever. Not even a clue from Phoebe that might serve as a lead.'

'It does appear that way, Sir,' Gilbert agreed. 'We have a woman seen by several, including the victim who got away, but no one can identify her. We have three ladies who have apparently sinned, and who are connected by their work at the charity shop and their church.'

'Yes. If we are to believe the letter writer is our murderer, then Miss Charity Buckley's sin was not honouring her father and mother, which resulted in her death. But Miss Buckley's parents died before her,' Harland said exasperated.

'But I suppose she may still have dishonoured them before their death and angered our killer,' Gilbert said. 'But that would imply the killer knew the family. Then, a week later, Miss Clara Garnham dies. Miss Astin did tell us that Miss Clara Garnham had stolen from the charity shop, and Father Taylor confirmed it, so that is a fact.'

'Even if it is a charity shop, and Miss Garnham needed charity. It is not as if she were using the money to do her Christmas shopping,' Harland said. 'How did the killer know of the theft but not know of her situation? Or have they no mercy?'

'And we know Miss Nora Waldren bore false witness against her neighbours; we saw evidence of that,' Gilbert said.

'She disparaged at least three people in our company,' Harland agreed with a small huff of laughter. 'All three ladies are connected through their volunteer work. Let us assume that the woman seen is the killer; from all descriptions, she would be robust enough to strike the girls with a sharp object. According to Phoebe, neither of the young ladies knew the woman, so she is not a friend nor a family connection. She does not work with them at the charity shop as a volunteer or manager. She must not be a regular donor to the store, as they didn't recognise her. So how was she privy to this information about their character?'

'We might assume she is a regular church attendee, Sir, and she is acquainted with Father Taylor,' Gilbert said as the men continued to share thoughts and throw around ideas.

'Yes. I thought of attending the masses on Sunday at St Mary's to see if I could spot any likely suspects, but as the priest said, I might end up with more than I bargained for with numerous ladies fitting the description.'

Gilbert agreed. 'Tomorrow, Sir, I should return to the charity shop and enquire about how many more ladies volunteer there, and warn them not to venture out alone for now.'

'That is an excellent idea, Gilbert.' He paced and stopped long enough to study the two notes given to Father Taylor. 'The writer has a very neat hand, we might assume she or he is educated.'

'It's beautifully written. It's not copperplate like we were taught at school, Sir.'

Harland looked at it again. 'Yes, you are right; I was taught copperplate too. Who could forget all the raps over the knuckles with the ruler when it wasn't to the teacher's standards?' Harland sighed, uncharacteristically sharing a bit of his history. 'This style is more fluid, but I wouldn't say it is feminine handwriting. I have known men with similar penmanship.'

'As have I, and it is lighter and more ornamental than what I was taught,' Gilbert said, studying the flourishing style. 'It is distinct, though. I wonder if it is taught somewhere. I will find someone who might know. May I keep one of these on me, Sir?'

'Of course,' Harland said, keen to have more concrete clues. He had learnt never to disregard his protégé's odd facts. They both thought in silence for a while and then Harland asked, 'It is possible the woman led the girls to a man, a partner in crime who killed them? Except that Miss Buckley's account to Phoebe seems to go no further than the woman herself. But why wait until now to punish the sinners? Has something happened in the killer's life to push him or her to these actions, or is it because Christmas and the birth of Christ is believed to offer salvation?'

'I think the former, Sir.'

'Why is that, Gilbert?'

'Well, the killer cites the Ten Commandments, and they are from the Old Testament, whereas the birth of Christ is in the New Testament. So, I am inclined to think something has unsettled our killer, and Christmas has little to do with it.'

Harland ran a hand over his chin. 'Interesting. I keep coming back to the notes themselves; I believe our strongest clues are from them. Our victims broke the commandments. How would the killer know those intimate facts?'

'She would only know by witnessing it firsthand or hearing it from other community members, friends or family,' Gilbert said.

'Exactly. So tomorrow, that is where we will start.'

With that, Harland headed to the club, and Gilbert ventured to collect Mr Brodie McGregor, the coroner's twin brother, for their night at the literary club.

Chapter 19

GILBERT PAYNE PUT ASIDE his detective work for now and arrived at the literary gathering twenty minutes earlier than the time he had arranged with the coroner's twin brother, Brodie McGregor, to ensure he was on hand for his arrival. Like Gilbert, Mr McGregor was a man not fond of tardiness and also arrived early.

Stepping down from the hansom, Brodie raised a hand. 'So kind of you to invite me tonight, Detective. I confess I much prefer a literary evening to a round of drinks and a fight in the ring.'

Gilbert grinned. 'As do I, and I hope you will find our gathering up to your standard.'

'I have no standards,' the congenial, reserved man, five years Gilbert's senior, said with a gentle slap on Gilbert's back. 'Shall

we dispense with the formalities and become official friends?'
he asked. 'Will you call me Brodie and I will reciprocate?'

'Indeed,' Gilbert agreed happily, and the men entered the
premises. Several of Gilbert's friends waved, and the two men
joined their tables, Gilbert undertaking the introductions of
the gathered party of all ages from all walks of life with a
shared love of literature. Drinks were ordered, and the night's
program discussed.

'I am afraid the poetry of Robert Burns will be part of
tonight's agenda,' Gilbert said, nudging Brodie beside him.
'You have sailed all this way from Scotland to hear poetry from
your own land.'

'Then I could not be happier,' Brodie said in his thick
Scottish accent. 'You will all then know the brilliance of the
Scottish bard himself.'

This was met with agreement all round and few challenges.
As the evening wore on and Brodie discussed his work in more
depth, Gilbert asked, 'May I seek your opinion on a clue from
our latest case if you don't mind being put to work on your
holiday? If not now, at a time of your convenience.'

'I would be delighted to help,' Brodie said. 'The study
of linguistics interests me at all hours, not just in my work
capacity. Ask me now.'

Gilbert looked around to ensure his friends were suitably
engaged and pulled the note left in the priest's confessional

from his pocket. He explained its significance quietly, so as not to be overhead talking about a current murder case.

Brodie regarded the note carefully before handing it back. 'You are right, Gilbert. It is not copperplate, but a Spencerian script. It is a graceful script and not as heavily shaded as copperplate. Where I am from in Edinburgh, some of the private schools continue to teach it. I cannot say whether that is the case here, but there has been a push to teach a uniform style. If that applies in Australia, then either your writer is old school or went to a school where it was the preferred script.'

'Most interesting,' Gilbert said, storing the information in his mind, as he did with all facts. 'What sort of person might choose to write in this hand?'

'Ah, a thoughtful question given the person you are looking for,' Brodie said, sitting back to think for a moment. 'I believe it would be a person who appreciates beauty, seeks perhaps to make their own mark by adding subtle flourishes and decorative elements. But perhaps likes order or structure; the lowercase letters are based on four fundamental strokes – a straight line, a left curve, a right curve, and a loop.'

Gilbert absorbed all the information. 'Thank you, Brodie, that is most interesting.'

'But of very little help, I imagine.'

'I would not say that,' Gilbert disagreed. 'It is impossible to know when a small piece of information will be the piece that fits the puzzle.'

'Well, I am glad to be of service. Please do not hesitate to ask again,' Brodie said. 'Ah, and it is time for Mr Burns.'

Both men smiled as a poet took to the stage, and his Scottish attire left no doubt of what he would read at the evening's gathering.

As he did every evening, Earnest Buckley said his prayers. Tonight, he felt inspired to say them in his sister's room, where he had spent several hours mourning her. After making the sign of the cross on his body, he rose from his kneeling position and surveyed tonight's labour.

Earnest had packed all of Charity's belongings into the cloth bags that Mrs Wilson from the church charity store had given him; all of her garments and shoes would be donated. He glanced around the now-spartan room. The timber wardrobe, the small table and chair with the attached looking glass, the thin mattress on a single bunk. Charity was gone, and so was everything that connected her to him.

'A life packed in three bags,' he said and sighed. 'It's as if you were never here, Charity. As if it were all a dream.'

He frowned, recalling a verse, and recited it aloud in a voice full of pathos: '"*All that we see or seem is but a dream within a dream."* If you were one of my students, Charity, you would recognise that poem by Edgar Allan Poe. One of his best short poems. But now you are gone, as if you were a dream; a memory.'

Turning to the figure behind him, Earnest shook his head. 'I don't wish to speak with you this evening; you have let me down.'

For a moment, he listened and then closed his eyes, as if calling for strength before opening them again and adding, 'You had that young woman. You had her in your grasp, and she escaped to sin again. If I were you, I would beg for forgiveness.'

Earnest refused to look, punishing with his indifference. He held up his hand and snapped, 'Say no more! If you are so very sorry, then you must make amends and quickly.'

He took a piece of paper from his pocket and looked at the list of names. Two had been marked off – his sister, Charity Buckley, and Clara Garnham.

'Leave Nora Waldren for now.' He read out another name. 'Mrs Martha Miller has broken the seventh commandment—Thou shalt not commit adultery—and has the audacity to come to church, to enter the house of the Lord. Married for less than two years, the woman has no virtue. Punish her.'

Chapter 20

Early the next morning, Charlie raced in from the back of the office and, remembering Ambrose had been chastised for hurrying in a place where one should be respectful, he slowed his steps.

'What's wrong, lad?' Randolph asked, seeing the young, slim man with the reddish hair, who had worked so hard and fitted in so well at *The Economic Undertaker*, hurrying up the hall.

'There's a boy my age here asking for Mr Astin, Julius. I think he slept in the stables; it's him, the one who was offered the job,' Charlie said, mixing up his words. He didn't say a great deal, but was delighted that he'd have someone to train in his job and there would be no delays to prevent him working with Phoebe as a mortician.

'Ah, good. I believe the young man's name is Mr Jacob Henley,' Randolph said calmly, consulting a slip of paper Julius had left him prior. He glanced at the clock. 'Julius hoped he would come and take up the position, but unfortunately I can't leave the desk right now. I'm expecting a client, and Phoebe has gone for the post.'

Mrs Dobbs stepped out of the kitchen. 'I'll make him welcome, Mr Astin, and then Charlie might be able to get him started on his duties?'

'I can, Ma'am,' Charlie agreed.

'As always, Mrs Dobbs, you are our most versatile employee and a lifesaver,' Randolph said, and she laughed.

'Go on with you, Mr Astin. I am happy to be of service.'

'Julius won't be long,' Randolph assured Charlie. 'He is visiting his accountant to sign some paperwork.'

'Let's see to this young man then,' Mrs Dobbs said. 'I'll take him a few biscuits. Have you had breakfast, Charlie?'

'Yes, Ma'am. My ma won't let me out of the house without a good breakfast in case I fall over from faintness or suffer some other similar peril.'

Charlie heard Mr Astin chuckling as he quoted his mother's words and waited for Mrs Dobbs to wrap a small bundle of food in a serviette.

'A sensible woman, she is,' Mrs Dobbs said as they headed to the back door.

They took the back stairs to the stables and found the lanky boy taking the initiative to sweep the floor. He stopped when he saw them, placed the broom down, and scowled as if expecting to be asked to leave.

'This is Mrs Dobbs,' Charlie said. 'She manages the kitchen and clients and lots of things. Mrs Dobbs, this is Jacob Hanley.'

'Good morning, Mrs,' he said and removed his hat.

'Good morning to you, young man, and welcome. Mr Astin is delayed this morning, but Mr Astin Senior, who is expecting a client and could not personally attend to you, said to welcome you warmly. Best you have these then,' she said and handed him the warm bundle. 'I think having biscuits for breakfast is a good idea now and then.'

He grinned and thanked her, hurriedly opening the bundle. Then, he offered one to each of them.

'I've eaten, but thanks,' Charlie said, and Mrs Dobbs declined.

'Thank you, dear, but I shall wait until morning tea. You have impeccable manners, young man,' Mrs Dobbs praised him. 'Now, I believe you are here to take on Charlie's role as he has been studying under Miss Astin's tuition?'

'Yes, Mrs, I am. Mr Astin offered it to me but I said no, and he said to come if I changed my mind, so I have,' Jacob said and took half of the biscuit in one bite.

'You can do other jobs if you want, work your way up,' Charlie said. 'Mr Astin encourages that.'

'I like animals and working with horses. I met Shadow the other night,' Jacob said, nodding to the horse as he continued to polish off the biscuits.

'Did you spend the night here?' Charlie asked, seeing the small sack in the corner.

Jacob's eyes widened, and he responded defensively, 'I touched nothing important; everything is still here. Mr Astin said I could sleep here if I take the job, so I was going to take it today, and then I can stay.'

'Goodness, you will do no such thing,' Mrs Dobbs said, and he looked as if he had been reprimanded. 'I have been rattling around in a big house all alone since my husband died, and I have often thought of having a boarder. My son and his wife are keen for me to do so.'

Jacob looked terrified at the thought. 'I couldn't do that, Mrs...'

'Dobbs,' Charlie reminded him.

'You don't even know me. I could be the devil himself,' Jacob said, shocked at the suggestion.

'Are you?'

'No.'

'Well, there you go, and I believe you are known to Father Taylor. There's no better recommendation,' she assured him.

'We won't get in each other's way – I have my cards group and church committee and work. And I will feel much safer having a man on the premises. I am only two omnibus stops from work.'

'I can't pay rent until I get paid. I can sleep here until then if Mr Astin gives me the job.'

'I believe you have the job,' Mrs Dobbs said kindly. 'We will work out a small rent once you get your first pay, and you can try it out for free until then. We will include board, meals and washing. How does that sound?'

'Mrs Dobbs is a really good cook,' Charlie added, and she chuckled.

'So, will you be staying, Mr Henley?' Mrs Dobbs asked.

'Jacob, just Jacob,' he said, 'and yes, thank you, Mrs Dobbs. I will.'

'Excellent. Well, Charlie will get you started before he must hurry inside to help Miss Astin, but from what Mr Astin said, you are a natural with animals.'

Again, Jacob looked surprised. The scowl that had been there earlier was replaced with a happier countenance. He returned Mrs Dobbs's serviette, thanked her again, and, looking a bit miffed at the speed of what just happened, got to work.

Phoebe couldn't focus on her work, or on the elderly lady who waited under the cloth to be made presentable for an early afternoon viewing. She was frustrated. Two murders had happened, and *The Economic Undertaker* had buried both ladies, yet she had learned nothing of significance to help Harland. Tomorrow evening, she was to see his house, and what if another murder happened beforehand? It would be tragic for the victim, and, feeling selfish, she did not want it to ruin their romantic plans. It was time to call for help.

'Uncle Reggie,' she whispered loudly and waited before trying again.

He appeared, resplendent in his riding gear and looking strikingly handsome; an untimely death at the age of 40 guaranteed he would not age. 'My dear great-niece, you called?' he asked, offering a small bow.

'Oh, Uncle Reggie, forgive me. I didn't mean to summon you, but I'm at a loss,' Phoebe said, leaving her work table and walking towards him.

'You may summon me anytime, Phoebe dearest. What is wrong?'

Phoebe told of her dilemma as Reggie paced the room, arms behind his back, listening.

'I see. That is a problem, especially as there are very few clues to share with your beau,' Reggie agreed with a small smile. 'How might I help?'

'Miss Charity Buckley never appeared to me,' Phoebe said. 'Miss Clara Garnham did and told me all she could, but I was hoping you might persuade Miss Buckley to visit.'

'I shall seek Miss Buckley and let you know of my success,' he said confidently, and Phoebe smiled.

'Thank you, Uncle Reggie. Of course, if she does not want to speak with me or revisit the trauma, I understand.'

He nodded, gave a small bow and disappeared. Feeling lighter and hopeful, Phoebe got to work. After all, the dead were in no hurry, but the living were restless to do right by them.

Chapter 21

THE OFFICE OF DETECTIVE Harland Stone and Gilbert Payne was busy early that morning with the two reporters in attendance.

'We have some information and thought we should check if you have anything you would like us to report,' Lilly said, and Harland's wry expression had her adding, 'or not like us to report but will let us, anyway.'

The men smiled at the likelihood of the latter.

'I have an interesting bit of information that might be worth storing away,' Ted Egan said with a glance to Gilbert, who stood by the notes on the board, poised to write. The senior journalist flipped through his notes. 'Small things noted by the witnesses can sometimes be useful.'

'Absolutely, thank you,' Harland agreed and nodded for Ted to continue.

'Mrs Wilson, the manageress at the Church Charity Shop, has five ladies who volunteer. Two are now deceased; one has been attacked. She has been privy to regular gossip by the ladies and advises that while it was believed Miss Clara Garnham stole the charity shop money for her unemployed father and struggling family, Mrs Wilson heard that Clara, in fact, gave the money to a friend. Mrs Wilson knew not which one, but I spoke with Clara's mother and her father, and they received nothing.'

'So where is that money now and which friend has it, I wonder,' Gilbert asked, making a note of it on the board.

'And why did the friend need it?' Harland added.

Ted Egan continued. 'Miss Nora Waldren, who is no stranger to gossip and escaped being a victim by good fortunate, claims your first victim, Miss Charity Buckley, was being forced to marry a man her parents approved of from their church. But with the parents gone, supposedly her brother wanted to honour the arrangement; Charity did not.'

'That is extremely interesting, thank you, Mr Egan,' Harland said, looking at the board. 'Miss Buckley was killed because she broke the fifth commandment and did not honour her father and her mother. We need to speak with her suitor and see if he is an angry young man with a firm grasp of the Old Testament.' He scribbled himself a note.

'His name, I believe, is Percival Triggs, but Earnest Buckley would be best to confirm that,' Ted said, reading from his notes.

'You are amazing, Ted,' Lilly said, admiring him. She had often wanted to investigate but, to date, had reported rather than sought her own facts. She was learning.

'Small stuff, Lilly my girl, and not all of it is useful,' Ted said.

'We have been surprised in past cases how the most obscure of facts can lead us on the right path,' Harland said.

'Then one more thing, detectives,' Ted continued. 'A witness to Miss Nora Waldren's attack, said the oddest thing. She could have sworn the lady with Nora was Mrs Buckley.'

The room fell silent.

'Mrs Buckley, as in Earnest and Charity's mother,' Lilly added in case the detectives had missed the connection.

'But she's dead,' Gilbert said, checking his board.

'She is indeed. Lilly checked that.' Ted confirmed.

Lilly nodded. 'We published her death notice, and she was buried by K.M. Smith Undertakers.'

Ted continued. 'But the witness, Mrs Upton, said she was walking behind Nora and this lady just before they entered the lane; that's when she parted ways from them. Mrs Upton said she stopped for a moment, about to call out a greeting before remembering Mrs Buckley was dead. She sat behind her at church for years and stared at the hat, which she could have sworn was on this lady's head. It was likely donated to the charity shop and purchased by someone else, but an interesting aside.'

Gilbert noted it and added with excitement in his voice, 'Mrs Wilson from the charity shop might recall who purchased it.'

'Thank you, Mr Egan, that's extremely helpful,' Harland said. 'I appreciate your sharing of information.'

'I worked closely with the police in my days on the beat, Detectives. It's good if we can help each other along since we both have a job to do,' Ted said.

'I have something of interest too,' Gilbert said. 'I cannot say if it will help us, but last night, I showed the written confession to Mr Brodie McGregor, a linguist.'

'The coroner's twin brother visiting from Scotland,' Lilly told Ted.

'That's him,' Gilbert nodded. 'He identified it as a Spencerian script that some of the private schools continue to teach.'

'I wonder if Earnest Buckley's school, St Joseph, teaches it,' Harland mused. We have a lot of leads to follow up. Thank you both for contributing. What angle will you take for your story in the late edition today?'

'Ted and I want to do a story asking, "Who is this woman?" It might bring forth other witnesses and rally the public to keep watch,' Lilly said.

'We might get the illustrator to come up with something, a sketch of the woman leading a young lady away,' Ted said, rising to depart.

'You are welcome to include the coroner's description of the murder weapon and the recent attack on another lady who escaped, but please do not identify Miss Nora Waldren, as yet,' Harland said. 'She also works at the church charity shop. However, should she be willing to talk with you and be identified, I have no objections.'

'Excellent, thank you, Detective Stone,' Lilly said, her eyes widening with delight as she made a note of Nora's name. 'I will attempt to speak with her this morning.'

'We will pay a visit to St Joseph's,' Harland said. 'Let's see which script they favour, and if Earnest Buckley will enlighten us about his late sister's suitor, Percival Trigg.'

'Kill two birds with one stone,' Ted agreed, 'and let us hope it is the last killing for the Christmas season.'

It was nearing lunchtime when Phoebe stood back, looked at the lady she had been working on and, satisfied, wished her well on her next journey. She carefully covered the lady's face and wheeled the trolley to the pulley system, ringing the bell for the body to be collected for viewing.

With a sigh, Phoebe turned just as Uncle Reggie, Miss Charity Buckley and Miss Clara Garnham appeared wearing the attire they were buried in, as Phoebe recalled from preparing the ladies.

'Oh, you are here! Thank you, Uncle Reggie, thank you for coming, Miss Buckley, and hello again, Miss Garnham.'

'I thought I would accompany Charity in case she needed support,' Clara said importantly.

'You were never very friendly to me when we were alive, you and Nora Waldren, but thank you anyway,' Charity conceded.

'I liked you, Charity, but Nora was... well, she pressured me, and I wasn't brave enough to go against her. I am sorry.'

Charity sighed. 'I understand, I do.'

Phoebe refrained from smiling at the impatient look on her uncle's face as if he had been caught in a stage drama.

'As I have delivered as requested, my dear great-niece, I shall be on my way for now. Good day, ladies,' Reggie said with a small bow and disappeared as Phoebe heartily thanked him. She turned her attention to the pretty Miss Charity Buckley.

'Miss Buckley, I was hoping to discuss with you your last memories before your demise; it might help to find the person responsible and stop them from taking the life of another before their time.'

'If I can help, I will,' Charity said, 'and I am sorry I didn't call on you earlier, Miss Astin. Clara told me to do so, but I didn't know I was the subject of discussion.' She looked at Clara and then back at Phoebe. 'I have very little recollection of what happened that night; it was all so quick, but I thought I was struck by a horse and cart.'

'You were found on the street, so it is possible that might have happened post-death, Miss Buckley,' Phoebe said and was about to offer the ladies a seat before realising there was no need to do so.

'But Mr Astin says I was murdered,' she said, looking at where Reggie previously stood as if he might appear again to confirm her statement.

'It is true. I am sorry. The coroner found a sharp wound to your skull. Miss Garnham died in a similar fashion,' Phoebe said, looking at Clara, who nodded.

Charity sighed, which always fascinated Phoebe as it was so lifelike for the deceased, and yet the spirits had no need to do so.

'I will try to remember what I can,' Charity said and took a moment before beginning her tale. 'I was walking home from the Christmas market. My brother insists I am home no later than eight o'clock, so I was on my way when this lady came up beside me. I didn't get a close look at her because the laneway was darker than the square, with few lights and full of shadows. I recall she took my arm, and I asked if she needed help.'

'That was kind of you,' Clara said. 'She just hurried me along.'

'She did that too. But she wouldn't look at me. She was just holding me so tightly that if I turned to look at her, I would have been looking straight into her neck, because she was taller, and I thought that was too close for comfort. I remember she said something about honouring parents, and I didn't know if she was talking about herself or me, because I was just trying to ease away and to get her to slow down.' Charity stopped and shook her head. 'I can't recall anything more. Perhaps that is when she struck me.'

'Did she seem familiar? Did she say her name or where she was going?' Phoebe grasped at straws.

'No. It was all very quick. I know that is not of much help.'

'It is, Miss Buckley, because it confirms the killer was most likely the same woman who led Miss Garnham to her death,' Phoebe said, and Clara Garnham shuddered as if she could still feel the cold or a chill could frighten her.

'I guess it has solved one problem,' Charity said and gave a small shrug. 'My parents wanted me to marry a man from our church, a friend of my brother's named Percival Triggs. I thought with their death I would be released from the commitment, but Earnest insisted I honour it. He didn't want to lose face with his friend. At least I don't have to now.'

'What a waste of money then,' Clara groaned, and Phoebe looked from one lady to the other.

'A waste of money? What do you mean? Will you tell me in case it is significant?' the young mortician asked as the two girls exchanged looks.

Clara looked shamefaced and said,' I stole money from the church charity shop, but I was going to pay it back.'

'No, I was going to pay it back,' Charity clarified. 'Clara stole it for me because if my brother insisted on the wedding, I was going to move away with the money and write my brother and Percival of my decision. I would then pay Clara back once I got work, and she could put it back in the tin, none the wiser.'

'But Mrs Wilson counts every pound and realised small bits were being taken,' Clara said with a roll of her eyes.

'May I ask why you did that for Charity if you were not close friends as you previously claimed?' Phoebe asked.

Clara pouted. 'Because I wanted Percival. He was sweet on me until he came into the store and Charity insisted on serving him.'

'That's because he has been pressing his attentions on me, and my parents and brother were keen for us to make a match.

How could I ignore him? Besides, I don't know what you saw in him.'

'I know he is not a handsome man, but we are like-minded and he has a secure job. I could do worse.' She added in a quieter voice. 'I am not as young or attractive as you, Charity, and have fewer chances, not that it matters anymore.'

'Oh, Miss Garnham, you should not have thought like that; you are very pretty and lovely of nature,' Phoebe instinctively said to the pert woman with large blue eyes.

'Thank you, Miss Astin, that is very kind of you. But he carried a flame for Charity, and he did not even see me that day in the shop. I thought if Charity ran away, he would see me again and might marry me,' Clara admitted.

Phoebe nodded and gave them both a sympathetic smile. 'It is hard when our hearts are committed elsewhere. I am not a detective, but might Percival have caused you both harm?'

The ladies looked at each other while they considered his nature.

'I could not say in all honesty,' Clara said, 'but if he did, who is that woman to him?'

'I do recall one thing,' Charity Buckley exclaimed. 'That woman said I was an angel, and I thought that was very kind, until she added a fallen angel and I did not get the chance to ask why.'

Chapter 22

JULIUS ASTIN LOOKED FRUSTRATED. It was a look that his family and staff were well familiar with, especially when Ambrose was present, but rarely seen during a funeral service.

'So you cannot see any spirits present at the moment?' Ambrose whispered.

Hot, uncomfortable, and weary of the same question, Julius turned to him. 'Must you ask me this at every funeral we attend?'

'I feel I must; it is just so interesting,' Ambrose said. 'I wish I could see them.'

'As do I,' Julius said drily. 'There is no point asking me; sometimes I don't know if they are real or spirits until they fade from sight.'

'Fascinating,' Ambrose whispered.

'Let's lower the coffin. The time has run over, and it might encourage the family to say their farewells.'

The Astin men stepped forward and, taking their positions, lowered the small casket into the ground. The result was not as Julius had hoped as several family members fell to their knees around the dug-out grave, while the reverend did his best, as did some family members, to console and pull back the affected relatives.

Julius and Ambrose, and the grave-digging father and son—the Redfords—waited. The sun belted down on them in their black clothing.

A subtle glance at his pocket watch told Julius the hour had struck eleven. The temperature had already reached 30 degrees, and the funeral that was scheduled for nine-thirty should have concluded well before now. Still, the grieving relatives remained, stalling the gravediggers, the reverend, the brothers from *The Economic Undertaker*.

'Let us remove ourselves to the wake,' a senior man suggested, and a dozen or more mourners readily agreed and started for the gates. But not all.

So they waited, and fifteen minutes later, Julius attempted to move them on again, advising that the cemetery staff must do their job, but the funeral of a child could not be rushed, nor the mourners expected to be rational in their emotions.

'It's all right, Mr Astin,' Mr Redford senior said. 'The lad and I can wait another half hour at most,' he said with a glance at his son. 'We'll wait in the shade over there. Why don't you depart? Your work is done here.'

Julius thanked him, but as they had nothing pressing, he would remain. He never left a job unattended until the body was in the ground and the earth upon it. The reverend departed, farewelling all present and offering some last words of consolation. The Astin men stood formally, waiting.

Suddenly Ambrose swayed, and Julius grabbed his arm.

'Sorry, brother, I must be letting the heat affect me,' the younger Astin said.

Julius studied him, quietly alarmed. 'Do not be sorry. This heat is ridiculous, and I should have sent you to wait in the shade earlier. Come, lean on me, and I will get you back to the hearse; you can rest there until it is time to go.'

The pair removed themselves to the hearse and horses waiting in the shade under several large trees, and Julius removed Ambrose's hat and worked the jacket from his brother's shoulders.

'Sit now. I shall bring you some water and attempt again to move the mourners along.' He looked up at the sound of horses. 'John Hislop is here with his hearse and a small crowd following. I hope they are near our funeral so they might disperse the crowd.' He raised a hand to acknowledge the rival funeral director who the brothers regularly encountered in the South Brisbane or Toowong Cemeteries.

'Grandpa said Hislop had a funeral scheduled for 1pm today; the notice was in the newspaper.'

'Dreadful. Perhaps the family requested it,' Julius muttered. 'Cannon and Crisps, along with K.M. Smith, are doing as we are – before 11am or after 3pm. K.M. Smith has one here today at 4pm.'

'Perhaps Hislop is so busy they have no choice,' Ambrose muttered.

'You could not conclude that from the notices they are running, but good luck to them if that is the case,' Julius said. 'We will not be booking funerals in the middle of the day. I would rather have the comfort and good health of my family and staff than bury people at noon.'

'That's not very businesslike of you,' Ambrose teased as he sat down in the shade.

'You cannot be too ill since you still find the energy to stir me. But next time, remove yourself, I will not blame you in this heat. I am sorry if you felt you could not do so.'

'Don't be. I didn't realise I was being baked until it came upon me. I will be more wary next time,' Ambrose assured his brother.

Julius moved away to get his brother a cup of water, retrieving a tin cup and screw-top water bottle from the hearse.

He filled it and checked the horses' water container at the same time. He returned to Ambrose. 'Here you go.' Julius retrieved his handkerchief, wet it and placed it on Ambrose's neck before pouring water from the container over his brother's head.

Ambrose spluttered. 'You enjoyed that.'

'Never,' Julius said, allowing himself the hint of a smile, given he had his back to the mourners. 'Oh good, Hislop has pulled up nearby, and our party are now dispersing.'

'Praise the Lord,' Ambrose muttered and staggered to his feet.

'Stay,' Julius pushed him down. 'I will see our mourners off and manage the gravediggers. Rest.'

He left his brother and bid the mourners farewell. Once the party was gone, Julius removed his jacket and helped the Redford men fill the grave despite their protests; with three able bodies, the job was done quickly.

'Thank you, Mr Astin,' Mr Redford said, wiping his brow and accepting the payment. 'We've got another at four o'clock today. We shall get out of the heat until then. I hope you can say the same.'

'No more today, mercifully,' Julius said. 'Just collections. If only we could do night funerals.'

'Not for the faint-hearted,' Mr Redford said with a laugh. 'Who knows what grave you might tumble into or what ghosts might come back from the dead and frighten us to be on our best behaviour.'

'If I thought that might work, Mr Redford, I would have done it years ago,' Julius said with a glance at Ambrose, and the men departed with a chuckle despite the solemnity of the occasion.

St Joseph's Boys College was like all other private boys' schools as far as Detective Harland Stone was concerned, and entering the grounds did not bring back any happy memories of his schooling years. Rather, he recalled the strict teachers, regimental routines and tasteless food of which there was never enough. He would not send his son—should he have one—to boarding school; he wanted to be there for every year, every memory.

The schoolboys walked past them in their formal uniforms, eyeing off the two men in their suits, as the detectives made their way to the administration area.

'Mr Buckley is on lunch break,' the matronly woman said from behind the counter.

'We assumed as much, Madam,' Harland said, 'which is why we came at this time so as not to interrupt his classes.

Could you let him know Detectives Stone and Payne wish to speak with him briefly, please?'

She moved away, looking unimpressed at having to do their bidding and interrupt something as important as a teacher's lunch break. Harland saw in her every woman at his old school – the stern, matronly types who young boys would not lose their hearts to as they came of age, or find any kindness to replace their own mothers while they were so far from home. Although there were always exceptions and several of the kitchen and laundry ladies were kind souls.

'Please follow me,' she said, returning and took them to Earnest Buckley's room – a small space with an envious view of the extensive playing fields.

'Sorry to interrupt your lunch, Mr Buckley,' Gilbert said.

'Not at all detectives, I imagine you have not lunched yourselves. What might I help you with? Have you made progress in finding dear Charity's killer?' He invited them to be seated on the chairs in front of his desk.

Harland closed the door and sat, feeling as if he were facing one of his teachers again.

'We have made some progress,' the senior detective assured him. 'We understand you were keen for your sister to honour your parents' wishes and marry a gentleman from your church parish?'

'She will not meet a better person than Percival Triggs. A man of principles, with a sound education and who can provide a suitable home for her. Percival was happy to honour the agreement made with my late parents.'

'But was Miss Buckley willing?' Harland asked.

'What does that matter?' Earnest snapped.

'Forgive me. I thought you and your sister were close and you would have wanted her happily partnered,' Harland said, bracing for the outrage he expected and hoped to see in order to assess the man's character. Earnest Buckley did not disappoint, slamming his hand down on his desk.

'You are questioning what is best for my sister? Her future happiness? Look what happened to her, Detective. If she had not fought me on this, had she been dutiful and not wandered around the market in the evening and gossiped with those girls from the charity shop, she would not have met such a perilous end. There is nothing charitable about that charity shop.'

'Why do you say that, Sir?' Gilbert asked, but the teacher waved his hand as if it should be obvious.

'The girls are too idle, and the chatter not in keeping with the church's doctrine,' he said, and Gilbert made a quick note of Mr Earnest Buckley's adherence to the "rules" of his faith.

'Where might we find Mr Percival Triggs?' Harland asked.

'Here, he is a fellow teacher at this very school.'

Harland and Gilbert exchanged surprised glances as Earnest Buckley continued. 'He is supervising the lunchtime activities today.' Rising, he turned to look out the window. 'You will find him near the sports oval.'

The men rose as Gilbert asked, 'One quick question, Sir. What kind of calligraphy do you teach at St Joseph's?'

'Spencerian script, although I believe there is disquiet among the teachers. Some wish to use Copperplate or adopt the Palmer Method. I prefer Spencerian.'

'That is all for now, thank you, Mr Buckley,' Harland said. 'We will call on Mr Trigg while we are here and keep you abreast of any advances in the case.'

'Thank you.' Earnest Buckley moved to the door to see the men out. 'You will find him heartbroken.'

The men moved down the corridor, past the administration desk, where Harland thanked the woman who was less than gracious, and onward to the sports field. Harland felt the stares and whispers of the boys in the schoolyard, which soon caught the attention of Percival Trigg.

He might have been a sincere and kind man as described, but Percival was not a handsome beau for a vibrant, pretty girl like Charity Buckley to show off – too thin, bespectacled, with thin lips and a look of fear at their approach.

'I am a broken man,' he told the detectives as they sat on a school bench out of hearing of the students. 'I had the approval of Charity's parents and her brother, and now I have lost the woman I thought would be my wife.'

'Did you propose to Miss Buckley, Mr Trigg?' Harland asked.

'I intended to do so, but when Charity's parents passed away, I had to respect her mourning. Earnest gave me permission to do so after three months.'

'Are you close to Mr Earnest Buckley?' Gilbert asked, and Harland gave a small nod of his head, telling Gilbert it was a good question. Might the men have conspired?

Percival looked uncomfortable.

'Our discussion remains in confidence,' Harland assured him.

'He is not a man whose friendship I would seek,' Percival said in a quiet voice. 'I find him regimented in his views; he cites that which is acceptable, does not challenge ideas; he likes what has always worked. But I believe Earnest has few friends, and no doubt thought as we would be brothers-in-law, we might be friends. It was difficult...'

'Why is that, Mr Trigg?' Harland pushed.

'He invited me to dinner recently, and I assume it would be a family dinner. But when I arrived, Charity was not there and had plans with her friends. I was quite annoyed, to be honest, but as dinner was cooked, I had no choice but to remain.

He gifted me a book that I would never read. I found the friendship forced.'

Percival Trigg looked as if he had swallowed something most unpleasant.

'What book may I ask?' Gilbert jumped in, and Harland schooled himself from looking frustrated at his protégé's interest in literature.

'"*The Picture of Dorian Gray*" by Oscar Wilde. A fairly recent release and not a book I would read.'

'Why Sir? It is a popular book,' Gilbert said, but Percival Trigg shook his head and offered no further comment.

Harland continued his questioning. 'Are you familiar with the Ten Commandments, Mr Trigg?'

The thin man laughed and looked at Harland as if he were absurd.

'Of course. I live them to the best of my ability, as every person should.'

'Was Miss Buckley of the same mindset? Did she live by them in the manner that her future husband professed to?' Gilbert asked.

'I could not fault her if she didn't. Once we were married, I would of course ensure that she understood my rules and was appropriately subordinate.'

Harland saw Gilbert's eyes widen in surprise. His protégé lived with a strong widowed mother, and his future fiancée was an independent working woman, as was Phoebe. But Mr Percival Trigg's view was within the bounds of society's legal framework and a view shared by many men.

'Sir, where do you attend Sunday Mass?' Gilbert asked.

'I was going to St Joseph's, but once Earnest introduced me to Charity at our school fundraising ball, I attended St Mary's every Sunday to have the pleasure of sitting beside her and Mr and Mrs Buckley.'

'Have you been to the Christmas market, Mr Trigg?' Harland asked.

'No, markets do not interest me, and now, I could not bear to go near them, near where Charity spent the last hour of her life before that brutal death.'

As neither detective had any further questions for the teacher, Harland thanked Mr Trigg for his time just as the bell rang to mark the end of recess.

'I hope you catch the killer, Detectives, and I hope he never sees the light of day again,' Percival Trigg said, his voice hitching. 'She was an angel.'

Chapter 23

T HE LADIES OF SPIRIT had left, and Phoebe was alone—well, almost—Rufus was keeping her company and stretched out on the couch, preferring the cool basement of Phoebe's room.

She hurriedly jotted a note to Harland outlining what Miss Charity Buckley had to say, noting the fallen angel comment and why Miss Clara Garnham stole the money. As she finished, Phoebe heard the sounds of the horses and hearse coming back into the grounds of *The Economic Undertaker*, and she sealed the letter, hoping one of her brothers might deliver it. She could give it to Harland herself this evening, but Phoebe didn't want tonight to be about work. There were more important discussions to be had, like seeing his house, hopefully receiving his proposal, and determining when they might marry. A rush of nervous excitement swirled in her stomach.

Her thoughts went to his house, and she hoped it was as lovely as he said, and that she could see herself there. It would be difficult to say that she did not like it when Harland made it clear he loved it. It would be equally challenging to live there if she disliked it but chose not to say anything. Another glance at the clock. Was today the longest day ever?

Considerable effort had gone into the choosing of her dress today, not that Harland would recognise that, but he liked pink or white on her, so she wore a white dress and red ribbon – a Christmas theme. If only her heart would stop drumming and her mind could focus on something other than Harland Stone and tonight's date. That wonderfully complex, kind, strong, forgetful, handsome, clever man.

The sound of footsteps above told her where each brother was, but she knew Ambrose would go straight to the kitchen and Julius would wash. Ten minutes later, Julius came down the stairs.

'Phoebe, Rufus, is all well?' he asked, his hair damp and sleeves of his shirt rolled up.

'Yes, we are both fine,' and Rufus agreed with a thumping tail as Julius leant over to pat him. 'But we have not been out in the heat. How are you and Ambrose?' she asked, concerned.

'Ambrose suffered from sunstroke today. He is all right,' Julius said, holding up his hand at Phoebe's concern. 'But I think he'd best have a few days inside. Mrs Dobbs is taking care of him now with cold drinks and cake.'

Phoebe smiled. 'That should do it. But who will do the funerals with you? Not Grandpa, surely!'

'No, definitely not. It is unfortunate Claude and Will are both away, but Charlie will have to don a suit and help. He is not the biggest lad, but he will manage. Failing that, Lucian might have a staff member who would be prepared to step in. Some of his carpenters are big men.'

'The new boy, Jacob, is tall. Do you think he might manage, or is that too risky given he has just started?'

'I wouldn't be prepared to risk our reputation on a newcomer. I will speak with Charlie; he will be fine, and it will be good for him to see that side of the business.'

Phoebe agreed. 'I am pleased Jacob accepted your offer.'

'As am I. I thought he might in his own good time. Now Charlie can teach him the role until you need assistance. I am also available if I am not attending a funeral.'

Phoebe thanked him and sat on a stool by her desk as Julius flopped onto the couch beside Rufus, who immediately rolled on his back to be stroked.

'I believe Harland intends to propose tonight,' Phoebe said and waited for her brother's reaction. To her relief and delight, he grinned.

'Ha, that is wonderful, Sister. What a good extended family we have – Violet, Harland, and maybe Miss Prout. We are lucky. You will say yes?'

'Yes, a thousand times yes,' Phoebe said and blushed with pleasure. 'We are going to see his house, which, hopefully, will become our home.'

'Ah,' Julius said, sobering.

Phoebe rolled her eyes. 'Do not worry. Nothing untoward shall happen. Did you want to chaperone?' she teased.

'Definitely not. But I will have a word with him... with your permission,' he added, and Phoebe recognised his seeking permission for the conciliatory gesture it was, given they had recently redefined their relationship.

'Thank you for caring, Brother, and yes, you may have the opportunity to do so if you have time to do me a favour?'

'Of course. What is it?'

Phoebe waved the letter and told Julius about her discussion with Miss Charity Buckley. 'I don't wish to hold this information in case it is of use, and I don't wish to discuss the dead or his business this evening.'

'Naturally,' Julius agreed. 'I shall have a cold drink, spend a moment checking on Jacob, and then I'll take your note and an omnibus to the police station, give the horses a rest.' He gave Rufus a rough up and rose.

'Be gentle with Harland, Brother,' Phoebe said, handing over the letter with her thanks.

'If he is to be my brother-in-law and the keeper of your heart, then I need to remind him I run a funeral business,' Julius said in jest, giving his sister a smile as he took to the stairs and Phoebe shook her head after him.

'Lucky we love him, Rufus, or there would be trouble,' she teased, and Rufus appeared to grin in agreement.

Harland pulled himself back into the hansom and instructed the driver to take them on to the Roma Street Police Headquarters.

'She is not in,' he responded to his protégé, having instructed Gilbert to hold the cab while he checked if Mrs Wilson was available at the church charity shop. Through the windows, they could see only two young ladies behind the counter. 'She is personally delivering several items that would be suitable for community members.'

'Most kind,' Gilbert said.

'We can return later.' Harland sat back with a sigh, catching the breeze from the moving hansom. 'I am disturbed by Mr Percival Trigg's parting comment.'

'She was an angel,' Gilbert agreed. 'Miss Astin told us those were the last words Miss Clara Garnham heard... an accusation of being a fallen angel. Miss Nora Walham said that woman said the same thing to her, but she lived to tell us.'

'I wonder if those were the last words that Miss Charity Buckley heard too,' Harland mused. 'But if Mr Percival Trigg is involved, what is his connection to this mystery woman?'

They spoke of the interviews just conducted and, on arrival at the station, Harland paid and thanked the driver, and the pair alighted. After a quick late lunch with what remained on offer in the police dining room, the men were once again in front of the board, as Gilbert added what they had learnt from Percival Trigg.

Harland paced as Gilbert studied the board.

'The only links we have between the victims are their volunteer work and parish, yet I believe we can be confident it is the same killer,' Harland said. 'Given his parting comment, and he is familiar with Spencerian script, Percival Trigg would be my prime suspect if there were just one death on our hands, that of Miss Charity Buckley. But what motive would Mr Trigg have to kill the woman he intended to marry, and to organise an attack on Miss Clara Garnham and Miss Nora Waldren's lives?'

'Perhaps it is his mother who did not like Miss Buckley. Some mothers will go to great extremes to protect their children, even adult children, if they think they have been slighted, and we have heard that Miss Buckley flirted with customers. Maybe Mrs Trigg caught her in the act,' Gilbert suggested. He gave a small shrug. 'Not a convincing argument, I know.'

Harland nodded. 'Nevertheless, it is a good thought and worth enquiring after Pervical Trigg's mother. I wonder if she recently bought a hat from the charity shop... Mrs Buckley's hat.'

'Oh, Sir, that is a thought. She might know the other girls from the shop.'

'Let us add that to the questions we ask Mrs Wilson at the charity shop. First, has she sold any of the late Mrs Buckley's hats and, if so, to whom? Second, does she know Mrs Trigg and can she describe her?' Harland said. 'That might save us a trip if Mrs Trigg is physically nothing like our killer.'

'There is a church connection that might not add up there, Sir,' Gilbert said, pondering the board. 'We don't know if Mr Trigg's family attends church. He told us he went to St Joseph's before changing to the St Mary's parish to be near Miss Buckley; maybe his parents changed then too if they are churchgoing. If the confession notes are being dropped to Father Taylor, then it is likely someone who attends St Mary's and writes using Spencerian calligraphy.'

'Very true. Mrs Wilson, as an attendee of St Mary's, might know. I doubt there is much that gets by her,' Harland said drily. 'Let's consider Earnest Buckley as a suspect.'

Gilbert started. 'The brother! He does prefer the Spencerian script. He knows the ladies from church and the charity shop, but why would Mr Buckley wish harm to his sister and the other young women, and who is this woman to do his bidding, if Earnest Buckley is the killer?'

'What if the two men were in this together?' Harland threw around the theory. 'But no. Why would Earnest kill his sister, especially if his friend was to wed her, and given Percival seemed genuinely in love with Miss Buckley, he would not stand by and allow it, surely?'

'Given that he did not seem to hold Mr Buckley in high regard, I can't imagine he would collaborate with him, unless his dislike was an act.'

Harland hesitated. 'This is an odd observation, Gilbert, and I do not mean to offend when I suggest it.'

'How could you, Sir? We have a killer to find.'

Harland gave a single nod and continued. 'Might Earnest Buckley be in love with Percival Trigg, and want the union of Mr Trigg with Miss Buckley so he can be closer to him?'

Harland expected his protégé to appear shocked, but was surprised to find Gilbert quite open-minded about the concept.

'I wondered the same, Sir. That is why I asked his reason for not reading the Oscar Wilde book. It is considered to have a narrative with those tendencies.'

Harland looked at the young detective, impressed. 'That is interesting, and from memory, he brushed off your question. I apologise. If I had known the context, I would not have hurried on with my questions. Why did you not raise this idea on the journey back?'

'I thought I might have been reaching, Sir, without knowing the character of either man.'

'I would prefer you to mention it, even if it seems far-fetched. I will never ridicule your observations,' Harland said.

'Thank you, Sir. Is it possible Earnest Buckley organised the death of his sister in a fit of rage because by rejecting Percival Trigg, she was denying him of the relationship – a friend, brother-in-law, lover? Although that doesn't explain the deaths of the other ladies.'

'Without knowing who this woman is and her connection to the victims and the church, I feel like we are chasing our tails, Gilbert. It all comes back to her.'

A knock on the door drew their attention, and Harland, who was nearest, opened it to find Julius Astin on the other side of the door.

'Julius, come in.' Harland sobered, concerned. 'Is Phoebe—'

'She is fine,' Julius assured him and entered, shaking his hand and doing the same with Detective Payne, as Harland closed the door behind him. 'I come bearing a note from Phoebe.'

'Tell me it will help our case?' Harland said. 'We are going around in circles.'

'I hope so; she was most insistent you have it, and I hoped to have a word too,' Julius said, and Harland froze momentarily.

'Ah, of course. Are you in a hurry?'

'Not at all.'

'Good, then let us read this first,' Harland said and opened the letter. And then he smiled. 'Gilbert, we might have found a motive.' He handed the letter to the younger detective and looked at the board, as Julius came to stand beside him.

Gilbert read it and hurriedly began writing what they had learned and placing after it the letter "H" in brackets. He glanced at Julius.

'That means it is hearsay, and we need to find evidence for ourselves, Mr Astin,' Gilbert explained. 'Not that Miss Astin has ever been wrong.'

'Of course you need proof,' Julius agreed.

Harland was staring at the board, his mind racing. 'So Charity was going to run away if forced to marry Percival

Trigg. That gives both her brother and pending beau a motive, if they knew this. Clara did not steal for her family, but to win back a man's affection. If either man found out about this, there's a motive to harm her for abetting Charity, if they were inclined.' He kept thinking out loud. 'Nora was attacked because she was a gossip, as such. If she knew of this and started speaking ill of Percival or Earnest, there is a motive to punish her.' He shook his head. 'The killer is easily aggrieved.'

'And the angel comment, Sir. Miss Charity Buckley told Miss Astin the last thing she heard was that she is a fallen angel. Now, all three ladies have said that. We can be in no doubt that we are dealing with the same killer.'

'But who is the woman?' Harland said, throwing up his hands.

Julius added, 'Phoebe said Miss Buckley could not say as she was drawn so close against the woman's body, all she could see when looking up was the woman's neck and chin.'

Gilbert placed his chalk down. 'Sir, if you wish to chat with Mr Astin, I shall pay a call at the charity shop and see if Mrs Wilson has returned.' He glanced at the clock. 'The store will close in an hour.'

'Excellent, thank you, Gilbert. Call it a day after that and pursue nothing further. Do not call on Mrs Trigg or follow any leads by yourself,' Harland warned.

'I won't, Sir.'

In a show of trust, Harland added, 'Gilbert, tonight I propose to Miss Astin; wish me luck.'

Gilbert's face lit up, and he shook his superior's hand. 'I am delighted to hear that, Sir, and I will save my congratulations for tomorrow when it is official.'

With that, the young detective bid them both farewell and departed, and Harland invited Julius to be seated.

Chapter 24

JULIUS RELAXED FOR THE first time today in the relative cool of Harland's office. 'It has been hell out there today,' he said, removing his suit jacket at Harland's invitation.

The two men sat opposite each other around the table, and Harland poured them both a glass of water from a pitcher on the table.

'I do not envy your work in the summer. I had several years working up north,' Harland reminded him. 'The heat never eases up, and trying to sleep at night was beyond me, having grown up in colder Victoria.'

'It is relentless, but the dead keep dying.' Julius thanked him for the water and took a mouthful as he studied the man opposite. They were both tall men, dark in features and of similar height. Still of nature, but not today, Harland had a restlessness about him which Julius understood.

He remembered the day he spent waiting to propose to Violet that evening in the Botanic Gardens. He was sure he could not say what had happened all day, so diverted was he, and then the proposal did not go as planned, but the result was what he wanted and hoped it would be.

'So tomorrow, we will be on our way to being brothers-in-law,' Julius said with a smile.

'I hope you are happy about that,' Harland grinned. 'I am. As an only child, I've always wanted to be part of a family, and soon I hope to have a wife, two brothers-in-law, grandparents, sisters-in-law, and many more in my life.'

'And as Ambrose and I will only have one brother-in-law, I am pleased it is you,' Julius said honestly. 'Do you remember the last time I visited you here in Phoebe's defence?'

Harland sat back and chuckled. 'Of course. I had slighted her at that doll shop where the murder took place and deeply regretted it. Then, on seeing you waiting for me on my return, I thought my chances of winning your sister's heart were over before they started.'

'I doubt I have that much influence, but I was riled up,' Julius admitted. 'She has a tender heart.'

'She does, but yet Phoebe is strong and determined,' Harland said, with the ghost of a smile on his lips. 'So what brings you here this afternoon besides Phoebe's note? I sense another warning is about to be issued.'

'You sensed right, and I have Phoebe's permission to speak with you,' Julius said, and Harland groaned.

'No, fear not, I am not about to lay down the Astin law to a man of law,' Julius said in jest. 'I know you will look after and honour my sister.'

'You can be sure of that. I would give my life for hers in a heartbeat, promise her loyalty and love to the grave, and she will want for nothing while I am still breathing.'

Julius raised an eyebrow in surprise.

'I know,' Harland said and shook his head. 'Gilbert is rubbing off on me, and I am becoming much more eloquent. Heaven help us all.'

Julius laughed, a rare and handsome sight that normally turned heads, and Harland could not help but laugh as well before sobering. With an exaggerated sigh, he added, 'Go on, say what you must.'

Julius leant forward. 'You are taking Phoebe to your house.'

'Ah, now we have it,' Harland said. 'Yes. I want her to see where I hope we will live. I want to propose to her on the doorstep so our happiest memories begin there. Nothing untoward will happen.'

'Will you give me your word that you will not take advantage of her if you are swept up in the moment? I wish to see her wed first.'

'You need not ask me, and I am surprised you feel the need,' Harland said, his tone bordering on anger.

Julius did not back down; his intensity was not diminished by Harland's offence. 'Our parents died when Phoebe was nine. I am five years her senior, and with an absent father, Grandpa and I have been her protectors. One day, you will have a daughter and understand and forgive my line of questioning.'

Harland sat back and exhaled. 'I understand it now. If I am blessed with a daughter, I will be at the door with a shotgun when she first brings home a suitor.'

Julius chuckled. 'Exactly. So, do not forget my profession. We have on occasion lost a body.'

Harland huffed. 'You have my word—not that you need ask for it—that I will honour your sister tonight and nothing untoward will happen. I will propose and, hopefully, she will like her new abode, and then I will bring her home to her grandparents straight after, no later than seven o'clock, to share our announcement.'

'Thank you. I shall let them know to expect you,' Julius said and rising, he clasped Harland's hand. 'I look forward to hearing the good news. Shall we share the ride?'

'Yes, thank you, Julius,' Harland rose. 'Thank you for bringing me into your group when I was new in town with no acquaintances, and thank you now for bringing me into your family.' Keeping it lighter, he added, 'Do you still wish Phoebe was to marry Bennet?'

'He would be home a lot more than you, but you'll do,' Julius said, and Harland chuckled, grabbing his hat and the two men departed together to *The Economic Undertaker* – Julius to collect his wife and dog, Rufus, and Harland to meet Phoebe to take her to their future home, and secure her love for good.

Detective Gilbert Payne was pleased to see Mrs Wilson through the shop window as he exited the omnibus. The store was due to close in thirty minutes, and fortunately, as there were no customers in the store, he was likely to get an audience.

'Detective, welcome,' Mrs Wilson greeted him on entering. 'Are you here for another Christmas gift or seeking information?'

Gilbert removed his hat. 'Good afternoon, Mrs Wilson. The latter, if you can spare me ten minutes? I am relieved to find you alone; I need to speak with someone who knows her

community well and could share some insights with me.'
He was prepared to flatter her if it assisted in getting a
murderer off the streets.

'I will do my best, my civic duty,' Mrs Wilson said. 'As
I am alone, I may have to serve a customer if one should
enter.'

'Of course.'

Mrs Wilson sat on a high stool behind the counter and
waved her hand at the stool near the makeshift dressing
room. Gilbert drew it closer, sat and took out his notebook.

'Mrs Wilson, do you know Percival Trigg personally?'

'I do indeed, and...' she hesitated.

'I assure you of my discretion,' Gilbert said. 'Our
conversation will remain between us and my superior,
Detective Harland Stone.'

Mrs Wilson nodded. 'He is an odd and abrupt young
man. I did not think him suitable for Charity. He is too
serious and dull, and she was a high-spirited young woman
whose head was easily turned by a handsome face, of which
Pervical Trigg was not one. I say that with some reluctance
as his mother is a good friend of mine.'

Gilbert's eyes widened with surprise and delight. That
would make securing an answer to his next few questions
much easier. 'Is Mrs Trigg a member of the St Mary's
community?'

'Martha? Yes, only of recent though. When Percival sought permission to court Charity, he moved his Sunday worship to St Mary's; his family followed. How Martha dotes on that boy, I am sure she can find no fault in him.'

'My mother would probably say the same of me,' Gilbert said with a chuckle, and Mrs Wilson gave him an affectionate look.

'We can be biased towards our beloved children,' she agreed.

'Could you describe Mrs Trigg for me, Mrs Wilson? Is she a large or small lady, tall, slim or broad?'

'I can indeed. She's a birdlike little lady. Slimmer than her wiry son and lucky if she tips five feet in height.'

Gilbert restrained a sigh. She was not the robust woman leading the girls away at the Christmas market. 'Did you know Charity did not intend to marry Percival Trigg and hoped that with the death of her parents, she was free of the promise?'

Mrs Wilson's lips narrowed, and she gave a sharp nod. 'I did. But of course I did not mention it to Martha. I thought Charity might change her mind to please her brother, Earnest. I saw no reason to cause the Trigg family distress.'

'I agree wholeheartedly,' Gilbert said and saw her glance at the clock. 'Just a couple more questions, if you permit, Mrs Wilson? I very much appreciate the help and insights you are giving me.'

'Of course. Go ahead.'

'Do you recall selling any of the late Mrs Buckley's hats through the shop and if so, who might have bought them?' He held his breath as the wearer of that hat was the closest the detectives might get to finding the woman who escorted the young ladies to their death.

'Well, that's the odd thing, Detective,' Mrs Wilson said. 'Only yesterday, Mr Buckley brought in his sister's clothing for the charity shop to sell. Very generous given the pain it must have caused him to pack up Charity's belongings and potentially see them on other young ladies in the community.'

'Most painful indeed,' Gilbert agreed.

'But I never received Mrs Buckley's clothing. I don't know why or where her dresses, shoes and hats went, but not one item came this way. Perhaps a family member benefitted.'

'None whatsoever, and Mr Buckley never broached the subject?'

'Not a word.'

Gilbert felt a rush of excitement, and a burning desire to see inside Mrs Buckley's wardrobe. 'I will take my leave now. Thank you, Mrs Wilson, for your time and generous community spirit. Oh, did Mr Buckley include a note with his sister's clothing by any chance?'

'Uh... yes, now that you mention it, he did.' She rose, opened a nearby drawer and pulled out several slips of paper, finding one near the top of the pile. 'Here it is, and very simple.'

She handed it to Gilbert, who read Earnest Buckley's words: 'I hope the church might benefit from the sale of dear Charity's clothes, Mrs Wilson. Yours faithfully,' and the signature.

'Thank you, Mrs Wilson, may I take this?'

'If you wish.'

He bid her good day and thanked the shop manageress again as he hurried out the door, the note burning in his hand. Mrs Buckley's clothes were not given away, and he was sure that if he put Earnest Buckley's handwriting next to the confessional letters, they would be a perfect match. Despite the light fading and the hour, Detective Gilbert Payne hurried back to the office to make the comparison for himself.

Mrs Martha Miller promised her husband of two years that she would not be late. Not that he would miss her; there was no great love between the older man and the young woman who was pressured by her father into the marriage to one of his aged friends. A business deal was secured shortly after, and the relationship with Martha was of a business nature as well. She was required to meet her husband's needs but not provide any additional company or comfort; she was lonely and desperate for love and affection.

If only her parents knew that every Sunday when she knelt in church, she prayed the young would be spared illness and the good Lord take her husband instead. He was, after all, in his sixth decade.

'I am just meeting my lady friends at the Christmas market and will be two hours at most. I will bring you home some of those jelly confections you love,' she called on departure. Mr Miller was happy to have his young wife out of the house and to indulge in his drink, smokes and other interests.

Martha departed, and as she rounded the corner, out of sight, stopped near a bench and hurriedly removed her dowdy hat and ribbon and replaced them with more attractive options. She was meeting the man who had stolen her heart several months ago, when she had collected a meat order for her husband's dinner. His family had a stand at the Christmas market, and they would only have a small window of time together when he took his break, but Martha would take it for the chance to see him, hear his voice, and feel the touch of his hand. It was so unfair that she could not be with him. Her father and her husband were brutes.

And so she hurried there, oblivious to the killer waiting for her, sitting in judgement on the young woman breaking the seventh commandment. Another fallen angel.

Chapter 25

UPON BIDDING FAREWELL TO Julius, Harland requested the driver await him in front of *The Economic Undertaker* while he entered to meet with Phoebe. She was in the foyer and hurriedly wished her grandfather and two brothers goodnight, conscious of everyone watching her given the importance of the evening.

The pair usually walked to Phoebe's house, but this evening, she accepted Harland's hand to enter the hansom. The different routine felt uncomfortable and exciting for both of them, knowing what was to come. Harland instructed the driver of the address before sitting back beside her with a sigh.

'Is everything all right?' she asked, and Harland could feel her eyes studying him as if he would bolt from the hansom at any moment and return to work.

'Yes, that was a sigh of relief. At last, I am beside you, and the day is done. I thought it would never end,' he said, reaching for her hand and holding it.

Phoebe smiled. 'I felt the same way.'

Awkwardness followed as both looked at each other, then out to the street at the falling dusk and people on their way home from their workday.

Harland cleared his throat. 'You look beautiful this evening. You always do, but I love this colour on you.'

'Thank you,' she said, a hand brushing down her dress. 'You might have mentioned that once or twice.' He laughed, and Phoebe squeezed his hand, bringing his eyes to her. 'Thank you for your heartfelt letter. I confess I read it many times before dawn. I have never had such a declaration and...' her voice trailed off.

Suddenly his heart stopped. 'Does it concern you, Phoebe? Do you not want to discuss our future yet?'

'Oh no, nothing like that; I am sorry to have alarmed you,' she hurriedly assured him, and his world fell back into place and he drew a breath again.

'What has you worried then?'

'It is just that...' she glanced away and not in a coy fashion but with a glance to the driver, who could not hear them with the evening noises, but nonetheless, she whispered, 'I know you are a man of the world, Harland, but I will not have the experience you are used to.'

His eyes widened with surprise. 'I love you, Phoebe. I am seeking a commitment for life, not instant gratification. We will grow together, and we will learn about each other.' He kissed her hand, loving her innocence even more, if that were possible.

She appeared to relax and gave him a small smile.

'Is that all that concerns you? You must be worried about my hours and my lack of attentiveness on occasion.'

'No. I will work odd hours too if need be, and as you said, we will learn more about each other. You are not worried about my... visitors?' she asked tactfully.

'No. They are most welcome,' he teased, 'within reason. There will be times when I am sure we won't welcome the interruption.'

She flushed and added, 'Of course. We would prefer them to meet me at the office during business hours.'

'Like crime, if only it would fit that pattern too,' Harland agreed. 'Is that all of your concerns? Please do not hesitate to mention whatever worries you. I am sure we can overcome it.' She was lovely, and he could barely take his eyes off her delicate features nor believe she was here with him. It was extraordinary. All he wanted was for Phoebe to say yes, and then, for the first time today, the feeling of restlessness would be gone and replaced by a sense of place, of being somewhere and someone's.

'Chester Street, Teneriffe,' the driver called down to them as they were approaching the turn into the street, and Harland busied himself to provide the fare, and assist Phoebe from the cab. His life was about to change, and feeling most unbalanced, he could not get to his future quickly enough.

'Oh, Harland, is this it?' Phoebe asked, her eyes wide with delight as she glanced at the large house in front of them, and the equally large residences across the street and on both sides; enormous yards separated the homes.

'Yes, it is this one,' he said, opening a gate set in a white picket fence and leading her into a garden that was well-established with a sizeable lawn. She could feel his strength beside her, the sheer manliness of him, and his pride in the home he hoped they would share.

It could not, however, be described as modest no matter how often he had said that to her; not this large and beautiful mansion. But how was Harland affording this on a detective's wage, Phoebe mused. It was a long, low-set home with decorative white steel lattice around a long bullnose verandah.

A high corrugated iron roof and stately timber French doors added to its charm, as it sat firmly in the middle of a large block with what appeared to be a considerable backyard.

'Is this what you spend your spare time doing? Mowing and gardening?' she asked with a laugh of surprise, and Harland grinned.

'No, I am fortunate to have an excellent gardener; he looks after the neighbour as well,' he said with a nod to his left, 'that is how I secured him. I have a cleaning lady too, so do not fear; the house should be presentable.'

'Harland, it is beautiful, much bigger than my grandparents' modest home. Mind you, Julius has regularly tried to improve their circumstances, but they are attached to their home full of memories.'

'I completely understand and hope we can say the same. Would you care to see inside? I assure you of my best intentions,' Harland said. 'Your brother has already threatened me with a six-foot plot.'

Phoebe laughed again. 'Dear Julius, ever the protector. Yes, please, I would love to see inside.'

They took the four stairs to the verandah, and Harland opened the door, leaving it open and asking Phoebe to wait in the hallway while he lit the home. When sufficiently done, he returned to her and, placing her hand on his arm, showed her through the large three-bedroom home with the VJ timber walls and twelve foot high ceilings.

'It is enormous,' she gasped, 'and the fittings and flooring are all so beautiful. It feels very new.'

He looked a little sheepish. 'It is relatively so. My father is a wealthy man, Phoebe, and gifted me this house when I said I intended to stay here some time. Of course, I did not accept,' he added quickly, 'but he insisted. So we agreed I would share half the purchase price. I know I am fortunate to have a good step up in life.'

'I am sure all parents would hope to do the same if they were in a position to do so,' Phoebe said. 'It feels so airy.'

'The high ceilings make it feel spacious. I can just imagine a large Christmas tree by that window,' he said, and Phoebe looked in the direction where he had placed a very small tree. Harland shrugged. 'It was the best I could do while busy.'

She grinned. 'A fine effort. I love your home, Harland. It is beautiful.'

With that, he dropped to one knee, and Phoebe drew a sharp breath in surprise. Her hand went to her heart as she felt the rush of fear, or was it excitement, or anticipation; all her emotions scattering in the truth of this moment.

'Phoebe, will you do me the great honour of marrying me?'

She was glad he did not say more; everything had been said already in his beautiful letter, and with no hesitation whatsoever, Phoebe responded a little breathlessly, 'Yes, Harland, there is nothing I want more in this world.'

He rose, his gaze never leaving hers, and removed a small box from his pocket. Opening it, Harland presented a sizeable diamond with a blue sapphire on either side in a dramatic setting. She looked up at him in awe.

'That is exactly the ring I envisaged.'

'Yes, I believe you told Violet, who told Julius, who told me,' he said cheekily. 'Your grandmother gave your grandfather one of your dress rings, who gave it to me so I could have it sized correctly.'

'It's a wonderful collaboration,' Phoebe laughed and watched in delight as he slipped the ring onto her finger. 'Oh, it is beautiful.' Tears welled in her eyes as she looked up at him. 'I have never known such happiness.'

'Let us make a future together, Phoebe, our own history,' he said, feeling such longing for her. For now, he kissed her hand and dared to touch his lips to hers. Pulling away, Harland hurriedly added, 'And now, I should get you home so we can share the news.'

Chapter 26

DETECTIVE GILBERT PAYNE RUSHED into the Roma Street Police Headquarters, greeting the night-desk sergeant, who had just started his shift, and hurrying up the hallway to his shared office. He knew Detective Stone would not be present, as he had the all-important business of a proposal to tend to, but this could not wait.

He removed his hat and hurried to the meeting desk, where a folder sat storing the evidence and notes gathered. Removing the confessional notes, he took them to his desk and pulled a lamplight closer before retrieving the note from the church charity shop. Placing them side by side and then underneath each other, Gilbert exhaled for what seemed like the first time in hours.

They were a match, right down to the small curves in each of the capital letters. Yes, the same design would be written by all students of the Spencerian script, but to write in the same size and apply the same pressure to some letters was unique, and Detective Gilbert Payne was confident he could now say, Earnest Buckley confessed to two murders – that of his sister, Charity, and her friend and co-worker, Clara Garnham. Plus, there was the attack on Nora Waldren.

'Detective!' A constable rushed into his office, startling Gilbert. 'Thank goodness you are here. It's about your case... the attacks at the Christmas market, there's a woman...'

'Another victim?' Gilbert asked, alarmed, and placed the notes in the folder, ready to depart.

'Yes, but she is here. She's alive. Shall I bring her in?'

'Yes please, right away,' Gilbert said, and in the absence of his superior, it was time to step up. He gathered himself as a young, attractive woman rushed in, the constable behind her.

'Help me, please,' she said and threw herself into the arms of Detective Gilbert Payne.

Maria Astin's hand went to her heart with fright as Ambrose raced into the hallway, banging the door and startling his grandmother. 'Are they here yet?'

'Goodness, I forgot you live here,' Maria said, taking a deep breath. She came out of the kitchen to address her grandson. 'No, but Julius said Harland promised to come straight here after the house tour and proposal.'

'They should be here any minute,' Julius joined them in the doorway. Behind him in the dining room, his wife helped lay out platters of nibbles for the celebration, and now all the Astins were on hand and awaiting the news.

Ambrose kissed his grandmother on the cheek. 'I brought a date. Is that all right?'

'Absolutely. I hope it is the lovely Miss Prout.'

'No,' Ambrose said as cousin Lucian entered after cleaning off his boots.

'Just me,' Lucian grinned. 'I heard about the proposal and wanted to be on hand. Forgive the intrusion, Aunt and Uncle, but Ambrose was sure I'd find a cold drink and a snack here as well,' Lucian said, shaking hands with his great uncle, Randolph, and kissing Maria on the cheek.

'Never an intrusion, darling, I am sure we can feed you, even if Ambrose has to miss out,' Maria said, matching her youngest grandson's cheekiness.

'We are delighted you are here,' Randolph said, taking more glasses through to the dining room and placing them as directed by Violet, ready for a toast to the happy couple.

'I hope they do come here and not detour to dinner,' Violet said as she and Randolph joined the rest of the party in the living room.

'Me too, I'm starving and will give them thirty more minutes only before I graze,' Julius said and smiled as his wife scolded him.

'I am so pleased for Phoebe,' Maria said. 'It feels like it was only yesterday when you two came straight from the Botanic Gardens to tell us of your betrothal,' she said, smiling at her eldest grandson and Violet. 'I am sure I did not sleep for a week with the excitement and relief of it.'

'Yes, it was a relief. We thought no one would have Julius,' Ambrose teased.

'Especially as he was soaked and looked like a drowned rat,' Randolph recalled.

'You were a hero saving young Alfie,' Violet smiled up at her husband, putting an end to the teasing. 'It certainly made for a unique proposal.'

'Now, we just need Ambrose to secure Miss Prout and your grandfather and I can consider our work done,' Maria smiled.

'What a relief that will be,' Randolph said and took a turn at glancing outside as everyone else randomly did when passing the window.

'Leave it with me, Grandma,' Ambrose said. 'As soon as Lucian proposes, so will I.'

His cousin groaned.

'Yes, your mother is most keen for that and very much likes Elizabeth, your young lady,' Maria said to her great nephew, and Lucian grimaced at Ambrose, while Julius insisted his extended wife take a seat and not over-exert herself.

'They are here!' Violet proclaimed, having just sat by the window, and the family gathered around her, ready to call out congratulations as they entered.

'Oh, she looks so happy,' Maria said, clasping her hands in delight.

'I guess she said yes then,' Ambrose said and grinned as his family riled him.

The pair came up the front stairs, and the family heard Phoebe open the door and lead Harland in. Her head appeared around the door, looking confused and curious.

'Congratulations,' they yelled in unison and mobbed the happy pair, kisses and handshakes flowing freely, as Randolph poured the champagne for a toast.

Phoebe told of the proposal and beautiful house, and Maria dabbed her eyes sentimentally as she saw the young man's eyes never leave his fiancée's face. It reminded her of her own engagement; she was a fool for Randolph Astin and could not wait to wed him. She cried again at the hug shared between Julius and Phoebe, the closest of siblings, and the slapping on the back of Harland, a new family member. A special moment indeed, and well aware of how life can change in the blink of an eye, she offered a silent prayer for the young couple's future.

'Miss, you are safe now, please try to calm yourself,' Detective Gilbert Payne said and led the young woman to a chair at the meeting table. He knew time was of the essence, and that her attacker had most likely fled the Christmas market by now.

'It was terrible. I've never been so frightened; I thought I was going to die,' she said hysterically without drawing a breath.

'Yet you have used your strength and good sense to survive,' Gilbert said, offering his handkerchief, which she snatched and wiped her face.

'Should I get the lady a cup of tea?' the constable asked, still lingering.

'That's an excellent idea, thank you, Constable.'

'Oh yes please, milk and two sugars,' she sniffed and gave him a grateful smile.

'And for you, Detective?'

'Nothing but thank you,' Gilbert said, pleased to be asked. Perhaps with the cases he and Detective Stone had solved, he was turning a corner and earning some respect from the officers below him who knew he had been accelerated into the position due to his late father's connections.

Gilbert fetched his notebook and pen and sat opposite the young lady with her dark hair, deep brown eyes and full lips. She wore a sizeable engagement ring and wedding band; her clothing was of good quality, and her grooming implied wealth.

'Now, Mrs?'

'Miller, Mrs Martha Miller,' she said, taking a deep breath.

'Mrs Miller, let's go slowly and tell me every detail you can remember of what happened to you and then, I will be on my way to investigate. Perhaps start with why you were there and who you were meeting.'

She nodded and coloured a little, as that would mean discussing her infidelity. Martha began. 'I went to the Christmas market to meet a friend. My husband is quite elderly and did not wish to come with me. I was to bring him home his favourite sweets,' she said as if justifying her outing.

'Did you wish to return home and have the support of your husband as I conduct this interview?'

'No!' she exclaimed and then calmed herself. 'No, he will be angry that someone attacked me. It is best I tell you so justice can be served.'

'Of course.' They paused as the constable brought in a cup of tea with a biscuit on the saucer, and Martha and Gilbert thanked him. The uniformed officer nodded and departed.

Martha sipped her tea before continuing. 'I promised my husband I would only stay two hours, and I met with my friend and did a little shopping.' Her eyes widened. 'I dropped my basket. It is somewhere in the lane.'

'Your safety was much more important. What happened next?' Gilbert encouraged her.

'Yes, you are right; it is not important,' she said shakily. 'I was walking towards the lane that cuts through to the main street so I could take an omnibus home, and this woman came up beside me. She was so close, detective, and she gripped my arm with such force. I am sure it will be bruised.'

'Did you see her face?'

'I tried to, but she wore a large dowdy-looking hat, and the night had fallen; the lane was darker than the market square. She hurried me down the lane towards a side lane and said...' Martha composed herself. 'She said I had broken a commandment and had to atone for it.'

'Did she say which commandment?'

'No. I don't know. Maybe,' Martha said, and Gilbert assumed she did not want him to know. 'I was so frightened because I read in the newspaper about a woman leading the girls to their death, and it was just like that. She said I was a fallen angel!' She took some deep breaths as her voice broke.

'Have a sip of tea, take your time, Mrs Miller,' Gilbert said in a calming voice but was interrupted by footsteps racing down the hallway, louder at this time of night as only a skeleton staff worked the night shift.

Miss Lilly Lewis raced into the detectives' office. 'Oh, thank goodness you are here, Detective Payne. There's been another attack; Bennet and I were just at the market and heard of it. Goodness, are you...?'

Gilbert rose. 'Miss Lewis, please come in, close the door if you will? This is Mrs Martha Miller. She has just had a terrible shock and might appreciate a lady present while sharing her story.'

'Oh, you're the reporter, Lilly Lewis!' Martha said wide-eyed. 'We all admire you.'

'That's very kind, Mrs Miller,' Lilly said, removing her hat and taking a place at the table with a nod of thanks to Gilbert. Taking Martha's hand, she said, 'I am so sorry you have had such a terrible fright.'

'Well, thanks in a way to your stories forewarning the public, I am alive,' Martha said.

'Please continue,' Gilbert said.

Martha swallowed and updated Lilly, who hurriedly grabbed for her writing implements and began to make notes.

'I was telling the detective that I went to the market to visit a friend and shop and was just departing when I met that woman you described in your stories in the lane. It was so frightening. She hurt me, gripped me so tightly and was dragging me along.'

Martha was becoming emotionally fraught, but Gilbert did not stop to calm her as he wanted the interview done, and Lilly was keen to hear the story at any cost.

'Then, she said I broke a commandment, and I didn't want to die, so I reached up and I hit her in the face, in the eye like my brother had taught me to do if I had to defend myself. She yelled, and just for a moment loosened her grip, and I ran. I didn't stop to see if she was chasing me; I ran screaming to the main street and found a constable who brought me straight here,' she said, finishing almost hysterically. 'But that's not all; something awful and scary happened.' Martha shivered despite the heat of the night. She wrapped her hands around the teacup and took a loud sip.

'Do tell, Mrs Miller,' Gilbert insisted.

Martha put the cup back on its saucer and acted it out. 'When I reached for her face after I poked her, I grabbed her hair, but it came off in my hand.' She gave a small scream and shudder. 'I was holding it! I threw it away and ran.'

'Good Lord,' Gilbert said, and he was a man who never broke the third commandment and took the Lord's name in vain. 'Mrs Miller, I will get the constable to take you home immediately. I have an arrest to make!' He rose and hurried to the door to call the constable.

'Let me come too, Detective, please,' Lilly said and then, remembering herself, turned to the young lady. 'You were so brave, Mrs Miller. May I quote your account?'

'All right,' Martha said, a little confused.

'Thank you. I will do you justice.'

With that, the constable assisted Mrs Miller, while Detective Gilbert Payne grabbed for his hat and, with Miss Lilly Lewis, hurried to collect Detective Harland Stone and put away the fallen angel killer for good.

Chapter 27

HARLAND STONE HAD BEEN to dinner at the Astin household many times over the past year while he had been courting Phoebe, and several times at Julius's house as well, but big family gatherings such as this still astonished him; it was such a far cry from his own upbringing.

He recalled one such family dinner during his time as a policeman in North Queensland; an invitation from a keen young lady who hoped a well-cooked meal and showing her family's wealth might win his heart. The excellent lamb roast swayed him, but on a policeman's wage and too young to wed, he came out of the situation unhitched. Harland had heard from a dedicated letter-writing friend that the young lady was now married with children and still an excellent cook.

To think of having missed the opportunity to meet and love Miss Phoebe Astin, struck the oddest sensation in him – that he might never have known the feeling of true and all-consuming love.

Harland's thoughts were interrupted by Randolph, the family patriarch, offering his soon-to-be grandson-in-law a chilled glass of Castlemaine beer that had been placed on ice earlier in the day for the occasion.

'The perfect beer for a hot day,' Harland thanked him. 'It was the most popular beer when I worked up north, and I have a taste for it now.'

'I prefer it to other beers, although I am more of a gin man,' Randolph said. Sitting at the table once again, the two men smiled as Phoebe showed off her engagement ring to her grandmother and sister-in-law and thanked them for their participation in its purchase.

Harland realised he had no reason to feel out of place. The family, who were so comfortable in each other's company, were a rowdy bunch, and he would rarely be put on the spot. Quite the contrary; he would have to fight to get a word in. Even Phoebe was more relaxed and talkative in the bosom of her family.

'Do you take your meals at work, Harland, or have a cook like Julius and Violet?' Maria asked, calling him by his Christian name now as requested.

'At work or at the club, Mrs Astin,' Harland said, uncomfortable calling the Astin grandparents by their christian names as invited, and he doubted he would ever manage to call them grandma and grandpa, although Violet had comfortably settled into calling her new in-laws as such.

'When did you find the time to buy your house?' Julius asked. 'You haven't been here that long.'

'I didn't buy it as such; my father found it. I mentioned in my correspondence that I was likely to remain here for some time, and he likes to take charge when he can. Now that I have been in my role for over eighteen months—'

'Already?' Phoebe exclaimed, rejoining the conversation.

'I remember when you first came to our business looking for one of your victims amongst our deceased,' Julius said with a smile. 'You were most official.'

'I expected resistance, not an invitation out for a drink as a newcomer,' Harland said with a grin, 'which, mind you, as a new face in town, I was grateful to accept.'

'You were saying about your house, Harland? It is very easy to be diverted by the Astin family,' Randolph said, adept at bringing conversations back on track.

'Ah, yes, thank you, Mr Astin. My father decided it best for me to invest in property, which I am grateful for now, as it appears I will remain in Brisbane.'

'Will you?' Ambrose cut in. 'Does our town hold any special attractions for you?'

Harland's gaze went straight to Phoebe, who blushed as everyone around the table smiled or laughed.

'Yes, one in particular,' Harland agreed.

'I, too, love our river,' Lucian joked. 'Oh, perhaps you did not mean that?' he ribbed Phoebe, who rolled her eyes at her cousin.

'I am sorry, Harland. It is impossible to finish a sentence or train of thought in this family,' Maria said. 'So does it need refurbishing?'

'No, Grandma, it is beautiful,' Phoebe answered before Harland could.

'But it needs a lady's touch,' Harland said. 'The interior decorations are practical at best.'

'How exciting,' Violet said. 'I love decorating a house. Choosing the floorings and curtains, but the little touches are more fun.'

'You've moved three times in the short time I've known you,' Ambrose said, 'so you have some experience.'

'Well, technically twice,' Violet said, 'as I moved back to my former home, so that does not count.'

'And now you are at home where you should be, Mrs Astin,' Julius said with a smile. Turning to Harland, he said, 'May we ask where your abode is located?'

'Of course. It is a modest home on Chester Street in Teneriffe,' he said.

Phoebe hid a smile. 'It is not modest, but you are, Harland,' she praised him and suddenly a sharp knock at the door had them all turning toward the front verandah.

'I'll get it, Grandpa,' Ambrose said and returned moments later with Detective Gilbert Payne. Harland rose to his feet, as did the guests, knowing a crime was afoot.

'Forgive the intrusion on this auspicious occasion, Mr and Mrs Astin, and Sir,' he said to Maria and Randolph and his superior. 'And congratulations, Miss Astin, Sir.' He beamed, and hands were shaken, and food and drink offered.

'Thank you, but no. Unfortunately, I need Detective Stone when convenient.'

'Another attack?' he asked.

'Yes, but she is not harmed, and I believe we now know who the killer is, Sir.'

'You must go immediately,' Phoebe said, heading to get his hat.

'I am sorry to run out—' he began.

'Not at all, it is good practice for the future,' Randolph joked, and the group moved to the front door to see the detectives off on their mission. Maria hurriedly bundled some pies into a tea towel for the men for the journey to keep their strength up.

With that, the celebrations continued without the intended groom, but it was soon about to end for the woman intent on slaying fallen angels.

Harland entered the hansom and exclaimed, 'Miss Lewis!' in surprise to find the reporter in attendance.

'Congratulations, Detective,' she beamed. 'I thought it best I wait here and let Phoebe tell me her exciting news when we are not in such a rush.'

'Miss Lewis arrived at the station not long after our victim, Mrs Martha Miller. I think it was of comfort to have another woman present,' Gilbert explained.

'No doubt. Tell me everything you know,' Harland said, getting straight to business as Lilly hungrily accepted a pie, and Harland took another for good measure.

Chapter 28

Detective Stone asked the hansom driver to stop at the South Brisbane Police Station en route and directed Gilbert and Miss Lilly Lewis to wait as he hurried in. Returning, he gave the driver the address of Mr Earnest Buckley's house nearby.

'The sergeant will get word to several of his officers on the beat and get them to Mr Buckley's house. I wish to have backup as it appears we have our man and an arrest might be imminent,' he informed them.

'His sister,' Lilly shook her head. 'If he is indeed the murderer, why would he kill his own sister?'

'Because she did not honour her parents' wishes, and most likely refused to marry Mr Percival Trigg,' Gilbert said. 'Commandment five. Or for the love of Mr Trigg.'

Lilly puffed her cheeks out and exhaled, explaining to Detective Stone, 'I was updated on the way over about the theory Earnest Buckley might love Percy Trigg and be jealous of the union. I am amazed that people continue to surprise me.'

'As am I,' Harland agreed. 'Now, Miss Lewis, you may remain if you stay in the hansom. We do not know if Mr Buckley is operating alone or how unbalanced he is. Nor do we know what the weapon is, but it will probably be on his person or in the house.' He saw her expression and added, 'I understand you discovered tonight's crime yourself while in the market, but I cannot focus on the crime afoot and an arrest if I have to protect civilians. We may have a very devious murderer on our hands. Are we in agreement?'

'Yes, Detective,' she sighed. 'But I will have the story and a quote from you?'

'Yes, I promise you that.' He turned to Gilbert. 'Excellent work securing Mr Buckley's note and the information from Mrs Wilson; now, it appears, the wig has damned him. When we arrive, I will lead, stay close by, and we will have each other's backs.'

'Yes, Sir,' Gilbert said, and Harland could sense his fear and excitement.

'The constables will not be far away. There is every chance he will deny everything and be sitting calmly in his lounge room as if he has been in residence all evening. We are dealing with a clever man here.'

'What will we do then, Sir? Question him at the house or take him to the station?' Gilbert asked.

'I will have the constables take him to the station so we can look through the house unhindered for the weapon and anything that will help our case... undelivered confessional letters, for example.'

The hansom pulled up, and Harland and Gilbert alighted. 'Driver, please remain. Miss Lewis, when the constables arrive, would you instruct them to stay by the door and not enter until I summon them? If they do not wish to believe you, tell them they will answer to me and quote my name.'

'I will. Good luck, detectives, stay safe,' Lilly said, exiting the hansom to stand closer to the horses and a curious driver looking at her for an explanation on the drama unfolding in what looked like a respectable neighbourhood.

Harland led the way to the two-level townhouse, noting neighbours were present on both sides; the glow of lamps appeared in the windows. There was only one light on in Earnest Buckley's house, and it shone from an upstairs window.

'We will do him the courtesy of knocking and request an audience with him in case he is playing the man at leisure,'

Harland said and tapped on the door. Gilbert waited slightly behind him as instructed. As expected, there was no answer.

'He is probably hurriedly changing upstairs, Sir, or panicking if he thought Mrs Miller saw his face,' Gilbert whispered.

Harland nodded and, taking a deep breath, turned the door handle, a gloomy premonition bearing down on him. He had come across unbalanced killers before; their violence and strength from some dark place within them was something to fear. To his surprise, the door opened, and Harland whispered, 'We will not announce ourselves now and see what the element of surprise turns up. Stay behind me, watch yourself, keep looking behind.'

'Yes, Sir,' a wide-eyed and nervous Detective Gilbert Payne nodded.

The men entered the dark hallway; Harland paused. There was not a sound to be heard. He waited a moment, allowing their eyes to adjust to the shadows so he could see no one was in the living room, nor the kitchen opposite. Harland nodded to the staircase down the hallway, and Gilbert stayed nearby.

The men took the stairs cautiously, listening, and stopping near the top to scope the area. Harland was conscious of his breathing as he heard the short, sharp breaths of his protégé behind him.

You are the young man's example; he reminded himself. *Stay calm, stay in control.* He glanced back and gave Gilbert an encouraging nod, as if all would be well and they were not in the house of a murderer ready to strike.

Harland continued; there was no one in sight, but a dim light shone from a room at the end of the top level. He started down the hallway and motioned for Gilbert to stop. There were voices coming from within the room. Harland put a finger to his lips, and the men moved closer to listen, hoping for an admission.

'You are a failure,' an unnatural falsetto voice said with a snarl. 'Your father and I have given you every chance to rise, but what has become of you? A teacher, unwed, who can't even control your sister and deliver our last wishes.'

A shaky male voice answered. 'I will make you proud. One day, I will be the principal of St Joseph's, and I punished Charity for her insolence, as you suggested.'

The female voice could be heard scoffing. 'Weak, you are weak.'

Harland moved forward, glanced into the room, and his expression relayed his surprise. He motioned to Gilbert to follow. The detectives entered. Before them in the mirror was a man dressed completely in a woman's attire – a sizeable man, which made the sight even more ungainly.

Earnest Buckley, the startling aberration of a man-woman, wheeled around. He spoke in his mother's voice, with an odd glee in his eyes as if the sight of them validated her rage. 'They have come for you. You could not even deliver the Lord's wrath without leading the police to your door,' he said in a high voice meant to be that of his mother.

The wig on Earnest Buckley's head was askew, a dowdy hat perched on top. Harland flinched at the sight of the man in a floral dress, his feet wedged into his mother's sensible heeled shoes, a drab coat open over the dress and a handbag hanging from his arm.

'Sir,' Gilbert whispered and pointed to the wall where a solid crucifix hung askew, casting an elongated shadow in the lantern light. A corner of the cross appeared to be marked, and the small dark red stain on the wall was most likely blood. The shape of the cross's corners fitted the coroner's description of the weapon that struck the two ladies' skulls.

'Mr Buckley,' Harland said calmly.

'He is useless,' Earnest Buckley snapped, and Harland started again, this time addressing the woman before him.

'Mrs Buckley, we need you to accompany us to the station. There will be no more delivering of justice. I am arresting you for the murder of—'

'I did not murder anyone,' the false Mrs Buckley roared. 'If I had, you can be assured justice would be done and all four women would be dead. My useless son murdered two of the girls. Two only.'

'Mother, please admit nothing to these men; they are detectives,' Earnest Buckley responded in his normal voice, but a quaver showed the fear he felt when talking back to this woman he perceived to be his mother. He glanced to the corner, behind the door, as if addressing someone there.

Harland gave Gilbert a subtle forward nod to indicate the younger detective should move nearer to the hallway, to flee for help if need be. With Gilbert in place, Harland stepped around to look behind the door in case they were not alone and someone armed hid nearby. He gasped, stepping back, and pushed the door to reveal the apparition. Gilbert cried out in fright at the gruesome sight.

Harland gathered himself to study the bony remains of a person sitting decaying in a chair. On its skull, a hat sat askew; a similar floral dress and shoes that Earnest Buckley was wearing now, hung from the decaying bones. Given there was no strong odour, Harland assumed the person, most likely Mrs Buckley, had died months ago in the cooler months and the body decomposition was almost complete.

Keeping Earnest Buckley in his sight, Harland issued an order to Gilbert: 'See if the constables have arrived and bring them here to handcuff Mr Buckley. Send the most senior man to summon the coroner; advise him the body is close to skeletal if he prefers it sent straight to the morgue.'

Gilbert nodded and hurried down the stairs, no doubt pleased to be out of the room. Harland wedged the door again to hide the sight from the constables.

'Did you do this, Mr Buckley?' he asked. 'Did you kill your mother?'

'She hated me, and I tried to be all she wanted. My sister Charity could do no wrong and I could do no right,' Earnest said, his eyes narrowing.

The strangeness of his voice coming from the man dressed as a woman unsettled Harland, who had seen many things in his years of policing. But not this.

'I told everyone at church she was away visiting her sister, and then she got an illness and died.' Earnest smiled. 'She didn't really get an illness. My father did, so I thought they could die together. She hated me,' he said again. 'But Robert loved me.'

'Robert?' Harland's ears pricked up. 'Who might Robert be?'

'Mr Kingston, a retired Latin teacher. He met me every week in the park; no one saw us. He loved me.'

Harland made a mental note of the name, wondering if Robert Kingston was still alive. 'What day and time did you meet?'

'After midday mass every Wednesday. I should have married him,' Earnest said, and Harland assumed he was speaking as his mother again. He had heard enough. This time, he issued the arrest to Mrs Buckley, as Earnest continued to believe he was his mother.

'I am arresting you for the murder of two women,' and before he could finish, Earnest Buckley swiftly grabbed for the crucifix.

'Sinner,' the man dressed as a woman roared and rushed straight at the detective, aiming the cross at Harland's head. Years in the rink had given Harland quick reaction skills, and he ducked and snapped out a punch straight to the man's stomach.

Earnest Buckley yelped and bent over in pain, gasping, and Harland whirled him around, restraining his arms as two constables hurried in with Gilbert. The cross fell to the floor with a thud.

'Retrieve the cross, Gilbert,' Harland ordered.

'Oh my Lord, it is a woman, no, what is this? A man!' Constable Wright, an experienced officer on the beat, cried out in amazement. 'The woman from the Christmas market is a man?'

Lilly Lewis appeared in the doorway. 'Oh my, what a great story this will be,' she said, mouth open and eyes wide in astonishment at the sight before her. She hurriedly grabbed her pad to write the details of the scene. The illustration to come from her memory would fascinate the entire town in tomorrow's afternoon edition of *The Courier*.

'Did he attack you, Sir?' Gilbert asked, shocked, retrieving the cross from the floor.

'He did, but I am not harmed. I almost did not react quickly enough. It is hard to strike a woman, even if a man is underneath the facade.'

The other younger constable shuddered. 'It is a frightening sight, Sir, not natural to see a man wearing a dress.'

'It is not a pleasant sight,' Harland agreed, as they bundled the killer to his feet. 'I will allow you to change under supervision, Mr Buckley, as you will be a target in the cells otherwise.'

'I am not changing. Let everyone know about my work. The church will be grateful,' he said, the wig and hat still askew. With that, Harland nodded for the constables to remove the killer from the room.

'Why did you call for the coroner, Detective?' Lilly asked.

'There is something in the room which I don't want you to see, Miss Lewis, but I will give you the details to report on it.' He turned to his protégé, and added, 'Gilbert, I will wait here for word from the coroner and lock up when done. You have had quite a shock. Head home now, and on your exit, authorise the constables to return to the station and put Mr Buckley in a cell. We shall charge him tomorrow and talk about all that happened then. Thank you for your excellent work.'

'Thank you, Sir. On the way here tonight, I prepared myself for the fact that Mr Buckley might be dressing up because of the wig, but to see him like that... and the body, the bones,' he said with a glance at the door blocking the confronting sight. Gilbert shuddered before quickly departing the room.

Normally, the young detective would have offered to stay, but Harland could not blame Gilbert for wanting to get well away from the gruesome find in the room. He gave Lilly her story. When finished, Harland was surprised to realise she looked more excited than concerned.

'Oh, let me see the corpse, Detective. I assure you I will brace myself, and it will be better for my writing to witness it firsthand.'

'I cannot in good conscience allow that, Miss Lewis. The image will never leave your mind.'

'But what I come up with to replace it will be far worse.'

Harland considered this and understood exactly what the young lady reporter meant. The mind was a powerful tool for creating an endless supply of ghosts and ghouls.

'At your own peril,' he agreed, and going to the door, slowly moved it to show the ghoulish sight. Lilly gagged and stepped back, her hand flying to her mouth.

'You were right, Detective,' she said, moving back toward the exit. 'I could not have imagined that. What kind of monster is Earnest Buckley?'

'One that suffered greatly at the hands of his mother, I imagine.'

Chapter 29

It was nearing nine p.m.; the night was still young, but Harland Stone thought it too late to return to the Astin household. Nor did he want to soil the earlier beautiful memories with the murder and despair he had witnessed this evening.

There was one thing he needed to do, and it was not too late. To close the case, Harland must check on the man Earnest or his mother professed to love, Mr Robert Kingston. Would he find him in the same condition as Mrs Buckley? The thought filled him with dread.

He withheld the information from Lilly Lewis for now and saw her off as he waited for the coroner. He might not release it at all if Mr Kingston is innocent of a crime and deserves his privacy. An affair was a breach of marital duty, not a crime, except to the church and its community.

Harland began searching for an address book in the Buckley household, which now had no inhabitants remaining. He rifled through the desk drawers in the study, then moved to Earnest Buckley's bedroom. In the bedside drawer, he found a small contacts book and within it, the address of Robert Kingston. He could easily be there in ten minutes on foot.

Out of curiosity, he moved to the closest in the man's bedroom and opened it. Hanging amongst Earnest Buckley's suits were numerous dresses, in the style of a mature woman. Harland had found Mrs Buckley's clothes that had not been given to the charity shop.

Hearing a cry from downstairs, Harland returned to the front door and found morgue staff and a trap to remove the skeletal remains; the coroner saw no reason to rush to the scene of the crime, and Harland could not blame Tavish. The detective had a confession, and the body was past sharing too many secrets.

Once the remains were removed, Harland locked the door behind him and departed the house. A feeling of dread filled him for the length of the walk to Robert Kingston's house, but his spirits buoyed when he came upon the small row of cottages and the sight of a light in the window at the house he was to visit. He rapped quietly on the door so as not to attract the interest of the neighbours.

'Who is there?' a craggy voice answered.

'Mr Kingston? Forgive the late call, I am Detective Harland Stone. May I come in?'

The door opened a little, and then a senior man with snow-white hair and a trim figure appeared and invited the detective in. 'I've just made a pot of tea.'

'I could use one, thank you,' Harland said.

After tea was poured and the men sat in a room that once appeared to have had the touch of a woman, Robert Kingston explained. 'I am ashamed to say, Detective, that Mrs Rosa Buckley and I enjoyed each other's company when we should not have. We met on a church committee. She was a spirited woman, full of opinions and energy, so different from my sweet wife, who passed two years ago. Rosa was lonely; her husband was a weak man, and I was bereft of company, being a retired widower. We met weekly.'

'In the park after midday mass on Wednesday?' Harland asked.

'Yes! How did you know?' he asked shamefacedly.

'Earnest Buckley told me.' He saw the look of fear cross the man's face and assured him, 'He has been arrested for murder and will probably never be released.'

'Oh, praise the Lord,' Robert Kingston said, his hand going to his heart. 'I was terrified of him.'

'Tell me what happened, please.'

Robert took a sip of his tea and sat back. 'Rosa was a God-fearing woman, but loneliness and attraction brought us together; she gave me purpose when I was lost. I don't know how her son found out, but he did, and Earnest proclaimed her a hypocrite and vowed to tell everyone.'

'Very brave for a boy who appears to be frightened of his mother,' Harland mused. 'Perhaps the hypocrisy was the trigger that brought on the killing spree after years of believing he could never live up to her moral expectations.'

'That is a sound theory,' Robert agreed. 'Not long after we had been discovered, I saw the death notices appear in the paper for Rosa and, the week prior, her husband, stating an illness had taken them. I dare not attend the funeral for fear Earnest would make a scene. But I was sentimental, and I returned at the same time and place to where we always met.'

'And so did Earnest?' Harland asked.

'Yes, dressed as his mother. You can't imagine my shock,' Robert huffed at the memory. 'I was frozen to the spot. He spoke in this odd falsetto voice; it still terrifies me. Then, I dared a glance at him and was aghast to see him wearing Rosa's clothes. His mother always said he was not a well boy, not well in the head.'

Harland did not interrupt; Robert Kingston was not a witness who needed prompting and gave his story freely.

'So I sat there and played along. I pretended that Rosa and I had met to offer each other advice and support, and I kept the conversation along those lines. It sounds odd, Detective, but he seemed to revere me, not despise me for my actions with his mother. He fell in and out of character, talking to me as a fellow teacher, and then as his mother. It was as if he were so desperate for affection, he chose to believe I loved him and even said twice that he knew I would love him more than his mother.'

'He did believe you loved him; he told me so tonight. I imagine that was in whatever form he took – himself or his mother.'

Robert gasped. 'I will be ruined when this comes out.'

'Mr Kingston, unless you have some information that bears on my case, I have enough evidence, and your history with Mrs Buckley is a private matter.'

Robert closed his eyes. 'Thank you, Detective, thank you.' He opened his eyes, took another fortifying sip of tea and continued. 'I met with Earnest twice. I was too scared not to come again the next week, and was quite frightened by his appearance. On our second time together, I told him I could no longer meet as my sister was ill and I had to do my duty by her. Fortunately, my sister is in fine health and lives far from here. I never returned to the park, and he never sought me. I also changed parishes and never returned to St Mary's Sunday service.'

'You did not think to come to the police?'

'And say what? I had no reason to think Earnest killed his parents; his father had been poorly for some time, and it did not occur to me that Earnest might be strong enough to harm his mother. I counted myself lucky to be away from what remained of the Buckley family.'

Harland finished his tea and thanked the elderly gentleman. 'You escaped with your life, Mr Kingston. Despite your loss, I hope that now with your good health and time on your side you can make the most of it.'

Miss Emily Yalden did not have visitors who called after nine o'clock at night. According to the deportment rules taught at the *Miss Emily Yalden School of Deportment*, that was definitely unacceptable, and so her heart raced in her chest as she approached the front door.

Her first thoughts went to Gilbert. She knew the man she loved might be harmed on the job; it was the price she paid for loving a man of the law. Fortunately, she had not bathed and changed into bed wear as she had been expecting word from Phoebe, and her dear friend had called in for a brief visit to share the happy news of the earlier engagement, and to advise Gilbert had collected Harland and they raced to the scene of a crime.

She opened the door, her heart pounding, her blood pumping in her ears, and there he stood on her doorstep; Detective Gilbert Payne.

'Oh, you are alive and well, the late call frightened me,' she exhaled and gave a small gasp as Gilbert rushed straight into her arms, embracing her fully, as she hurried him in a few steps and closed the door, for propriety's sake.

'Please forgive me, Emily,' he said, pulling away and removing his hat.

'No, there is nothing to forgive,' she said and quickly closed the gap, holding him again. They remained that way for a brief time. 'Are you injured? Did something happen?'

'The "Fallen Angel" killer has been arrested, and I desperately needed to see my angel,' Gilbert said and then smiled, embarrassed. 'I hope that one day early in the new year, I will come home to you every night.'

'And I will always be here, waiting for you, ready to provide solace and company. Do you wish to tell me what has you so rattled?'

'No. I want to protect you from that, and not put that image in your head or burden you with it. I want to preserve your goodness,' Gilbert said, and Emily felt the full extent of his love from the way he grasped her hands, and the sincerity of the expression on his face as he looked into her eyes. She was tall, only an inch shorter than him, and her dark eyes studied him with compassion and care.

'Come, let us sit. I will make tea unless you would like something stronger? Perhaps a drop of brandy with your tea?' she offered.

'This evening, I think I will accept that offer, but rest assured I am not one to imbibe when stressed,' he said, following Emily into the kitchen.

'A little brandy will relax you,' she said. 'I am not as delicate as you think, but I thank you for wanting to keep the world at my door. You can speak to me about anything.'

Gilbert took a seat at the table as Emily placed two cups and saucers, a small jug of milk, teaspoons, a sugar bowl and a dash of brandy before him. A plate of shortbread followed.

'It was an ugly case on many levels,' Gilbert said. 'As I get more experienced, I am sure that the depravity of people will shock me less.'

'Let me ask then,' Emily said, removing the boiling water and pouring it into the teapot, 'Do you think you wish to remain in a profession that will harden you?'

Gilbert exhaled as if the brandy had already worked its magic, and he gave a small nod. 'I have thought the same often, but it is satisfying to bring justice to those often without a voice.'

'I imagine that is how Phoebe feels sometimes too,' Emily said, placing the teapot between them and taking a seat at the table opposite her beau.

'Miss Lewis was there, so you will read the horror for yourself in the newspaper tomorrow,' Gilbert recalled.

'Lilly? Good grief, how did she know to be there?'

'She was at the Christmas market with Bennet and heard of the attack.'

Emily smiled. 'So she raced straight to the station hoping to find either of you in attendance, and there you were.'

'Yes, she was fortunate. I normally would not have been there that late, but I had found a vital clue—a sample of Mr Buckley's handwriting—and so I returned to the office to compare it to the ransom notes. It was the same. Miss Lewis was with me when we retrieved Detective Stone but did not want to intrude on Phoebe's family gathering. She remained in the hansom then, and also when we entered the premises, but came in after the arrest and got her story.'

'Did she see the same scene that disturbed you?' Emily asked, sipping her tea.

'Yes. You will read all about it tomorrow, no doubt,' Gilbert said and hastily added, 'I don't mean to withhold—'

Emily raised her hand. 'Forgive me for stopping you, but I understand. Let this be a haven of peace for you.'

'The dark and the light, love and loss,' Gilbert agreed. 'I imagine an artist who paints, writes or performs must experience the extremes to be truly good at what they do. Perhaps if I wish to be serious about my poetry, then it gives justification to my job.'

'Yes, as long as there is plenty of light, more so than the darkness. Was it Aristotle who said, "The aim of art is to represent not the outward appearance of things, but their inward significance," if I recall correctly?'

Gilbert brightened and looked at Emily with great admiration. 'Indeed, you did. Why, Miss Emily Yalden, you never cease to amaze me.'

'I shall keep working on that then,' she teased.

'Thank you, Emily,' he whispered, sending her pulse racing and her heart fluttering as he reached for her hand across the table. The pair sat in the silence of a perfect union.

Chapter 30

The Courier – Afternoon edition

SHOCKING MAN–WOMAN MURDER CASE
DETECTIVES' FRIGHTENING ENCOUNTER WITH
THE INSANE
CHRISTMAS MARKET WOMAN A MAN
DECAYING BODY ON PREMISES

An exclusive report and interview with the killer by Lilly Lewis
and Ted Egan

In a shocking revelation and arrest made by Detectives
Harland Stone and Gilbert Payne, the woman at the centre

of the "Fallen Angel" murders is in fact a man, Mr Earnest Buckley, a well-respected teacher from St Joseph's College.

The frightening scene that confronted the detectives and your reporter Lilly Lewis is not one that will easily be forgotten. Mr Buckley was dressed in his deceased mother's clothes – a grey wig and women's hat atop his head, a floral dress and his mother's shoes on his person. He spoke to himself in the mirror and, most shockingly, to someone who appeared to be sitting behind the door.

The detectives moved the door to reveal the decaying remains of a person, believed to be Mrs Rosa Buckley, sitting on a chair, with a lady's dress and stockings hanging from the bones.

Mr Earnest Buckley—or rather his mother—berated himself for not succeeding in taking the life of Miss Nora Waldren and Mrs Martha Miller in unsuccessful attacks at the Christmas market, the latter taking place earlier last evening.

That he imagined his mother was before him, punishing him for his failures, can only engage sympathy, had not his sister, Miss Charity Buckley, and her friend, Miss Clara Garnham, lost their lives at his hands.

On the wall, a crucifix hung crookedly with a stain of blood on the wall behind it, and is believed to be the heavy weapon that cracked the skulls of both young ladies.

Miss Nora Waldren and Mrs Martha Miller were lucky to have escaped with their lives, as Mr Buckley believed they, and his first two victims, had broken commandments, and that he was the deliverer of judgement and divine retribution.

In an exclusive interview this morning with your reporter, Ted Egan, Earnest Buckley was himself again, and spoke of his torment. A child repressed by a zealot mother and a weak father, Mr Buckley was whipped, locked in cupboards, starved and belittled if he did not live up to his mother's standards and beliefs. His sister did not share his fate; Earnest Buckley, the only son and the eldest of the two siblings, carried the burden.

On the death of his father from illness, Earnest admitted to taking the life of his mother, the manner yet to be determined by the coroner. Mr Buckley told your reporter that he removed the body of his mother from her coffin, replacing her weight with earth, and closed the lid before the funeral directors collected the body.

However, in his fragile state of mind, he assumed her persona. His sister knew nothing of the corpse in her brother's bedroom, but on the death of their parents, Miss Charity Buckley felt liberated, and no longer wished to honour an engagement that she did not abide by – to marry Mr Percival Trigg.

Her brother did not agree to releasing her from the commitment and, not being of sound mind, believed she must be punished for dishonouring her parents. Torn between his faith, his love for his sister and the domination of his mother, Mr Buckley believed he did his mother's calling when he took Miss Buckley's life and confessed in note form to Father Taylor of St Mary's Church.

Earnest Buckley also punished Miss Clara Garnham, whom he learnt had stolen money to assist Charity to escape the commitment of the unwanted marriage. He took Miss Garnham's life for breaking the eighth commandment of stealing and admitted to knowing this due to overhearing Miss Nora Waldren speak of it, and telling of another young lady's infidelity, as she laughed among her friends. Miss Waldren was attacked but survived. Her sin, commandment nine – bearing false witness. In an earlier interview with your reporters, Miss Waldren vehemently denied the charge.

The detectives believed Earnest Buckley to be a suspect, but the role of the woman seen at the four attacks stumped them until hours prior to his arrest. Then, they discovered the confession was written by Mr Buckley's hand, and that his mother's clothing had not been surrendered to the church charity shop, but his sisters had been.

Meer hours later, the last victim solved the mystery of the woman seen at the Christmas market. When escaping, Mrs Marther Miller fought for her life, and the wig on the woman's head came off in her hand. The detectives knew exactly who the wearer was and swooped.

It is unlikely that Earnest Buckley will see the inside of a prison cell. According to Detective Harland Stone, the man is on his way to the Woogaroo Lunatic Asylum at Goodna.

Ted Egan was confident in the quality of the story he and Lilly had delivered; but one could never tell with these younger editors what might please them. And so, with the youthful Lilly Lewis beside him, the pair sat waiting for the acting editor, Lionel Faherty, to finish reading their copy. Blissfully, they did not have to endure the cigar smoke of the absent editor, Alex Cowan.

Lionel put down the copy and with a smile, he said in his endearing Scottish accent, 'What a bloody good yarn that is.'

The two reporters exhaled and grinned.

'It was a sight, Mr Faherty, seeing Earnest Buckley there dressed as a woman and sprouting retribution. Frightful. Topped only by the skeleton behind the door,' Lilly said excitedly.

'I can imagine. The illustration will cement it. How did you get the exclusive interview?' Lionel asked.

'Lilly has developed an understanding with the two detectives and works closely with them,' Ted said.

'And Earnest Buckley wouldn't talk with a woman, hardly surprising given what his mother put him through, but Ted sounded like a priest willing to hear his confession, and Mr Buckley agreed to speak with him,' Lilly said with a laugh.

'Whatever it takes, Lilly, my girl,' Ted grinned.

'You are a dynamic pair,' Lionel said. 'And speaking of which, I thought we might make it permanent.'

Both reporters stared at him, surprised, and Lionel held up his hand to ward off the questions and continued. 'I have spoken with Alex, who will return to this chair next week, and he agreed with me it is a clever pairing.'

Lilly clapped her hands together. 'Oh, Ted, I would love that. I have always wanted to do investigative reporting, not just report news as it happens, and I am learning how to from you. Plus, you can introduce me to your contacts and teach me how to work with them. Would you be willing?'

Ted grinned. 'I would love to return to my reporting roots; the fire never leaves the belly, and you are a breath of fresh air, Lilly; your energy lifts me, I will learn from you too.'

'Excellent,' Lionel said, smiling at both.

'But what of Fergus?' Lilly said loyally. 'I would hate to let him down.'

Lionel shook his head. 'Alex has been thinking of shuffling the entire reporting team portfolios for sometime; keeps everyone on their toes.'

Ted nodded. 'He does it now and again. It's hard to rebuild contacts, but it keeps the stories fresh and avoids corruption.'

'Corruption?' Lilly exclaimed. As the newest on staff, she could not imagine such a thing going on.

'It happens more than you know,' Lionel agreed. 'Payments for stories, a nudge here or there to forget a detail in return for a favour. As it so happens, Fergus knows a great deal about the arts; his father once took to the stage, so that will be his new role.'

'How exciting,' Lilly said.

'Plenty of variety,' Ted said. 'I imagine he will still have after-hours work, but with a young family, the hours will be more predictable than those of crime reporting.'

'Alex and I agree,' Lionel Faherty said. 'It's done then. Go chase up the illustrator. Give me another update on this story tomorrow; the readers will be insatiable for a while. Chat some more to the young lady who escaped last night. The wig in her hand is worth some column space.'

Ted nodded and added to Lilly, 'We can chase up that witness who identified Mrs Buckley's hat and almost called out a greeting to her as she led one of the young women away.'

'Oh yes, we didn't write that up at the time as it seemed irrelevant given Mrs Buckley was dead.' She turned to the acting editor. 'We told the detectives, though, which led them to enquire about her clothing. Thank you, Mr Faherty,' Lilly said, rising.

'Thank you, Lionel,' Ted said, and the men shook hands. On departing the office, Ted teased, 'Well, how about that, Miss Lilly Lewis, reporter?'

'We're going to be amazing together, Ted,' she agreed grinning, and then she departed to chase up the illustration, and Ted strode back to the desk that was now going to be his as he returned to doing what he excelled at – investigative reporting.

Detective Harland Stone finished his report and read it over once more. Nearby, Detective Gilbert Payne cleaned the board, packed their notes and evidence into a box and marked on the nearby lid, "The Fallen Angel case – Mr Earnest Buckley" and dated it.

Rising, Harland asked, 'Will you read this and check I have left nothing out?' He brought the report to Gilbert. 'Then,

I shall take a lunch break and quickly visit my fiancée to apologise for my rapid departure last evening.'

Gilbert grinned. 'Some cheerful news, Sir, amidst our daily drama.'

'Indeed.'

'There is a flower seller on the corner, Sir, and you can get a hansom from there.'

'Sage advice indeed, thank you, Gilbert,' Harland said with a chuckle. He would not have thought of taking flowers.

While Gilbert sat and read through the report, Harland looked out the window to the street at the passing carriages and foot traffic, thinking of his proposal and Phoebe's delight in his house. He found himself smiling, and his mind went to the future until Gilbert brought him back to the now.

'It's thorough and accurate, Sir,' he said, rising, and returned the report to his superior's desk. 'I am pleased Mr Kingston's story will not be in the newspaper. It would serve no purpose.'

'I agree,' Harland said. 'I can't help but wish he had come to the police and mentioned the boy was wearing his mother's clothes and was unbalanced. Uniformed officers might have checked on Mr Buckley and found the corpse earlier. Even if they did not see Mr Buckley as a killer, they might have found him ill in the mind. He could have been incarcerated earlier, and two young ladies would be alive now.'

'But he was very good at appearing normal, Sir. We did not know he was unbalanced from our interviews with him.'

'Very true,' Harland conceded. He passed their meeting desk and stopped to lift Mrs Buckley's dowdy and modest hat from the case box awaiting its lid and a carbon copy of the final report to the inspector. 'Poor wretched fellow.'

'I cannot help but feel sorry for him too, Sir. I thought my father was strict, but as an adult, I know all my punishments were justified.'

'I can't help but wonder what you might have done to earn the wrath of your father, Gilbert,' Harland gave his protégé a smile.

'I blew up the letterbox with firecrackers once, Sir. My best friend and I wanted to see if it would work. I got strapped severely that time.'

'I'm assuming then that it worked.' Harland laughed and returned to his desk, retrieved the report, and thanked Gilbert. 'Take a lunch break while you can, and hopefully the inspector will give us a reprieve for the two days before Christmas Day and not land another case immediately upon us. I shall return after seeing Phoebe in an hour or two.'

'Yes, Sir,' the young detective smiled. 'I might see if Brodie wishes to have lunch?'

'I'm sure Tavish will be pleased to have his twin occupied. Gilbert, I hope I have not dampened your proposal news; I thought you were intending to ask Miss Yalden soon,' Harland said as the men headed toward the door at the same time.

'I am intent on doing so, Sir. Emily mentioned she loved the start of a new year and all it promised, so I decided to plan a special picnic for New Year's Day and get on bended knee then.'

'Excellent,' Harland grinned and lightly slapped his protégé on the back as he departed one way with the report, and Gilbert headed to the exit with his hat.

Chapter 31

PHOEBE WAS IN A state of pure happiness; she had not slept a wink for thinking of the proposal, her beautiful new home and all that was to come. It felt so grown-up to soon be having a husband and a home. The only thing that dampened her happiness was leaving her family home and knowing her grandparents' would now have an empty house. Perhaps they were relieved, given they had raised three children they did not expect to inherit, and yes, Ambrose still lived in residence, but was rarely there, and was now seeking to purchase his own home.

She smiled as she dressed this morning; as she sat on the omnibus beside her grandfather on the way to work; as she applied powder to the elderly lady for the afternoon viewing. And every so often, she sighed with contentment.

Phoebe had already engaged Miss Mary Pollard at the dress store next door to make her wedding dress and happily accepted Mrs Dobbs' offer to make the wedding cake. She would soon meet Harland's parents if they made the trip to Queensland for the wedding.

'You look very happy for a young lady working on the dead,' a voice said beside her, and Phoebe laughed, unstartled. Regular visitors were a normal part of her day.

'Very true, Uncle Reggie. If I were attending a funeral, Julius would have to berate me instead of Ambrose for a change.'

'Congratulations, dear Phoebe. You have secured the love of a noble and decent young man.'

Phoebe looked up at her uncle. 'Thank you, Uncle Reggie, I do believe so too. I could not be happier; it would be impossible.'

'No doubt my brother is delighted to have two of his grandchildren happily settled, and the third on his way towards engaging a young woman,' Reggie said and sighed.

'Are you all right, Uncle Reggie?' Phoebe asked, pausing in her work. 'I imagine you miss Grandpa, but every time you speak of him, I sense your melancholy. It is that time of the year too where those without family are more conscious of it.'

Reggie strolled around the room, hands clasped behind his back. 'Very true, dear niece, but my melancholy is all my own doing. I put my lovelorn feelings before my family, rightly or wrongly. I could have had both; I should have waited and lost my heart to someone else.'

'Like Ambrose did when he did not win Lilly's heart but found Billie and is now very happy.'

'Exactly so. But I was an impetuous young man intent on reading the verses of poet Robert Browning as if they were the gospel and imagining myself so badly done by.'

'He has some beautiful verses,' Phoebe agreed. 'Was there one in particular that you took to heart? Let me guess, the one with the lines, "Grow old along with me, the best is yet to be?" Yes?'

'No,' Reggie gave a shake of his head and came to stand opposite her at the worktable. 'I never advanced far enough to make that request of a lady. It was a poem, some lines in particular that Browning published in the year of my death, that advanced my passion.'

'Do you recall them? Will you tell me?'

'Oh, I recall them,' he said with a heartfelt voice. 'It feels like it was only yesterday that I read the poignant words and my heart broke knowing Maria would belong to my brother and not me. Did you know that I loved your grandmother?'

Phoebe gave a small nod. 'I learnt about it recently. What were the lines that pained you so much, Uncle?'

He recited:

'What's the earth, with all its art, verse, music, worth—
    Compared with love, found, gained and kept?'

Phoebe exhaled and asked hesitantly, 'And did you decide since love was not yours to be gained and kept, that the earth was worth nothing?'

Reggie gave a small bow and disappeared without saying a word.

Detective Harland Stone did not get as far as *The Economic Undertaker*. As he passed *Beyond the Veil*, tapping on the window and a hail of good wishes stopped him in his tracks, and he entered the premises to receive the congratulations from the staff but found only Miss Mary Pollard and Mrs Jane Moss present and looking most excited, and Miss Pollard was hurriedly donning her hat to depart.

'Thank you, ladies,' he said, making no effort to hide his delight. 'But where are my future sister-in-law and Mrs Shaw?' he asked with a glance around on not seeing Violet and Nellie Shaw.

'There is much excitement, Detective; Mrs Astin has begun her labour just now. Nellie is accompanying her; they are outside preparing to depart,' Mrs Shaw said.

'And I am off to fetch the midwife. I will be back as soon as possible, Jane. Good day, Detective,' Miss Mary Pollard added, having said more than she normally did in the presence of a male, but forgetting her nerves in all the excitement.

'I shall see if I can assist,' Harland said, holding the door for Miss Pollard before hurrying to the store next door. Despite the adrenaline, as he always did, Harland gently opened the door of *The Economic Undertaker*, in case mourners were present, but he found chaos instead.

Phoebe had just arrived breathless at the top of the stairs. Mrs Dobbs was directing her to the backyard, where Mr Randolph Astin had just hurried outside to assist, and fortunately there were no clients in-house.

'Hello Harland,' Phoebe said, her face lighting up. 'I need to check—'

'I will come with you,' he said, placing the flowers on the reception desk, and greeting Mrs Dobbs as the pair rushed down the hallway and opened the back door to find Julius's well-rehearsed plan in action.

Violet was being helped into the trap, and Nellie Shaw followed, sitting beside her. Charlie was at the reins. Randolph was issuing orders to the new lad, Jacob, who appeared to have hurriedly dressed in a suit and was to accompany him in the trap to take Julius's place at the funeral as Randolph took his grandson home.

'I am all right; do not be concerned,' Violet assured her worried grandfather-in-law.

'I've got this under control, Sir,' Charlie said when all were on board. He slowly turned the horse.

'Make haste but safe progress, Charlie,' Phoebe said, as she blew a kiss to her sister-in-law.

'Mr Astin, don't worry about securing the other trap. I will take Jacob in a hansom, leave him at the funeral with Ambrose and bring Julius home to Violet, if you wish to stay here,' Harland stepped up.

'A perfect solution, thank you, Detective, and timely,' Randolph said and exhaled with relief. He instructed Jacob, 'Do your best at your first funeral service, lad. Do as Ambrose tells you.'

'Yes, Sir, I will make you proud,' the gangly young man said.

With a quick smile to Phoebe, Harland and the young man raced around to the front of the premises to hail a hansom on the main street and make their way to South Brisbane Cemetery.

Perhaps it was because the Astin family trap did not appear at the funeral Julius Astin was officiating with his brother,

Ambrose, that at first Julius did not react. He saw in his peripheral vision a hansom arrive and, moments later, his new employee, Jacob Henley, alight followed by Harland Stone; Julius stood momentarily frozen.

Beside him, Ambrose saw the men, his eyes widened, and he nudged Julius. 'It is time, go brother. I will see you at your home.'

Julius inhaled sharply and departed immediately. Not a glance to his brother, who wore a small smile, nor to the funeral party whose members not in deep grief watched with some interest as one funeral director left and a tall young man replaced him.

Hurriedly arriving by Harland's side, he asked, 'Violet?'

'Yes, all is well,' Harland nodded. 'I have given the driver your address, come, I will take you straight home.'

'Thank you,' Julius said and entered the hansom first. Harland followed quickly behind him, and the vehicle started to the nearby home of Mr and Mrs Julius Astin and Tom.

'When?' Julius asked, his face pale with concern.

'Just now. Mrs Shaw is with her, Charlie is at the reins and young Miss Pollard is fetching the midwife. All is going as you planned,' Harland said, keeping his voice calm.

Julius nodded and sat silently. Not a word, his gaze fixed on nothing and everything in the passing view as his mind raced. A cold shard of fear wedged itself in his heart, and he knew all that was at risk. There was no future without Violet, and he knew only too well how life could change, how easily a life could go off the tracks. She could be taken from him in a heartbeat, and he would not survive that loss, would not want to survive it.

His stomach whirled with anxiety; his mind raced with the possibilities, the dangers, what lay ahead. He felt vulnerable and hated the feeling. Julius closed his eyes and exhaled, his fists clenched. After a moment, he realised Harland had spoken, and opened his eyes.

'I'm sorry, what did you say?'

'Nothing of importance. Just the ramblings of a man who can contribute nothing to the situation.'

The answer surprised Julius, and he laughed. 'Yes, that's exactly how I feel. I don't enjoy not being in charge of the outcome.'

'Nor I,' Harland agreed. 'But sometimes, we must trust others to do their best.'

Julius nodded and took a deep breath. 'Yes, you are right. All I can do now is have faith.'

'Then we shall do it together. I am sure Ambrose and Tom will soon join us, four brothers, although one is in waiting,' he said referring to his own unofficial status. 'We will do what men do at a birth... wait until you have a child to announce.'

Julius gave him a grateful look and resumed his stance, seeing nothing and silently panicking as the world went by.

Chapter 32

SEVERAL DAYS LATER...

It was a Christmas day of admissions and omissions, of family absent and new members present. Across town, Jacob Henley enjoyed the day with a family he did not know this time last year when his parents were alive. Now, living with Mrs Dobbs, he found himself in the company of her son and daughter-in-law and three grandchildren under ten, who insisted he play cricket and partake in all manner of activities.

Mr Bennet Martin, who was lunching with Miss Lilly Lewis and her family, arrived bearing gifts for Lilly, her parents, five brothers and the two girlfriends present. As always, he was treated like royalty. Not because he was the beau of the only girl in the family, but Mr and Mrs Lewis—still amazed that their reporter daughter, would attract any man while working, let alone a man of the quality of Mr Martin—would not rest easy until Lilly became Mrs Bennet Martin.

Miss Emily Yalden arrived on time and beautifully presented at the home of her beau, Detective Gilbert Payne, to enjoy lunch with mother and son. Naturally, as manners dictate, she brought a homemade cherry tart and gifts for the pair. The lunch was a lovely, intimate gathering with witty conversation and a delicious spread of dishes, made better by Gilbert not being called away to a ghastly crime on Christmas Day.

From mid-morning, the Astin family guests arrived at the home of hosts Randolph and Maria Astin. Of course, Ambrose and Phoebe were already in residence, but in this year of 1892, for the first time, Ambrose did not share Christmas with his family. He was to join Billie and her family to celebrate the day but lingered to welcome everyone as he was not due at Billie's father's home until midday.

His seat at the table would be taken by Harland Stone, who arrived with gifts, amazing the family that he had time to shop for them with the "Fallen Angel" case consuming most of his time. He did not let on that he had left it until last evening—quite common for men to do so he was told—and with a list of names, Harland engaged for a small fee, a stall owner's daughter at the Christmas market to assist him to shop. As if born to the task, she hurried him from stall to stall, a basket in hand, and within an hour, he had a small gift, nicely wrapped, for all in attendance.

Arriving with much fuss and welcome, came the new heir of the Astin family. Rufus leapt out of the carriage first, heading straight to the backyard to inspect and sniff, as was his duty. Tom jumped down next to take his baby nephew from his sister's arms, as Julius assisted Violet down. She was remarkably well despite 12 hours of labour only 48 hours earlier, but happily welcomed the seat offered once inside, and smiled as everyone in attendance insisted on holding the Christmas baby boy.

'See, all turned out very well,' Harland said, standing in the corner with Julius watching the scene before them.

'I don't know if I can go through it again,' Julius huffed.

'I can only imagine how taxing it was for you,' Harland agreed with a laugh. But he was soon captivated by the sight of his fiancée holding the newest member of the Astin family.

Phoebe looked so beautiful with the baby in her arms that he was not aware he was staring and smiling or that Randolph had arrived beside him until the senior Astin said, 'That might be your situation next year then, Harland.'

He whipped around in surprise to see Randolph smiling at him, and said, 'I hope so, Mr Astin. I hope so.'

Phoebe handed the baby to Ambrose and joined Harland at the window; her brother and grandfather moved away, talking of work matters. Harland took her hand and placed a kiss on it.

'I am so glad you are here, Harland. Our first Christmas together as an engaged couple,' Phoebe beamed up at him.

'You cannot know how glad I am to be here, Phoebe, and hopefully the criminals will have the day off or at least hide their crimes until Boxing Day.'

She laughed at the notion. 'A family Christmas lunch might drive a few to crime.'

'It is highly likely,' he agreed. The pair moved to sit on the large bay window seat where they watched the family interact. 'I have gone from being on my own to having a beautiful fiancée, the promise of our own family and being welcomed into your family as if I were an Astin. I never thought I would know such happiness.'

'This time next year, we will have our own Christmas tree.'

'In our house,' Harland said, smiling at her.

Ambrose's banter cut into their conversation as he walked with the baby in his arms near Violet and Julius. 'I am truly surprised you did not name him after me. Ambrose is such a lovely name, and I was there when you met. That should have put me well ahead of all the other contenders.'

Julius rolled his eyes. 'I put up with you all day at work. Am I to go home and be reminded of you all evening?'

'I understand your disappointment, Ambrose,' Violet teased. 'But we are fortunate to have so many good men in our family, including my late father, Edward, and your father, Montague, our grandfathers Randolph and Henry, and brothers, how could we choose?'

Julius agreed. 'If we had gone that way, our baby's name would have been Randolph Henry Montague Edward Ambrose Tom Astin. I would have expired from exhaustion by the time I called him for dinner.'

The family laughed at Julius's nonsense and marvelled at his light-heartedness born from pure happiness.

'I think your name choice is perfect,' the matriarch Maria said. 'He is of a new generation, and it is a perfect name for this young man, especially at Christmas. It was the Archangel Gabriel who delivered the news to Mary that she was blessed with a divine child.'

'All that is very well,' Ambrose said addressing the baby in his arms, 'but Master Gabriel Astin, as you don't have my name, I only hope you have my looks,' he said and laughed at his family's reaction.

'Before Ambrose departs, shall we have a Christmas toast?' Randolph said, and Phoebe rose to help hand out glasses of champagne. Julius accepted his son from Ambrose and the champagne from his sister, and joined his wife for the toast.

Together, they raised their glasses. Randolph could not see his late brother present, but Julius and Phoebe silently greeted Uncle Reggie as he stood happily amongst the family. Reggie was on the senior Astin's mind, though, as Randolph started the toast: 'To those who are absent but present in our hearts, and to the family present today. To those who will soon join the family,' he said, pointing his glass at Harland, 'and to those who will carry on our name. Welcome, young Gabriel. Merry Christmas. To family.'

'To family,' they toasted, and as Julius lifted his son to his shoulder, Phoebe saw Gabriel lift his little hand to grasp the fingers of Uncle Reggie, who stood behind the man he imagined for his own grandson, Julius. The long-deceased uncle smiled with delight as the child laughed with him, and then the spirit faded, leaving the day and its celebration to the living – the mature and faithful, the newly in love and promised, the new family and the future.

THE END

Afterword

Thank you yet again, dear reader, for visiting the Astin family with me. This story was loosely inspired by a true Australian tragedy that played out in the late 19th and early 20th centuries. Eugenia Falleni was born a woman but desperately wanted to be a man. That was unacceptable in that era, and while Eugenia did not set out to kill anyone, she did commit murder. Eugenia dressed as a man and called herself Harry Crawford. She married a lady and, not long into the marriage, murdered her.

Today, it would seem impossible to imagine how a man could marry and his bride not be aware that he is actually a woman, but in "those days" pre-marital relations were frowned upon and most relationships were not consummated or intimate until after marriage. In the modesty of a dark room, a lady may be none the wiser if the husband was diligent.

Dressed as Harry Crawford, Eugenia was a respectable-looking man; neat and conservative. Eugenia hailed from Italy and, as a child, often dressed as a boy. She left her homeland as a baby; the family immigrated to New Zealand, and Falleni arrived on Australian shores, aged approximately 23, in 1898 (six years after *The Fallen Angel* novel is set).

Eugenia arrived with a daughter, Josephine. The story goes that as Eugenia began dressing as a man, her horrified and confused family disowned her. Taking on the male persona, she worked at sea until "the captain of the ship discovered she was a woman. He brutally raped her, and she was offloaded in Newcastle."[1] This was how her daughter was conceived, and young Josephine was put into the care of a childless Italian family in Sydney.

No doubt traumatised physically and mentally, Eugenia continued life under the male alias of Harry Crawford, and occasionally Jack Crawford. She managed this successfully for 22 years, working in Sydney hotels, laundries and meat factories. She fell in love with the beautiful widow Annie Birkett, and accepted Annie's son, also named Harry. Annie had some savings, which also made her an attractive prospect.

Soon they wed, and Eugenia Falleni was living the life of a family man. It was February 1913, a year before the war broke out, and the couple opened a confectionery shop in Balmain, Sydney. Within four years of their marriage, Annie disappeared after a spring picnic in September 1917. Harry told her son and all who would listen that Annie had left him for another man, receiving sympathy and support from friends and neighbours alike.

Time passed, but there was no word from Annie—her family and friends forgotten by her—but her son, Harry, did not believe his mother would abandon him. Three years after his mother's disappearance, Harry, now aged 17, ran a missing notice in the Police Gazette.

Believe it or not, Eugenia/Harry took another wife, one day short of the two years since Annie disappeared. He married a hotel office worker, Miss Elizabeth King Allison, on 29 September 1919. The following year, in 1920, burnt remains were found and identified as that of Annie Birkett. Soon the police came knocking at Harry's door, and he was arrested on the 5 July 1920, on suspicion of murder. One can only imagine the shock to then-wife, Elizabeth.

But what became of Annie? Did she discover Harry's secret, and he killed her in a spur-of-the-moment rage? Or was it a planned picnic outing for the purpose of murder? We'll never know, as Harry maintained to the end that he did not kill

Annie and had never been to the area in Lane Cove where the body was found.

Harry was put in a lineup as witnesses tried to identify the person they saw in the area several years prior and after, was charged with murder. When threatened with the prospect of being sent to the men's prison, Harry had to come clean and reveal her identity as Eugenia Falleni. She asked to be housed with the women prisoners. The man-woman scenario drew enormous interest from the media and the public, and at her trial, Eugenia dressed as a female.

The public spotlight was cruel, and Eugenia was often referred to as the 'Man-Woman' in headlines, and the court was crowded with people trying to get a glimpse of her.

The late Annie's son, Harry Birkett, and Eugenia's daughter, Josephine, were both present at the trial and testified. Josephine appeared with her face covered by a veil. Then, aged 22, she shared: "My mother has always gone about dressed as a man."

Some of her comments were quite damning, including the reflection on Harry and Annie's marital relationship. Josephine said: "They occupied the same bedroom. They quarrelled a great deal. Mrs Birkett had discovered that she [Harry] was a woman."[2]

Annie's son, Harry, who was now a tailor's apprentice, told the court how Harry/Eugenia took him to The Gap (an ocean cliff on the South Head peninsula in eastern Sydney, well known as a suicide spot for its dangerous drop-off) and Harry went inside the fence and invited young Harry in too. "He began throwing stones over the cliff, and asked me to come and throw some over. I wouldn't go inside, so he came out."[3]

Harry Birkett also recalled when seeing the newspaper, Harry, who could not read or write, asked him anxiously if there was "anything of a murder over at North Sydney. So I looked, and finding a little piece, I read it to him... Up to that time 'he' had not said anything about my mother."[4]

When the experts stepped in, Annie's autopsy revealed, "Many fissures or fractures in the skull, mainly due to the heat of the fire, but the coroner could not tell whether she was dead before the fire started... A large linear crack to the back of the skull was discovered under X-Ray."[5]

Eugenia was convicted after the jury deliberated for two hours and was condemned to death. Her appeal was rejected, but the sentence was commuted to life in prison. After serving eleven years in prison, the work of her support network and her failing health resulted in Eugenia Falleni's release in 1931 on the condition that she lived as a woman. She assumed yet another name, Jean Ford, and worked as a landlady.

Seven years later, Eugenia was struck by a car, lingered for a while but died in Sydney Hospital on 9 June 1938. Ironically, the accident was on Oxford Street, where today, Sydney's Mardi Gras passes along annually. Eugenia is buried in an unmarked pauper's grave in Rookwood General Cemetery, Sydney, New South Wales, Australia.

My story, as mentioned, was loosely inspired by Eugenia's journey to find love and acceptance, as my fictional character, Earnest Buckley, struggles to be accepted by his mother, yearns to be loved by Percival Trigg, and desperately seeks affection even if it while dressed as his mother in the company of Robert Kingston. Both chose to end the lives of the innocent when their goals were thwarted.

Images follow:

Harry Crawford (left): New South Wales. Police Dept (1920). Eugenia Falleni, alias Harry Crawford, special photograph number 234, Central Police Station Sydney, 1920.

Eugenia in prison dressed as a woman (right): New South Wales. Dept. of Prisons (1928). Eugenia Falleni, alias Harry Crawford, criminal record number 741LB, 16 August 1928. State Reformatory for Women, Long Bay, NSW.

Mrs Annie Birkett (bottom left): Annie Birkett headshot from: Find A Grave, database and images (https://www.findagrave.com), memorial page no. 87467197; maintained by graver (contributor 47037760).

*Top left: Eugenia as Harry Crawford.
Bottom left: first wife and victim, Annie
Birkett. Right: Eugenia's prison photo.*

For those who know their Bible, for this story, I have referenced the *Exodus King James* version.

In 1890 Australia, companies did not offer paid annual leave, but many closed for the holiday season. Retail shops in Brisbane city closed on Christmas Eve and did not re-open until after Boxing Day, giving their staff a good few days' rest. Government offices and banks observed the same.

There were several good motherhood books available to women in the 19th century, including *The Mother's Book* by Lydia Maria Child (1831),[6] which Phoebe mentions to Julius. You can read this book for free thanks to Project Gutenberg. Click on the link to review. Also, the wonderful author Mimi Matthews has a blog page titled *'The Victorian Baby: 19th Century Advice on Motherhood and Maternity'.*[7]

The news article Lilly and Ted wrote is based on several true crime articles featured in the newspaper in 1894. The manner of writing in those days was almost like storytelling and strung the reader along with the tale. Dramatic headlines—always at least three—were most captivating.

Copperplate and Spencerian scripts were taught in 19th-century schools, ensuring the students graduated with the penmanship required to succeed in the letter-writing world. Often, the style chosen was the decision of the school or teachers and their preference for particular scripts. By the 1890s, there was a push to standardise education, but it was not fully implemented, particularly in private schools. The art of good penmanship is fast becoming a skill lost to the world today.

The beer that Harland and Randolph enjoyed was very much a part of our culture in 1890. Mr J.H. Fitz, the local agent for Castlemaine Beer, recommended it to the readers of the *Northern Miner* newspaper, Queensland, claiming it was "the best beer in the market."[8] The Castlemaine Brewery was established in 1857 by Edward Fitzgerald, and soon his brother, Nicholas, joined him in the business. Over the years, it has developed with multiple stakeholders and brands, and in Queensland, it is the Castlemaine Perkins company we know today.[9]

The Teneriffe estate in Brisbane in the 1890s, where Harland's house was located on Chester Street, was in a state of growth. There were grand, palatial homes for professionals and smaller homes and cottages for trade workers. The area was serviced by a horse-driven tram until electric trams came into being later in the century. Harland's father was a wealthy man, and there was nothing modest about Phoebe and Harland's future fictional home. As an example, house prices in this era (1890s) ranged from 85 to 160 pounds. 15 years ago, on the same street, a house built in 1886 and still standing sold for $4.5 million.

Finally, for fellow authors who might be reading this novel, a shout-out to a great resource, the "Random British Name

Generator"[10]. You can choose name combinations and mix them up from the current date or 1881. It is the source of many great first and last names for characters.

Until the next book, dear reader, I thank you for your company. Take care.

Also by Helen Goltz

If you like the Astin family, you might enjoy:

Miss Hayward & the Detective Series (historical mystery/romance):

Murder at the Carnival

The Artist's Missing Muse

Mystery at the Asylum

The Mortician's Clue (introducing Phoebe and staff from The Economic Undertaker)

Murder in Bridal Lane

The Clairvoyant's Glasses (supernatural/romance)

Volume 1 – A vision unexpected

Volume 2 – Time has a shadow

Volume 3 – Love knows no bounds

Volume 4 – Fate comes to call

Volume 5 & 6 – coming soon, The Raven's Son.

The Jesse Clarke series (cosy mystery):

Death by Sugar

Death by Disguise

Death by Reunion

The Mitchell Parker series published by Next Chapter (crime thrillers):

Mastermind

Graveyard of the Atlantic

The Fourth Reich

Writing as Jack Adams (psychological mystery/suspense):

Poster Girl

Delaney and Murphy childhood friends series:

Asylum

Stalker

Cult

Hitched

Carnival.

Coming soon... Forgotten.

With journalist Chris Adams, The Grave Tales series (non-fiction) x 9 titles:

Grave Tales: Brisbane Vol.1

Grave Tales: Great Ocean Road – Geelong to Port Fairy

Grave Tales: Sydney Vol.1

Grave Tales: Bruce Highway

Grave Tales: True Crime Vol.1

Grave Tales: Queensland's Great South West

Grave Tales: Melbourne Vol.1

Grave Tales: Queensland's Scenic Rim & Surrounds

Grave Tales: Tasmania.

Grave Tales: Cold Cases (an amalgamation of stories from existing titles)

The Lady Mortician's Visions (historical mystery/romance/paranormal twist)

The Missing Brides

The Fake Child

The Dastardly Debutante

The Deathly Dolls

The Potent Perfume

The Watery Grave

The Vanishing Groom

The Fallen Angel

And one last story to come...

Writing as Ally Adams:

The Saints team (contemporary romance):

Team Lucas

Team Tomas

Team Niklas

Team Alex

Stand-alone titles:

The House on Findlater Lane (mystery/romance paranormal)

The Forgotten House (historical romance)

Three Parts Truth (mystery suspense)

Morphers (middle grade fiction).

About the author

Helen is a hybrid-published, Amazon best-selling author. Post-graduate qualified in English literature, media, and communications from universities in Queensland, Australia, Helen has worked as a journalist, producer and marketer in print, TV, radio and public relations. She also obtained a counselling diploma along the way. Born in Toowoomba, she has made her home in Brisbane, Australia, with her journalist husband, Chris, and Boxer dog, Baxter. She is published by Next Chapter, Podium Entertainment, and her own imprint, Atlas Productions.

1. Discovering Eugenia: One of Australia's most unusual murder cases, SBS. Retrieved 30 January 2019 from U R L : https://www.sbs.com.au/news/thefeed/story/discovering-eugenia-one-australias-most-unusual-murder-cases

2. "THE MAN-WOMAN." (1920, August 20). The Register (Adelaide, SA : 1901 - 1929), p. 6. Retrieved January 30, 2019, from http://nla.gov.au/nla.news-article62922342

3. ANNIE BIRKETT'S DEATH (1920, August 17). Barrier Miner (Broken Hill, NSW : 1888 - 1954), p. 2. Retrieved January 30, 2019, from http://nla.gov.au/nla.news-article45539383

4. ANNIE BIRKETT'S DEATH (1920, August 17). Barrier Miner (Broken Hill, NSW : 1888 - 1954), p. 2. Retrieved January 30, 2019, from http://nla.gov.au/nla.news-article45539383

5. Eugenia Falleni - convicted murderer, State Archives and Records, NSW State Government. Retrieved 29 January 2019 from URL: https://www.records.nsw.gov.au/archives/magazine/galleries/eugenia-falleni-convicted-murderer

6. https://www.gutenberg.org/ebooks/69345

7. https://www.mimimatthews.com/2016/05/08/the-vict
   orian-baby-19th-century-advice-on-motherhood-and-m
   aternity/

8. The Northern Miner. (1890, May 14). The
   Northern Miner (Charters Towers, Qld. : 1874 -
   1954), p. 3. Retrieved September 7, 2024, from
   http://nla.gov.au/nla.news-article76974735

9. Castlemaine Brewery. (2024, June 23). In *Wikipedia*.
   https://en.wikipedia.org/wiki/Castlemaine_Brewery

10. https://britishsurnames.co.uk/random